The Untoward

Assassin

Also by Janet Kellough

The Palace of the Moon
The Pear Shaped Woman
The Legendary Guide to Prince Edward County
The Bathwater Conspiracy

The Thaddeus Lewis Series:
On the Head of a Pin
Sowing Poison
47 Sorrows
The Burying Ground
Wishful Seeing
The Heart Balm Tort

The Untoward
Assassin

A Thaddeus Lewis Novel

Janet Kellough

F
KEL   M,C

Issued in print and electronic formats.
ISBN 978-0-9937200-9-3 (print) 978-1-9990022-0-6 (ebook)

Cover image: peter-forster-373964-unsplash
Published 2019 by Janet Kellough

To everyone who asked for more Thaddeus

Chapter 1
Wellington, Canada West 1854

The bitter November wind blowing across Lake Ontario made the cabin of the packet steamer uncomfortably cold, even though the stove was stoked up and radiating heat in waves. But Thaddeus Lewis couldn't get a seat as close to it as he wanted, and to make matters worse, a woman in a large black hat blocked his view through the window. The lake was choppy, and the lack of a reference point on the horizon made him a little queasy as the steamer rolled and bumped it's way toward Wellington. Or maybe it was the prospect of the difficult conversation ahead that made him feel sick.

This wasn't a journey he wanted to be on. His intention had been that he and his granddaughter, Martha Renwell, would stay with his sons in Huron County until after Christmas. Two weeks into their visit, however, a blistering letter arrived from Martha's father, demanding that Thaddeus return home with her immediately.

Francis Renwell had known about Martha's involvement in the Cobourg murder case. Martha wrote to her father after it happened, and then there had been all the reports in the newspapers. Thaddeus's name was mentioned only once or twice and Martha's not at all, even though one of her insights proved to be a key piece of evidence that kept an innocent woman from the gallows. It wasn't the Cobourg case that had Francis riled.

Thaddeus had hoped that news of the subsequent events in

London had been eclipsed by the dreadful railway accident at Baptiste Creek. After all, what was one small kidnapping stacked up against a mountain of dead and injured passengers? But details of the murder investigation were reported widely after all, and there was no denying the fact that Martha had been snatched off a London street by a killer, and that it was as a direct result of Thaddeus being in the employ of a Toronto barrister. The reports had reached Wellington and now Francis was furious.

Martha didn't want to go home.

"We just got here," she said, when he told her about the letter.

"Francis sounds pretty angry," Thaddeus said.

"I don't want to go back to Wellington." Martha's face was stubborn. "You said I could stay with you."

"I know what I said, but he is your father, after all. And he wants you home."

"I'll write back and tell him I'm not coming and that it has nothing to do with you."

"I'm not sure he'll believe that. And you're putting me in an awkward position."

"I suppose." Her face softened a little as she considered this.

"I'm going to have to go talk to him whether you come or not," Thaddeus pointed out. "And the talking is going to be a lot harder if you're not there to back me up."

"Fine. I'll go with you. But it's just for a visit. I'm not staying."

"You can tell him that yourself when you get there," Thaddeus said. And then he added, "but if you're determined not to stay, I strongly advise you to come up with a reasonable alternative."

It had been a glum journey, Martha grumpy and poor company the whole way.

As the steamer approached Wellington harbour, the other passengers in the cabin began stirring, gathering up parcels and pieces of baggage that had not been checked, corralling children and buttoning up their coats. The vessel had not yet reached the wharf when people began shuffling toward the door.

"We might just as well wait here for a while," Thaddeus said to Martha. "Even after we reach the dock, it's going to be some time before we can get ashore." He was in no hurry to disembark.

Janet Kellough

They were amongst the last to leave the cabin. Even so, there was still a crush at the gangway as friends and relatives of passengers swarmed on board to help with parcels and packages, and a porter leading an elderly woman down the plank presented an even further obstacle. Thaddeus stepped sideways past the bottleneck and moved toward the stern of the vessel. He looked behind him to see if Martha was following, but her exit was blocked by a very fat man carrying a huge, overstuffed valise.

He turned away to scan the wharf, looking to see if Martha's father had come to meet them. Suddenly, a sharp jab in the small of his back knocked him off-balance. He shouted, and reached out to steady himself by grabbing the rail, but the blow was still hard enough to knock him down on one knee. Martha shoved her way past the fat man and rushed over to him.

"What happened?" she asked. "Did you fall?"

"No, somebody elbowed me and I lost my balance."

A tall man in a brown suit who had been standing nearby reached out a hand to help Thaddeus to his feet.

"That was a near thing, wasn't it?" the man said. "You might've toppled over the rail."

"We should have waited in the cabin a little longer. I didn't realize there would be such a mob. A couple of people jostled me, and then someone gave me a good hard jab in the back."

"The deck is a bit slippery," Martha said. "You must have lost your footing on it."

"Yes it's starting to ice up in the cold," the tall man agreed. "We'll need to be careful going down the gangplank."

"Are you all right?" Martha said.

"Yes, I'm fine. And now the way is clearing out and I can see your father waiting for us."

Martha scanned the crowd on the wharf and located Francis Renwell. He waved, but Martha didn't wave back.

Thaddeus lifted his hand instead.

"You've got a hole in your coat," Martha said. "I can see it when you move your arm."

"Where?"

"In the back. You must have caught it on something when you

9

fell."

"How bad is it?"

"I think it can be repaired. But I don't know what you ripped it on." She looked around. "There don't seem to be any sharp edges on this part of the deck."

"Maybe it wasn't an elbow that jabbed me," Thaddeus said. "An umbrella? Something with a pointy end."

"I'll have a look at it later. I think I can mend it. If not, we can take it to a seamstress or a tailor."

Finally the exit cleared and they made their way down the plank.

Francis was waiting at the bottom. He hugged Martha tightly for a few moments and then he held her away from him and looked her over anxiously. "Are you all right?"

"I'm perfectly fine," she said. Her tone was cool.

Thaddeus held out his hand. "Francis! Good to see you again."

Francis glared and ignored the outstretched hand. "Martha, could you please go over there and wait for your trunk while I have a word with your grandfather?"

"All right," Martha said, and walked over to where the porter was wrestling with baggage. A gentleman in a tweed suit and the woman in the black bonnet were waiting as well, but they were standing a little further down the wharf, closer to Francis.

Thaddeus had been prepared for a certain amount of unpleasantness, but he was taken aback by the lack of any sort of welcome.

"I know you're provoked with me," he said to Francis in what he hoped was a diffident tone.

"You're correct," Francis said. "I am. Very. I assumed that you'd keep her out of trouble. I suppose I should have known better. You're always falling through the ice, or getting hit on the head, or shot at or chased, or some damn thing – but I had hoped that having Martha there would make you think twice about getting involved in things that don't concern you."

His vehemence took Thaddeus by surprise. Francis was ordinarily mild-mannered and he had never before heard such strong language from the man. Now was not the time to comment on it, but he was glad that Martha had been sent out of earshot.

"I'm sorry. It was my fault entirely."

"Yes, it was your fault. How could you let her get involved in a murder investigation?"

"It wasn't so much a matter of "let", Thaddeus pointed out. "It was more a matter of "try to stop her.""

"You were supposed to be taking care of her. She could have been killed."

Francis' voice was rising with each accusation and from where he stood Thaddeus could see that Martha had sidled over to stand beside the other two passengers. She was close enough that she could probably hear most of the conversation. He frowned at her, but she ignored him and stayed where she was.

"Yes, you're right. I'm sorry," he mumbled. "I should never have let her help." He hoped that his apology would soon end this all-too-public discussion.

But Francis wasn't done yet. "Not to mention allowing her to associate with a known criminal."

"Which known criminal?" Thaddeus was genuinely puzzled. There had been plenty of criminals to go around, but Martha hadn't really had much contact with any of them. Except for the man who had kidnapped her, of course. Maybe Francis had a point.

"I'm talking about Clementine Elliott. The woman is nothing but a huckster."

Two of the carters' heads shot up at this. Apparently Martha wasn't the only one who could hear the argument. And Clementine Elliott must still be a name that could set tongues wagging in Wellington.

"Well, yes…but…" Thaddeus wanted to say that Clementine was an extremely charming huckster who had been very kind to Martha, but he knew that it would just aggravate Francis more, and Francis was aggravated enough as it was.

"Martha doesn't listen to anything I have to say. She really only listens to you. But that means that you have an even greater responsibility to keep her out of harm's way. A responsibility that you seem to have completely disregarded. I honestly don't know what to say."

He had said quite a lot already, and there was little of it that Thaddeus could disagree with. It was a conversation that he'd already had with himself. Unfortunately, it was a conversation that everyone on the wharf now seemed privy to as well. The man who was standing beside Martha had a grin on his face, and even the black-clad woman beside him appeared to have cocked her head to listen.

"If I didn't owe you so much I'd tell you to get right back on that steamer and sail to the devil for all I care."

Thaddeus was stunned. He hadn't expected a warm welcome, but the fact that Francis would threaten to exile him was an indication of just how truly angry he was. Martha's argument for continuing to live with Thaddeus was going to have to be very persuasive indeed.

"I'm sorry," he mumbled again.

"You can say you're sorry until the cows come home, Thaddeus, and it won't change anything. It's one thing if you want to take reckless chances on your own account, but it's another entirely when it involves my daughter. You have severely tried my patience sir!"

Thaddeus judged it wisest to say nothing at all at this point.

"Now, apparently, your luggage has been delivered. Let's get a cart and go." Thaddeus was relieved that he seemed to be included in this instruction. But Francis wasn't quite finished yet.

"You and I need to have a serious discussion about what happens from here."

"Yes, I think that's a good idea."

"Good. Then that's understood." He strode off to where the porter was standing guard over a mound of trunks and cases. "And pardon my language," he muttered as he walked away.

Martha walked over to stand with Thaddeus while Francis negotiated the delivery of their baggage.

"Are you…?"

"Shush," Thaddeus said. "Not now. Don't worry – everything will be fine."

He hoped he was right.

Chapter 2

When they reached The Temperance House Hotel, they found Martha's stepmother Sophie waiting for them on the top step of the verandah. She shot a glance at her husband, then swooped down to hug Martha and Thaddeus both. Then she chivvied them all into the kitchen where she had tea waiting.

They no sooner sat down than the wagon arrived with their baggage.

"I'll see to it," Francis said. He got up and walked through to the hall.

"So…" Sophie said, looking at Thaddeus. "Is everything all right?"

"Not yet," Thaddeus said, "but it will be."

Sophie nodded, then turned her attention to Martha. "You've done your hair differently. You look wonderful."

"A friend of my grandfather's showed me how to do it," and then she blushed. Judging from what she had overheard, she figured it wouldn't be wise to specify that it was Mrs. Elliott who had helped her with her hair. She was sorry now that she'd mentioned Clementine in her last letter home.

"But tell me what's new here."

Sophie launched into a description of village news – who had died, who had given birth, who had married – and Martha was surprised to hear that this last category included a girl she had gone to school with. The village constable retired, Sophie said, but a new one had not yet been appointed. All in all, Martha thought, only the details of village life had changed. The basic story remained the same.

Just then a young woman Martha didn't know came into the kitchen with a bowlful of peeled potatoes. She nodded at them and set the bowl beside the stove.

"Martha, Mr. Lewis, this is Letty Brooks. She's been helping in the kitchen the last couple of weeks."

"Hello," Martha said, and the girl nodded her head and smiled shyly.

Martha wondered if it had been her absence that had necessitated hiring extra help in the kitchen. "It's getting close to suppertime," she said. "Could I help set the tables?"

"No, no, you sit," Sophie said. "It's done already and you must be tired after your journey. You've come such a long way. What was it like, riding on a train?"

"Exciting at first. It's noisy and the cars jolt around, but then after a while it stops being exciting and it puts you to sleep."

Francis returned with a bundle of letters, one of which he handed to Thaddeus, who glanced at it with a puzzled look and tucked it into his pocket.

"We're not too busy right now so we've put you in the two front rooms on the third floor," Francis said. "I can manage the valise and the small case, but I'll need some help with Martha's trunk."

Thaddeus rose. "It's the least I can do," he said. "And I haven't been gone so long that I don't know that it would be best to get out of the way while you feed your guests."

Sophie smiled at him. "You know the drill. Come back for your supper when the dining room clears out."

"While you're doing that, I'll take your coat and have a look at the tear," Martha said. "There's no point in leaving it."

But when Thaddeus turned to follow Francis, she gasped. "There's a rip in your frock coat as well. Whatever poked you went right through your winter coat."

Thaddeus stopped and shrugged out of his jacket. There was a second tear and when he reached around behind him, he realized that there was a small hole in his waistcoat as well.

"It's no wonder you went down," Martha said. "Something really walloped you."

"When was this?" Francis asked.

"Just as we were getting off the steamer. Everyone was crowded around the gangplank so I stepped out of the way. It felt like someone elbowed me."

"Pretty sharp elbows to make a hole like that."

"It's a good thing you were wearing your greatcoat, otherwise you might have been hurt," Martha said. "If it hadn't been for all the layers of cloth, whatever it was might have gone straight through to the skin."

"How very odd," Thaddeus said. "I'll change and bring the things to you. Sorry to be the cause of so much mending."

"I'm happy to do it. But I'll get out of the way and take everything upstairs where I can spread it out."

And, she figured, if he brought the things to her room, they could discuss what Francis had said and go over the plan one more time.

As soon as he and Francis deposited Martha's trunk, Thaddeus went to his room across the hall and changed into his old black waistcoat, the one he had worn when he was preaching.

He rummaged through the pockets of his frock coat and retrieved several coins, a handkerchief, the stub from his steamer ticket, a small wooden box and the letter that Francis had handed him.

He didn't recognize the handwriting on the outside of the letter, but when he opened it he discovered that it was from his former neighbour in Cobourg, the lady with whom he had left an old dog.

Dear Mr. Lewis,

I thought I should tell you that Digger is gone, but not in the way we all expected. Mrs. Howell and her daughter returned to Cobourg a couple of weeks after you left. They didn't stay long – Mrs. Howell said they'd sold the farm and were just there to get the dog and would be returning to the States on the next steamer. I didn't want you to make a whole trip back here for nothing, just to retrieve something that isn't here any more. Hope you are well.

Mrs. Jacob Small

It was only a little over a year since Thaddeus had become infatuated with Ellen Howell, but now it seemed as though it had happened a long time ago, so he was surprised at the little twinge of disappointment he felt at not seeing her one more time. Apparently she didn't want to see him. She had made her feelings clear enough at the time, but surely he hadn't been so odious that they couldn't have carried on a civilized conversation over the fate of a dog.

He also wondered how she managed to arrive in Cobourg just at a time he was guaranteed not to be there. He could think of only one answer to this question – his erstwhile employer, Towns Ashby, must have informed her. Ashby had known he was heading off to Huron to visit his sons. Thaddeus also knew that Ashby was in touch with Ellen - he had undertaken to sell the Howell farm for her. He must have let her know that she could return to Cobourg, fetch the dog and complete the sale of the farm without the risk of an awkward encounter. Ashby meddling in everyone's affairs again.

Although to be fair, Thaddeus was reasonably certain that Ashby knew what had happened in London with Clementine Elliott. Thaddeus had noted a couple of amused glances sent his way, and then, when they all thought Clementine had been killed in the railway accident, Ashby had displayed more sympathy to him than was warranted for the loss of someone who was nothing more than an acquaintance – and an argumentative one at that. Ashby must have reasoned that Thaddeus's involvement with Clementine meant that he had put Cobourg behind him, and that any further contact with Mrs. Howell would be an embarrassment to both parties. Maybe he was right.

There was really nothing Thaddeus could do about it anyway, even if he decided he wanted to. He had no idea where Ellen had gone, nor would she appreciate any effort on his part to find her. He should put her out of his mind. He should put both women out of his mind.

And with that resolve, he gathered up his damaged clothes and took them to Martha's room.

"I thought you'd like to know that Digger's gone," Thaddeus said when Martha answered his knock. "The letter was from Mrs. Small."

"Oh. Well, we kind of expected it didn't we? He was so old."

"No, he's not dead. He's gone. Mrs. Howell retrieved him after we left."

Martha wasn't sure how to respond. Her grandfather's interest in Mrs. Howell had caused him a great deal of grief, she knew, but she assumed that he'd more or less got over it after what happened with Clementine. Except that he didn't know that Martha knew what had happened with Clementine.

"Are you all right?" she finally ventured.

"Yes. Just a little annoyed with Ashby. He must have told her I wouldn't be in Cobourg."

"Yes, I suppose."

He shrugged. "Just as well, I guess."

"Yes."

"There was no point in it anyway, was there?"

"No, I suppose not."

"Well. I thought you'd like to know about Digger, that's all."

"Yes. Thank you."

"See you at supper, then." He nodded at her and left. She'd have to wait until later to discuss her father's extraordinary tirade and how she should counter it.

Francis seemed a little friendlier toward Thaddeus when they finally sat down for the family supper. He'd had his say and had time to calm down, although Thaddeus knew that the anger would probably sputter into life again at moments here and there. It would be a pale imitation of the original outrage, though, most of the fury spent in the initial onslaught. Francis didn't have the necessary temperament to sustain a grudge.

"So how are Will and Moses getting on?" Francis asked. "It's hard for me to think of them as grown men with families of their own. They were just lads when…" His voiced trailed off. Francis first met Thaddeus's sons when he started courting their sister, but now he seemed reluctant to invoke his first wife's name, perhaps out of deference to his second, perhaps because none of them wanted to remember that Sarah had been murdered. It was an unfortunate subject in light of what had almost happened to Martha.

"Moses is a good farmer and doing well," Thaddeus said. "That was to be expected. Will is a terrible farmer, which is also as expected, but Moses basically works both farms anyway, so Will does all right too."

"That's the way it always was. Moses always picked up Will's slack."

"Will's household is a shambles, but Moses and his wife pick up that slack as well. Fortunately, nobody seems to mind and all the children seem equally at home in either place. It would drive me mad, but as long as everyone is happy, I see no harm in it. Things may change though – Will is dabbling in politics and paying even less attention to the farm than he did before."

Francis looked alarmed, and it was only then that Thaddeus remembered that Francis too had been caught up in politics as a young man. He paid a heavy price for it. His years in exile cost him Martha's childhood.

"It's nothing too radical," Thaddeus hastened to add. "He's thrown in with the Clear Grits. They're finding a lot of support in the western part of the province."

"Who are the Clear Grits?" Sophie asked. "You'll have to excuse me – I don't pay much attention to these things."

"A new would-be party that wants representation by population, amongst other things," Thaddeus replied. "They've all lined up behind George Brown, the editor of the *Toronto Globe*."

"But what an odd name," Sophie said.

"The only members wanted in the party are those who are 'all sand and no dirt, clear grit all the way through" Thaddeus explained. "Or at least that's what I read in the paper."

"Their idea of having local officials elected by local councils isn't a bad one," Francis added. "Right here in Wellington we're currently without a constable because we're waiting for someone in the legislature to get moving and appoint one. If it had been done locally, it would have been taken care of long since. There are plenty of things that need fixing, that's for sure, but there are so many parties and alliances and movements in Canada right now, you have to wonder if a brand new one stands any chance of success."

"Time will tell, I suppose," Thaddeus said. "They need to come up with a better name though. Grit sounds like something you need to clean out of a pipe."

They all laughed, and as they had finished the main course, Thaddeus jumped up to begin clearing plates.

"I haven't forgotten how to do this," he grinned at Sophie. "You trained me well."

And by the time dessert was served, the conversation had again turned to family and the state of farming on the Huron Tract. They talked until the teapot was empty, then Francis took the rest of the dishes through to the sink room. Thaddeus followed him.

"I can manage," Francis said.

"I'll give you a hand. I can at least earn my keep while I'm here."

Francis shrugged and began dipping hot water from the stove reservoir into a basin. Thaddeus tempered it with cold water from the pump and then sliced a few slivers of soap into the basin. He rolled up his sleeves and began washing a tray of glasses. Francis dried, but the two worked in silence until Thaddeus finally said, "You know, I never minded washing dishes. It seems like a fine thing to wipe a plate clean so you can put something new and tasty on it."

Francis didn't answer for a moment, then in a low voice he said, "I'm sorry, Thaddeus. But I've been very angry with you."

"That's all right. I seem to recall that at one point in time I was very angry with you. Now we're even."

Thaddeus had once held Francis Renwell responsible for his daughter Sarah's death, but they had long since sorted out the truth of the matter.

"Just tell me one thing," Francis said. He was hunched and tense. "Was Martha interfered with in any way when she was kidnapped?"

"No. That's not what he was after. And we found her right away anyway."

"So the newspapers had it right? He was just trying to get away?"

"Yes." Thaddeus thought his answer was truthful, but he wasn't entirely sure. He didn't really know what would have happened if more time had elapsed. "I wanted to bring her back home, Francis, but she refused point blank. She said she hadn't seen enough of the world yet, and if she couldn't come with me, she'd just have to go off on her own."

"She defied you?" Francis seemed startled by this.

"Yes. But it was done very matter-of-factly. She must have known what I was going to say and had given her response some thought."

"What on earth did she think she was going to do?"

"She had a whole great long list of things she thought she could do. And you know, some of them weren't that far-fetched. She's probably more employable than I am."

"And then you gave in." Francis snorted. "That's exactly what her mother used to do to you."

"I know," Thaddeus said. "I don't seem to have any defence against it."

"Your sons used to complain all the time, you know, about how you were always so much easier on the girls. First Sarah, then Martha."

"I know." There didn't seem to be anything else to say, because Thaddeus knew it was true.

Francis sighed. "Am I such an awful father, that she'd run away rather than live with me?"

Thaddeus felt a wave of pity for this man, who had never been able to take his rightful place as a parent.

"No, of course not. It has nothing to do with you. Martha loves you. But she's looking for something that she can't find here."

"I miss her more than I can say. But even I can see that there isn't enough here to keep her busy."

"No?" Thaddeus was puzzled. "But you've hired extra help."

"You mean Letty Brooks? There's more to that than hired help. Letty is about to become my sister-in-law. She and Sophie's brother plan to marry in the spring, they just haven't made the news very public yet. And the hotel, is, after all, half Martin's, so he's well within his rights to expect an income from it. Letty's just getting a head start on what will be expected of her, that's all."

"So even if Martha stayed, there would be less for her to do than there was before she left?"

Francis nodded. "Yes. I'm not at all happy that she's getting tangled up in your escapades, but I don't have much of anything to offer her in lieu of them. And I don't want her to marry the first fellow that comes along just because she's bored."

Thaddeus didn't bother mentioning that the first fellow had already come along, and Martha had sent him packing.

"I don't know what to do," Francis went on. "Under ordinary circumstances, I'd ask for your advice, but I'm afraid I've lost confidence in anything you have to say."

Thaddeus continued washing plates in silence until Francis broke the tension that stretched between them.

"But against my better judgment, I'll ask anyway. I'm sure you've thought about it."

Now was as good a time as any to mention what he and Martha had hashed out. There wouldn't be many opportunities that offered such a natural opening. "I've often wondered if she should get some more education," Thaddeus ventured. "She's very bright and she's only had the basics at the village school."

Francis shook his head. "I can't afford to send her. Business isn't that great to begin with, and soon the hotel will have four of us to support. I can't stretch things far enough to cover the fees at a finishing school."

Thaddeus took a deep breath. It was now or never. "What about the Normal School in Toronto?"

"What's the Normal School?"

"It's the provincial teacher's college that Egerton Ryerson started a few years back."

"I thought you didn't like Egerton Ryerson?"

"When it comes to church matters, I don't. But as Superintendant of Education he's had at least a couple of good ideas. The Normal School is supposed to improve the general state of education by providing trained teachers for the common schools. There are norms and standards set for the whole province. Or at least that's my understanding," he added hastily. "It could be an opportunity for Martha to further her education and she'd be able to earn some money afterwards, if that's what she's determined to do."

"How much would it cost?"

"I don't know, but I can find out. It can't be a lot, since they actively recruit from the ranks of regular folk. They seem to be looking for people who are willing to go off and teach in the country schools."

"And they take girls?"

"Apparently."

Thaddeus could see that Francis was giving the idea serious consideration.

But then he shook his head. "I don't like the idea of her being all alone in the city. And even if the fees are modest, they must still charge for board. I'm not sure I could manage it."

Thaddeus hesitated. He had reached the critical point in the proposal, and everything could well fall apart if Francis reacted badly to it. "I'm going to Toronto anyway, " he said tentatively. "I need to find some work and that's easier to do in the city. She could stay with me."

Francis threw down his towel and whirled to face him. "You've had this planned all along, haven't you?"

"As you pointed out, I've had time to think about it," Thaddeus allowed. There was no use denying it.

"And what will you be doing in Toronto?"

"I don't know. I haven't figured that part out yet."

"Are you going to work for that barrister again?"

"I haven't heard a word from him." Thaddeus didn't add that he was hoping he might. "In any event, I can support both of us until I find something. Mr. Ashby paid me very generously for the work

I've already done."

"No chance you'll go back to preaching?"

"No."

"Oh well, I don't see that it matters much," Francis said. "It didn't ever keep you out of trouble anyway."

Thaddeus judged it wisest to hold his tongue and let Francis mull the proposition over, which he did while Thaddeus finished washing the plates and started on the pots.

"I'll think about it," Francis said finally. "I haven't spoken with Martha yet. And I won't make any sort of decision until I talk it over with Sophie."

"Fair enough. And Martha needs to make up her mind about whether or not this is really something she wants to do. There's no point in making arrangements unless she agrees."

"Evidently no point at all," Francis muttered. "I'll think about it. But you should bear in mind that I'm still very, very angry and that may well colour my decision."

Thaddeus had pushed his argument as far as he dared for the present, and the two men finished the dishes in silence.

"I need to go to Scully's," Martha said to Thaddeus the next morning at breakfast. "I tried to fix the tear in your coat last night, but Sophie says I need to tack a piece of cloth in behind it so it won't pull apart again."

"I'll go with you," Thaddeus said. He knew she wanted to know what he and Francis had talked about the night before, but he wanted to tell her away from the hotel, where they could discuss it without being overheard.

"You don't suppose you could pick up the bread order while you're out?" Sophie said.

"Of course. Anything else?"

"And a lemon, if you can find one?"

"Happy to be useful."

"I'd like a word with you at some point this afternoon," Francis said to Martha. "Maybe after we get dinner out of the way?"

"Of course."

"You'll have to be careful not to stretch too much until I can reinforce the tear," Martha said as they were getting ready to leave. "Just don't wave your arms around or anything."

"It's warm enough I don't need a winter coat," Thaddeus said. "That way I won't have to worry about it."

It was, indeed, a warm, sunny day for December. The temperature had shot up overnight and now the sun glinted off the rapidly-melting snow and water dripped from the eaves of the hotel. Martha, too, decided against her heavy winter cloak, and wrapped herself up instead in her paisley shawl.

Thaddeus expected a spate of questions as soon as they were out of the door, but he was surprised at what Martha said first.

"Am I being selfish by wanting to go away again?"

"In what way?"

She sighed. "It always seemed like there wasn't anything to do here. But I must have been doing more than I thought. I mean, they've had to get Letty to help in the kitchen and everything. Have I just been thinking of myself, and not them?"

"No," Thaddeus said, "but bless you for thinking it. This is confidential at the moment, so I'll ask you not to repeat it, but Letty and Sophie's brother are engaged. After they're married, she'll be pitching in at the hotel. She's just getting a head start on learning the ropes, that's all. So nothing would change if you stayed."

"Oh. That's good, I guess."

"Have you changed your mind now that you're back? Would you rather be here after all?"

"No, not really. I just need some time to get used to the idea that there will be someone else at the hotel, that's all. Francis would like it if I stayed though, wouldn't he?"

"Yes, he would. But not because of the work you do. For some strange reason, he likes having you around."

Martha laughed. "He has to. He's my father."

"No he doesn't. I'm your grandfather and I don't have to like having you around. But I do."

"Well, that's something, I suppose." Then she sighed. "I was hoping he hadn't heard about the kidnapping."

"It was in all the papers," Thaddeus pointed out.

"I'm sorry he blamed you for everything. It's not fair."

"Don't worry, I've been yelled at before and I survived."

"So what did he say? Last night, I mean."

"Oh now, let me see," Thaddeus pretended to think for a moment. "He said that I'm far too soft on you."

She giggled. "Only because you like having me around, right?"

"Maybe. He also said that you're just like your mother."

"Am I?"

"Yes. You wheedle your way around me just like she did."

He could see that this pleased Martha, even though she could have no memory of Sarah.

"That's surprising. You always say I'm just like grandma."

"Oh no," Thaddeus said. "Your grandmother never wheedled. She just told me what to do and if I had any sense, I did it." He grew more serious then. "You already know that Francis is not at all happy about what happened in London. But he isn't sure what he should do about it. He knows there isn't enough to keep you busy here."

"So…?" Her tone was guarded.

"I had to do some fancy talking, and it's by no means settled, but he's willing to consider the Normal School idea. The part he's not so sure about is me. He's not convinced that I'm a reliable guardian. And he may be right."

Martha began to protest, but Thaddeus stopped her. "There's no question that decisions I made put you in danger. He's well within his rights to be upset with me."

"But he didn't say no?"

"He didn't say yes, either. He said he'd consider it. But you need to really commit to it – and not just to get your own way. Otherwise it's a waste of time and money and we'd be right back in the same boat at the end of it. So I'm asking you one more time – is this really something you want to do?"

They walked along in silence, Martha deep in thought. One or two people who passed nodded a greeting at them. Wellington didn't seem to have changed at all in the time Thaddeus had been away. Same houses, same shops, same people. He felt a sudden sympathy for Martha's desire to see new vistas.

| The Untoward Assassin

"It's been a lot to consider in such a hurry, but yes, I'd like to do it," Martha said. "As long as you're coming too."

"Francis has the last word on that. But if at all possible, I'll come too. It will be easier to find work in the city."

"Maybe Ashby will have something more for you to do."

"If your father agrees to this – and there's no guarantee that he will – the one thing you will not do is get involved in any of Ashby's business. If that were to happen, you'd find yourself back here in the blink of a lamb's eye, and I would personally deliver you to the doorstep. Then you'd be on your own. Is that clear?"

"Yes boss."

"I opened the door, but it's up to you to convince Francis that you'll stay out of trouble."

"And at the end of all this I can get a job teaching school?"

"There's no point in doing it otherwise. And then we can talk about how well you're going to keep me in my old age."

She smiled. "I suppose it's my turn, isn't it?"

By then they had arrived at Scully's dry goods store. They were greeted by Meribeth Scully, the tiny seamstress who constructed dresses for most of the women in Wellington.

"Mr. Lewis! Martha! What a pleasure to see you. I hear you've been having some adventures."

Meribeth circulated most of the gossip in the village, living vicariously through her customers. Thaddeus wasn't surprised that she knew about his latest exploits. If Francis had heard, it was inconceivable that Meribeth hadn't.

"Another murder!" she went on. "My goodness, it seems as though you find crime wherever you go, don't you, Mr. Lewis?"

"It's not surprising," Thaddeus said. "There's plenty to find."

"And I hear that you found Mrs. Elliott as well. Now that is surprising."

"Yes, it was."

He had no intention of supplying any more detail than had been written in the papers or overheard on the wharf. The world knew enough of his business as it was.

"We need a small piece of buckram to reinforce a patch," Martha said. "My grandfather ripped his coat and I need to mend it."

The seamstress rummaged under the long table where she worked and pulled out a scrap of material. "This is cotton, which should do nicely. I have linen as well, but it's a little dearer."

"The cotton will be fine, thank you."

"You're looking very well, Martha," Meribeth said. "That bonnet really suits you. And your wrap is lovely."

"Thank you," Martha said. Thaddeus could see that she wasn't prepared to offer any more information than he had.

"Indian paisley is all the fashion just now. I had a lady in here yesterday who ordered one just like yours."

"It's nice to know I'm in style," Martha said. "How much do I owe you for the buckram?"

She named a price and Thaddeus handed over a few pennies in payment, and then they went out the door, leaving Meribeth's curiosity unsatisfied.

"I wish your father hadn't mentioned Clementine's name quite so loudly," Thaddeus muttered. "It would be better if no one knew we'd seen her again."

He turned his head to make this remark to Martha and failed to notice a man in a plaid suit walking directly in front of the door. Thaddeus had to stop abruptly to avoid a collision with the result that Martha ran into the back of him and dropped the parcel she was carrying.

"Sorry," he said. The man nodded at him and went on.

"That was the man on the wharf the other day, wasn't it?" Martha said.

"Yes, I believe so," Thaddeus said. He stooped to pick up Martha's parcel. As he straightened, he noticed a woman in a big black hat watching them from across the street, but as he had never been able to see past the brim of the hat, he couldn't be sure that it was the same woman who had blocked his view out the steamer window.

Chapter 3

After the guests had all been served and the family had eaten their noontime dinner, Francis beckoned Martha into the dining room. Sophie joined them.

Thaddeus helped Letty wash the dishes, then he casually wandered into the small sitting room at the front of the hotel. It was right across the hall from the dining room, but from there he could hear only a murmur of voices. At least Francis wasn't yelling. All of his anger had been reserved for Thaddeus.

He picked up a newspaper and attempted to read an article about the life and recent death of Lord Arthur, the autocratic one-time Lieutenant-Governor of Upper Canada, but his mind kept wandering to the subject of what he would do if Francis tried to make Martha stay in Wellington. Or more to the point, what Martha would do. Thaddeus had no wish to get into the middle of an argument between his granddaughter and his son-in-law, but he could scarcely sit idly by and let her go off by herself as she had threatened to do.

Finally he decided that the conversation wasn't going to end anytime soon and that it would probably be better if he wasn't discovered sitting right across the hall attempting to listen to it. He'd go for a walk and hope something had been resolved by the time he returned.

Disinclined to exchange small talk with anyone, he avoided Main Street and headed down to the harbour. He wandered through the rows of fishing vessels that had been hoisted up onto cribs for the winter, their exposed keels bare and forlorn looking. This was a favourite place for the village children to play hide and go seek in the wintertime. There were good hiding places, and one could elude the seeker simply by sliding in and out of the shadows cast along the ghostly rows by the bright winter sun.

But this was a school day, and no one was about except for old Bert Marshall, come to check the tarp that covered his fishing boat.

They nodded at each other.

"Nice day," Thaddeus said.

"It is," Bert returned. "Glad to see the end of the wind."

Thaddeus walked past him, to stand a little further down the shore. The cold temperatures and bitter winds of the week before had pushed the waves up into frozen jumbles of ice near the shore, but now pools of water were collecting in low spots as the sun softened them.

Thaddeus spent some time looking out across them, lost in thought about the future and what it might bring. If she made her case with Francis, Martha's plans would relieve him from making any important decisions for a year. If she didn't, he would have to develop some sort of plan of his own. He had no idea what it might be.

A scrabbling noise behind him and somewhere off to his left brought him back to the present. Another fisherman, come to check on his boat? He couldn't see anyone. A rat, maybe, they were common down here at the harbour. He thought he caught a glimpse of someone stepping into a shadow, but when he peered closer he wasn't sure that there was anything at all.

It didn't matter. He had used up a considerable amount of empty time. He'd make his way back to the hotel and see if anything had been decided.

As he turned to go, he once again thought he heard something, but he ignored it and walked back to the main street.

Everyone was in the kitchen when he returned. Sophie had made tea and as he walked into the room, she placed a plate of cookies on the table. Martha looked up and smiled at him, but it was impossible to tell from her expression whether she was pleased or not.

And before long, it was time to begin preparing for the supper service.

"I'll set the tables," Thaddeus said. He wasn't surprised when Martha offered to help.

"He wants to talk to you again," she said when they were alone in the dining room. "It's not settled yet, but I stuck to my guns. Your turn now."

And sure enough, when their own supper was finished, Francis rose and looked at Thaddeus.

"A word with you?"

Thaddeus followed him into the dining room and took a chair in the corner, away from the door, just in case a guest should happen to wander back down the stairs from his room.

Francis remained standing, and got straight to the point.

"I had a long talk with Martha. She seems determined to go off somewhere and do something and there seems to be little I can say to stop her. She was very polite about it, and made it very clear that it had nothing to do with any unhappiness with me, but she was clear nonetheless. She says she likes the idea of being a teacher, and I have nothing else to suggest anyway, so it seems as good a plan as any. I'm sure she'll do well, and as you pointed out, it will provide her with a respectable way to earn a living if she's so determined not to stay in Wellington."

He glared at Thaddeus, his anger surfacing again. "My concern is you. I would be a lot more comfortable with this, Thaddeus, if I knew what you'd be doing in Toronto."

"I'm sorry, I don't know what to tell you. I don't know yet."

"You've been adrift for a long time, you know. I thought you'd sorted yourself out when you went back to preaching, but I'm not sure your heart was ever really in it after Betsy died."

"I'd have to agree with that." It was a fair enough statement. Thaddeus had known it at the time.

"Martha isn't Betsy. You can't expect her to keep you company forever."

"I know."

"I have some stipulations," Francis said, and Thaddeus knew

that Martha had won him over.

"I expected nothing less."

"Should you find yourself involved in another one of your adventures, you will keep Martha strictly out of it."

"I can't imagine what adventure there would be," Thaddeus protested. "My aim is to lead a quiet life and help Martha with her studies."

"If I know you, sooner or later something will crop up. I don't care what you do about it, but I do not want Martha involved in any way."

"I have no difficulty with that." Thaddeus said. "I'd already decided that anyway."

"Then that's understood. Now - where would you be living?"

"Either a small house somewhere near the school, or I suppose we could take rooms somewhere in the general neighbourhood." He hesitated for a moment before he added, "That way if Martha should run into difficulties of any sort, Luke is nearby."

Thaddeus's son Luke was a doctor in the small village of Yorkville, just to the north of Toronto, and not far from the Toronto Normal School.

Francis looked dubious. "Luke the confirmed bachelor? What does he know about looking after young girls?"

"Not much, I suppose. I'm just saying that if something were to happen to me, Martha could call on him. And I have friends nearby as well. They'd be happy to assist Martha should she need it."

"I'd prefer that you find a respectable boarding house. One with inflexible rules."

"I can ask Luke to find us one."

"And I need to know what happens if this all falls apart. What if she isn't admitted to the school, or if, for some reason, she has to leave?"

"Then I'll bring her back here. What happens after that will be up to you and Martha."

"And if she completes the course, she'll go off somewhere to teach?"

"If you allow it, yes."

"What will you do then?"

"I don't know. But this is about Martha, not me."

Francis looked bemused. "It seems odd, to send her out to work."

"She once said to me that women work no matter what they do. They just don't often get paid for it."

"Sophie said the same thing. And she's right, I suppose. I couldn't run this place without her. She thinks this is a fine idea and that Martha will make a wonderful teacher. They ganged up on me this afternoon," he said a little sheepishly.

"Women will do that."

Francis walked over to the window and stood there for a few moments, looking out at nothing. Finally he sighed and turned to look at Thaddeus.

"Martha has always been yours. I was gone too long and missed my chance to be a father to her." He held up a hand when Thaddeus began to protest. "Oh, I know, she holds me in fine enough regard, but I'm a poor second best to you and I always will be. All I want is for her to be happy, but I don't see how she'll ever be happy here, and the devil of it is that she'll never forgive me if I try to make her stay."

"I told her that the decision is yours. I won't gainsay you Francis." Thaddeus felt his heart could break for this man, who lost a wife and forfeited a daughter.

"It's all right. Go ahead. Take her to Toronto." And then he glared again. "But for God's sake, look after her this time."

Thaddeus found Martha in the sink room helping Sophie wash the supper dishes.

"You go sit down, Sophie. We'll finish this off."

Sophie handed him the dish towel. "Thanks," and then she patted him on the arm as she left.

Martha looked at him wordlessly.

He grinned at her. "Looks like you're going to be a teacher."

Francis left it to Thaddeus to make the arrangements. He wrote to the Headmaster at the Normal School, and when a response arrived, he could see nothing in the stated requirements that would prevent Martha from attending.

Applicants needed to be at least sixteen years of age and certified to be of good moral character. As well, they were expected to read and write intelligibly and be acquainted with the simple rules of arithmetic. All prospective teachers were required to pass a basic entrance examination to demonstrate this proficiency before they would be allowed to enter the program.

Other than that, all Martha really had to do was declare her intention to teach school upon graduation.

To Thaddeus's surprise, both tuition and books were provided free of charge and the school also offered a small amount towards board for out-of-town students. It was another point in favour of the plan, although he was quite prepared to use the entirety of the generous payment he had been given by Towns Ashby to see them through the year. He was reasonably certain he had enough, but anything extra, even a small amount, would ease the financial pressure.

The subjects covered were the usual ones taught in any village school - reading, writing, grammar, composition, arithmetic, history and elementary science with a few more advanced courses in algebra, geometry, trigonometry, drawing, and the elements of logic.

Also listed was something called agricultural science. Thaddeus wasn't at all sure what this was, but as the letter indicated that there was a botanical garden on the grounds, he figured it must have something to do with farming. Practical teaching experience was offered in a model school setting. The course was split into two five month sessions, one beginning in January, the second in August.

As the granddaughter of a Methodist minister, the headmaster wrote, Martha sounded like an ideal candidate.

That would remain to be seen. Thaddeus's notoriety had apparently escaped the notice of anyone at the school, which was a relief, but Martha's experiences had made her far more worldly and independent than the usual run of minister's children. On the other hand, he supposed, any girl who was interested in becoming a teacher must have at least a little gumption.

He tucked the letter back into a pocket and turned his attention to the second piece of mail that had arrived that afternoon.

It was from Thaddeus's eldest son Will. Correspondence with his sons had always been sporadic. It didn't seem to occur to any of them to pass on the details of their lives unless something extraordinary happened, like the birth of a child or a severe illness. Their wives wrote to their own families, not to Thaddeus.

Will's letter was brief, to the point and more than a little facetious.

Dear Pa,

Last week I travelled down to London to attend a meeting connected with organizing the Grits in this riding and was astonished to discover that you are quite well-known in the town. I suppose that's not surprising given your involvement in the recent murder trial there. I was astounded, however, to discover that you are the object of a great deal of sympathy because of the tragic death of your wife in the Baptiste Creek Railway accident.

We knew that you had some sort of romantic entanglement while you were in Cobourg, and have endeavoured to be sympathetic to your difficulties, but I find it extraordinary that you failed to mention a subsequent marriage and bereavement since then. We would like to have known that we had a stepmother, even if it was only for the briefest of times.

I didn't know what to make of what I was told, and my informants must have considered me a singularly unfeeling son when I didn't respond in an appropriate manner.

This is, of course, your own business, and you are under no obligation to confide any details, but I must admit I remain,

Your puzzled son
Will

Complication upon complication. Thaddeus should never have let the rumours about he and Clementine Elliott get so far out of hand. It had seemed amusing at the time, but he had known even then that it was bound to cause difficulties down the road. It really was amazing how much trouble she could generate. He must come to terms with this, somehow, but the prospect of explaining it all to his family was more than he could deal with at present.

He shoved the letter in beside the first one and set off to tell Francis what the headmaster had written.

Thaddeus decided to use the time remaining until their departure for Toronto to prepare Martha for everything he thought she might need to know in order to pass the entrance examination. On stormy days they would claim a corner of the dining room after the guests left and he would set mathematical problems for her to solve, and refresh her memory on how to properly parse a sentence. He kept the arithmetic firmly focused on the practical, since he guessed that this would be emphasized in any course designed for country schools – how to calculate compound interest, for example, and how to express fractions as percentages. Martha had a ready talent for numbers. This didn't surprise Thaddeus. In his years as a teacher, he had found that it was most often the girls who were good at arithmetic, but they were seldom encouraged to learn anything beyond the basic bookkeeping skills needed to run a household.

On the days when the weather was fair, they would walk, most often to the village outskirts and then along a section of the Danforth Road that ran north of the village. It was a busy thoroughfare, but the frequency of carriage travel meant that its surface was well-packed and easier to negotiate than the back ways where snow had frozen into humps and bumps. As long as they were vigilant about approaching traffic, and stepped well to the side, it was by far the most pleasant place for a stroll.

As they walked Martha would reel off the capitals of the world or recite the names of the kings and queens of England. Thaddeus taught her a mnemonic that would help her remember the last. "Willie, Willie, Harry, Stee, Harry, Dick, John, Harry Three," she would chant, as she marched along, drawing curious looks from the people they passed.

"But why is there no mention of Matilda?" she asked one day. "The list is incomplete without her, isn't it? And what about Lady

Jane Grey? She wasn't there long, but she was there."

"I don't think either was ever officially crowned," Thaddeus said. "In any event, it's unlikely to come up in the initial exam. Maybe later, when you get into history in depth." But he was pleased that it occurred to her to ask the question.

He guessed that she would have no difficulty with the rudiments of logic course that she would take in the second half of her year at Normal School.

He guessed that she would have no difficulty with any of it – she had been well-grounded in the basics, and showed an ability to grasp concepts quickly.

By the end of the second week, Thaddeus felt that Martha was well-prepared, but he enjoyed their sessions and was reluctant to curtail them, so he expanded their review past what would be initially expected of her.

"What is the corollary of the statement 'All men are evil by nature?" he asked as they walked along one afternoon.

Martha was in a playful frame of mind. "All women are good?" she said and then laughed at his reaction.

"That's the sort of argument Mrs. Elliott used to put forward," he said. "Logical on the surface of it, and complete nonsense at its core."

"About Mrs. Elliott..." Martha began, but before she could complete the question a small buggy fitted with sleigh runners came careening around the bend in the road. They were well past Wellington's limits by this time, into the section of the Danforth that wound through meadows and woods, the shoulders of the road crowded with scrubby brush. Both Martha and Thaddeus stepped to one side to let the buggy pass, but there was no room to get off the road completely. As the buggy neared, instead of swinging out to give them a wide berth, the horse appeared to head directly for them. Thaddeus grabbed Martha by the arm and pulled her into a stand of sumac. As they crashed into the bushes, a thick branch walloped the side of her face.

The buggy didn't even slow down, but continued its breakneck pace toward Wellington, the horse spurred on, Thaddeus noticed, by the application of a whip.

"Are you all right?"

"I think so." Martha rubbed her cheek, where the branch had hit her. "Is there a scratch there?"

"No, it's just red, but it may swell up. You need to put a cold cloth on it."

He retrieved his hat, which had been knocked off when they plunged into the bushes.

"Whatever possessed the driver to go so fast so close to the village?" he said, brushing bits of twig out of the felt.

"I can only hope he slows down when he reaches the main street."

"If he can," Thaddeus said. "Maybe the horse got spooked and was out of control."

"Maybe." Martha said. "Let's not say anything about it, all right?"

"Why?" Thaddeus was puzzled.

"Because Francis will be sure to think it's somehow all your fault."

She had a point.

Francis was no longer combative, but he seemed distracted and grumpy, even with Martha, and especially when she made some casual reference to Toronto, and what she would be doing there.

"This place is turning into the Thaddeus Lewis post office," he grumbled when a bundle of letters arrived for Thaddeus one afternoon.

Since Francis was in such a cranky mood and everyone else was busy preparing dinner, Thaddeus took them to his room to read.

There were a couple of letters from members of Thaddeus's former congregations, people who had become friends and who still kept in touch. These, he knew, would be full of news of births, deaths and marriages, and the welfare of mutual acquaintances. He set these aside to read after dinner.

There was a letter from Bishop Smith, but when Thaddeus opened it, it was only a courtesy note to inquire as to his well-being. He wasn't sure what he had expected, or that it mattered anyway. Had Bishop Smith written to tell him that all of the Presiding Elders of the Methodist Episcopal Church of Upper

Canada were clamouring to have him return to preaching, his answer would have been the same: no thank-you. He'd write back at some point to thank the Bishop for his concern, and to let him know that circumstances had not changed.

The third letter was from his son Luke. Thaddeus had written to ask Luke's assistance in finding a suitable boarding house somewhere near the Normal School and Luke had replied promptly, but the contents of his letter were both gratifying and problematic.

Dear Pa,

There is no reason for you to go to the expense of taking rooms when you can reactivate your old arrangement here. Your bed is waiting for you in my sitting room, and as for Martha, we can move a bed into the little sewing room at the top of the stairs, since it is used at the present for nothing more than storing boxes.

Yorkville is close enough to the Normal School that she can walk in fair weather, otherwise there are regular omnibuses that will take her nearly to the door.

Dr. Christie is delighted at the prospect of having you here – in fact, he was the one who suggested it when I mentioned that you were looking for rooms. Apparently he misses you. I am, as he puts it, "exceedingly dull company". He is intrigued by Martha, and looks forward to meeting her.

Most importantly, our housekeeper Mrs. Dunphy has no objection either. In fact, she said, in her usual dour way, that "it's about time there was another woman about the place."

Let me know if this will suit. If so, I'll put Morgan Spicer's twins to work getting rid of boxes.

Feel free to come whenever you like – there is no need to wait until the term starts. In fact, it might be a good idea for Martha to get used to the city before she plunges into her studies. And Dr. Christie will be pleased if you come sooner rather than later.

Your Loving Son,
Luke

It would more than suit. Thaddeus had stayed with Luke and his eccentric employer while he preached on the Yonge Street Circuit two years ago. He enjoyed Dr. Christie's company and looked forward to sparring with him over the dinner table, and Martha might well appreciate the company of another woman, as uncommunicative as Mrs. Dunphy could sometimes be. They would be far more comfortable there than in bare rooms somewhere. Best of all, it would be far cheaper. He would contribute toward the household expenses, as he had done before, but this would amount to much less than it would cost him to stay at a boarding house. As far as Thaddeus was concerned, it was ideal.

But he would have to sell the idea to Francis.

Thaddeus waited until after dinner, when there was a lull in the day's chores.

Francis was immediately suspicious.

"Did you have this part of the plan all sorted out ahead of time as well?" he asked.

"No, I didn't. I honestly intended to find a boarding house, as you requested. I only wrote to Luke to ask his advice. But surely this will be even better. Luke will be right there. And Dr. Christie and Mrs. Dunphy can keep an eye on things as well."

"If that's the case, then why do you need to go at all?"

Thaddeus hadn't anticipated this argument. "I don't, I suppose, except that's what we already decided. I'm not sure Luke has time to take full responsibility for Martha, and I think the invitation was extended on the assumption that I was coming too."

"As long has somebody takes responsibility," Francis muttered and Thaddeus heaved a sigh of relief.

"If it's all right with Christie, I suppose I should be grateful," Francis went on. "Yes, go ahead, if you think it will work."

Thaddeus had been prepared for more discussion, and it was only when he relayed the conversation to Martha that he found out why Francis had given in so easily.

"I think Sophie's expecting again," she said. "And I think Francis is worried sick. There have been so many disappointments. He's got a lot on his mind right now."

It would certainly explain Francis's uncharacteristic irascibility. Thaddeus could only hope that things would go well this time, or at the very least, didn't end in disaster, which was always a possibility when it came to women and childbirth.

He sent up a prayer for Sophie's safety, and for the child's as well. And then he added an extra one for Francis, who wanted so badly to be a father.

Just before they were to leave for Toronto, another piece of mail arrived for Thaddeus. It was a package wrapped in brown paper with no return address. Puzzled, he ripped the package open. It was a Bible. An old Bible, bound in cracked brown leather. He opened the cover to check the flyleaf. There was no name or dedication, only a brief inscription: *ecalp efas a ni siht peeK Keep this in a safe place.*

Thaddeus knew of only one person in the whole world who could have written it. He had seen her do it once, when she was duping a customer into thinking it was a message from the spirit world. She'd started in the middle, a pen in each hand and wrote in unison toward the edges of the page, one side a mirror image of the other.

"It's quite a party trick, you know," she'd said. "It's the one thing I do that is truly impressive." The package could only have come from Clementine Elliott.

"Who's that from?" Martha asked.

"An old friend." Thaddeus glanced around the kitchen, but nobody else was paying any attention. He'd examine the Bible more closely when he could do it in private.

As soon as he could without drawing undue attention to the action, he rose and went to his room. Why would Clementine want him to keep a Bible in a safe place?

He sat down on the bed and thumbed the pages. The book fell open to reveal a fifty dollar American banknote. The message suddenly made sense. He held the book by the spine, spread the pages out with his fingers and shook as hard as he could. Seven more banknotes fluttered onto the bedspread. Then, just to be sure, he flipped through the pages again, but he'd apparently found them all. He stacked them in a pile and studied them while he considered what to do.

She must be in a jam. "A real pickle", as she had once put it. He'd promised he would help her if that happened, but when he'd promised it he thought it would entail galloping to the rescue somehow - to save her from a lynch party, perhaps, or to help her get out of town in a hurry - not to act as her banker.

What had she got herself into? And where had this money come from? From no honest source, of that he had no doubt. Four hundred dollars was a lot of money, by Thaddeus's standards. But not a lot by hers, if the quality of her hats and dresses was anything to go by. Had she sent it as a hedge against a rainy day, in case she ran through all her other funds? But if that was the case, why hadn't she simply put it in a bank account where it would be safe until she needed it? And then Thaddeus answered his own question. Because she wasn't sure she would be able to retrace her steps to get it, that's why.

He looked again at the brown wrapping the Bible had arrived in. The postmark was blurred, but he thought it said "Baltimore". She'd intended to go to Chicago. How had she ended up in Baltimore? She was on the move for some reason.

The more important issue, at least for Thaddeus, was his own role in this. If the money came from a criminal activity, was he complicit in the crime if he kept it for her? And if he didn't keep it safe for her, what should he do with it instead?

Thaddeus could think of only one person who would have an answer to this. As soon as he got to Toronto, he would go to Towns Ashby's office and ask. And even if Ashby had no answers for him, it was far too much money to leave lying around. Maybe Thaddeus could give it to Ashby for safekeeping. Surely that would protect him from any legal repercussions.

And in the back of his mind there was a tiny little niggle of happy anticipation. Sooner or later, he knew, Clementine would come looking for her money, and then he would get to see her again.

Chapter 4
Toronto, January 1855

At first, Martha had agreed to go to school because it meant that she wouldn't have to stay home. But now, as the coach pulled out of Wellington and turned west toward Toronto, she found that she was excited by the prospect of becoming a teacher. A major point in its favour was that it didn't entail any cooking or cleaning, or even any sewing, but as she thought about it more, she realized that if she could successfully complete the course and earn a certificate, she could lay claim to a profession. Almost like a doctor or a lawyer. Not quite so prestigious, perhaps, but of a higher status than any other occupation that was open to her.

But best of all, agreeing to go to school meant that she could be with her grandfather, and part of whatever adventure befell him next. And she was sure that there would be adventure. Adventure followed Thaddeus around.

She looked over at him and grinned. "Here we go," she said. "I'm glad our plan worked out."

He frowned at her. "You really are incorrigible you know." But there was no sting to the words. She could see that he was just as pleased as she was that they were, once again, setting off together.

The roads were solidly frozen, and the stage seemed to fly across the rock-hard surface.

"At least we won't have to get out and push," Thaddeus remarked as they went through Brighton, "but I wish they'd hurry up and complete the rail line. It's such an easy way to travel, now that I've done it."

Martha had to agree. The cold that had frozen the roads had also iced up the ports, but not even the steamers compared with the ease and comfort of traveling by train. But although the Great Western Railway had established a route from Toronto to points westward, the Grand Trunk was still struggling to complete its line from Montreal to Toronto, and winter travellers were forced to rely on the province's network of stagecoaches.

After what seemed like innumerable stops, they reached the staging inn at the north end of Toronto, found a carter to take them to Yorkville and arrived at Dr. Christie's house, bruised and exhausted, just in time for supper.

"I think I'm more nervous about this than going to school," Martha said as they approached the doctor's door. "I've heard so much about Dr. Christie, I'm not sure what to expect."

"No one is sure what to expect from Dr. Christie," Thaddeus said. "But my prediction is that he'll find you fascinating. Just don't be alarmed at anything he says to you. He tends to be a little direct when he's curious about something."

Thaddeus was surprised when Christie himself answered their knock. He never answered the door if he figured someone else was around to do it, and almost never even when there wasn't.

He gave them a typically exuberant welcome. "Lewis! Wonderful to see you! Come in! Just leave the baggage in the front hall," he directed the carter who had trundled them north along Yonge Street. "We'll get the baggage up the stairs ourselves."

Since the carter had no intention of doing anything else, he obligingly dumped Martha's trunk in front of the first step.

"I have no idea where your rapscallion son has got himself to," Christie said, taking their coats and flinging them over the newel post. "Never around when you need him. Never mind, we'll have a jolly time all by ourselves, now, won't we?" He stopped and peered for a moment at Martha. "Oh my goodness, this must be your granddaughter. How do you do, my dear?"

"Dr. Christie, this is Martha Renwell, Martha, Dr. Christie." The formal introduction was entirely unnecessary as Christie was paying no attention to Thaddeus. He grasped Martha's hand, and studied her face intently.

"I'm pleased to meet you sir," Martha said, and gave him a demure smile.

"I say, Lewis. You really outdid yourself with this one. Third generation bred better than the second, eh? Why have you been keeping her to yourself all this time?"

Then, before Thaddeus could answer, Christie turned toward the back of the house and bellowed.

"Mrs. Dunphy! Sherry!"

"'Get it yourself!" a voice shouted back. "I can't cook dinner and get you sherry all at the same time!"

"Ah well," Christie said. "There you go. Come into the parlour and have a seat and I'll get the sherry."

"Please don't bother on our account," Thaddeus said.

"Oh don't worry, my dear man. I haven't forgotten your temperance sensibilities. If you don't mind though, I'll bother on my own behalf. Please, sit. Sit." He waved them into a small parlour off the hall.

Martha giggled and followed Thaddeus into the room, which hadn't changed in any respect since the last time Thaddeus had been there. The furniture was still shabby, there were newspapers scattered everywhere and books had been shoved haphazardly onto a shelf along one wall. Martha paused in front of these, scanning the titles. She was still looking at them when Christie returned, glass in hand.

"A reader? My heavens, Lewis you have surpassed yourself," Christie said. "All this loveliness, and an interest in books as well. But of course, you're going to be a teacher aren't you, my dear? Hard to pass knowledge on if you can't read."

"It doesn't always follow," Thaddeus pointed out.

"No, I suppose not." This had apparently never occurred to Christie before.

"Come to think on it, one of the masters at the Normal School is a bit of an odd fellow. Ormiston. Goes to my church. Can't say I've ever been impressed by him. I must ask him some time if he knows how to read. I fully expect his answer will be in the negative, but evidently it hasn't prevented him from becoming a schoolmaster."

Martha looked at Thaddeus, unsure how to respond to this remark. Fortunately, the front door opened before a response seemed necessary, and Luke Lewis walked into the hall.

"Where have you been boy?" Christie boomed. "Out lollygagging around I warrant, and here your family is, anxious to see you."

Luke shrugged out of his coat, doffed the rather elegant hat he wore and smiled at them. It was a smile that immediately made you want to smile back. He moved with an easy grace as he walked over to his father and embraced him in a big bear hug, then he turned to Martha.

"You're all grown up!"

Luke and Martha's paths had not crossed often. Luke had gone with his brothers to the Huron Tract while Martha was still quite small, and upon his return, went to Montreal to study medicine. He had taken a position with Dr. Christie after graduation and had been in Yorkville ever since.

"She seems to have grown up rather well," Christie said. "Don't you think so, Luke?"

"If appearances are anything to go by, yes. And since my father was largely responsible for her upbringing, I'm confident of her character as well."

Thaddeus was startled. This was an eloquent little speech for Luke, who when he first arrived in Yorkville had often stuttered and stammered in Christie's presence. But now, although his youngest son's appearance seemed hardly to have changed at all since he was a student, his manner had acquired a confidence and polish that had been absent before.

Martha, however, was not content to be discussed as though she wasn't in the room.

"Yes," she said, "I'm far too old to sit in a bed of hollyhocks anymore," and Luke laughed.

"We did sit in the hollyhocks, didn't we? And then we skipped stones down by the shore. You were very kind to me that day, and I don't think I ever thanked you for it."

Fortunately, before anyone was obliged to comment that this had taken place on the same dreadful day that Betsy Lewis died, a voice called out from the dining room.

"Dinner's ready."

"We'd better go in," Christie said to Martha. "Once she's produced a meal, Mrs. Dunphy doesn't like to see it sit on the table for too long."

He led the way in and plumped himself down in his usual spot at the head of the table. Luke pulled out the chair to Christie's left for Martha, an action that appeared to startle the old doctor.

"Well done, boy, well done. Mustn't forget our manners with a lady present."

Martha stifled a fit of the giggles. Luke sat beside Martha and Thaddeus took the chair on the other side of Christie, the seat he had occupied when he'd stayed before.

"Just like old times," Christie boomed. "Just like old times, only now we have three Lewises at the table instead of just two." He beamed at Martha. "And I have to say that the third is by far the most pleasant. No offence to either of you," he nodded in the direction of Luke and Thaddeus, "but it has been many a year since I've had a lovely young woman sit at my dining table."

"Thank you, sir," Martha said. "I'll endeavour to contribute to the conversation as well as I can, but you'll forgive me if I become a little lost at times. You are all so well-informed I don't know if I can keep up."

Mrs. Dunphy plodded in with a tureen of soup before Christie could reply to this. To Thaddeus's amusement, she placed it in front of Luke, and then plunked herself down in her chair with only a nod at the rest of the company. Luke graciously served Martha, and then Mrs. Dunphy before he helped himself and proffered it to Thaddeus. Christie's eyes followed the bowl as it passed around the table and looked a little put out when it finally reached him last.

"You're looking well," Luke said to his father as Christie ladled his bowl full.

"Not having to ride has done wonders for my leg," Thaddeus said. "It can still flare up from time to time, but it's quiet most days."

"You've had some adventures since you left, I hear."

"Stumbled into one, went looking for the other," Thaddeus said. "I shouldn't have got involved in the case in Cobourg in the first place, but I have to say it led to some lucrative employment."

"Ah yes, Cobourg," Luke replied, and Thaddeus knew that he'd heard all about it. He wondered if Luke had been apprised of developments in London as well. He would have heard about the murder and kidnapping, of course. After all it had been in all the newspapers and even Francis knew about it. There really was no reason to think that Luke knew about anything else, unless Will had written to tell him.

The remark remained unanswered as Christie zeroed in on Martha. He seemed mesmerized by her.

"You had a very unsettling experience I hear," he said. "Kidnapped, they tell me."

"Yes, it was quite alarming. But I knew my grandfather would come for me and that helped."

"And you are quite recovered now?"

"Oh yes, no ill effects."

Christie leaned in closer. "You made the acquaintance of a phrenologist, I hear. Did he have skulls?"

"Yes, although most of them were plaster casts. He had a small collection of real ones, but he said they had been dug up from ancient battlefields."

"The newspapers said that there was an infant that had been pickled in a glass jar. Did you, by any chance, get a good look at it?"

Luke attempted to intervene in the macabre conversation. "Um...Dr. Christie...I'm not sure this is a subject that Martha will find comfortable."

Christie looked astonished. "But she says she's quite recovered!"

"Still..."

"It's all right, Martha said. "I don't mind. Yes, I saw the baby," she said to Christie. "But I was a little preoccupied at the time, being tied up and all, so I can't say I took a really close look."

"But it was intact? Well-preserved?"

"It appeared so. Mind you, her shoulder had been dislocated, so she floated rather...um... oddly."

"And what happened to it afterwards?"

Thaddeus answered for her. "It was handed over to the grandparents and given, I trust, a Christian burial."

"After dinner, maybe you should show Martha your bones so she knows why you're asking her all these strange questions," Luke said. "Otherwise she's apt to think that you're a madman."

"Would you be interested in seeing them, my dear?" Christie asked.

"Of course. My grandfather says they're extraordinary."

"Does he now? Does he?" Christie beamed at Thaddeus. "Your grandfather really is an excellent fellow."

"Yes, Martha said. "He is, isn't he?"

Luke rolled his eyes, then turned to his father. "How are Will and Moses getting on?"

Thaddeus knew that this was a valiant effort on Luke's part to deflect the dinner conversation away from bones and babies.

"Nothing much has changed since the last time I was there. Moses does most of the work and Will dabbles. The only thing that's different is that Will is dabbling in politics. He's all mixed up with the Grits."

"You'll have to explain that to me," Luke said. "I'm so busy I don't pay much attention to these things."

"It's a political movement that's gaining a lot of traction in the west. Essentially, representation by population, universal suffrage, expansion into the northwest territory, that sort of thing."

"Anarchists!" Christie suddenly pronounced. "Nothing but anarchists! The idea that some uneducated, illiterate man should be able to make a decision about who should govern is complete nonsense. They should all be hanged!"

For the first time, Martha looked alarmed. "It's all right," Luke said to her. "The noose is Dr. Christie's solution for almost everything."

"And an excellent solution it would be!" Christie said. "Get rid of the problems once and for all!"

"There's one thing I don't understand," Martha ventured. "Suffrage means voting, right?"

"Yes. And universal suffrage means that every man would get a vote regardless of whether he owns property or not," Thaddeus said.

"But what about women? Do the Grits want to give the vote to women too?"

"No, I don't believe so."

"Then how can they call it universal? Universal means everybody doesn't it?"

Christie threw his head back in a great roaring laugh, slopping a spoonful of soup onto the already stained tablecloth.

"A most logical conclusion! Well done, my dear. Marvelous! Not about to happen anytime soon, mind you, but bravo for thinking of it! It's clear to me, Mr. Lewis, that your intelligence skipped over your son and has been bequeathed to your granddaughter. You must see to it that as fine a mind as this is properly educated. It doesn't do to ignore the girls, you know."

"But..." Martha said, "I'm ..."

Luke shook his head at her, as if to say that there was little point in protesting that education was precisely the reason she was in Toronto, and that Christie had already commented on the shortcomings of one of the masters.

To everyone's astonishment, Mrs. Dunphy spoke. "I'd like to vote."

"Would you really, Mrs. Dunphy?" Christie asked.

"I have more education than most men and I work for my living. Why shouldn't I have a say?"

She didn't wait for an answer, but cleared away the bowls and plodded into the kitchen with them.

'My goodness," Christie said. "I had no idea she felt that way."

"I have to say I agree," Thaddeus said. "Mrs. Dunphy is an eminently sensible woman. She'd make eminently sensible choices."

"But what about the women who aren't sensible?" Christie said. "We'd be burdened with their choices as well."

Martha bravely jumped into the conversation again. "I know

more sensible women than sensible men. Perhaps it would be an improvement."

Mrs. Dunphy returned just then with a pot pie and Christie was deflected from the argument as he waited for her to dish it out.

"The soup was delicious," Martha said to her.

She seemed startled by being addressed. "Thank you, my dear. Himself seldom notices, although he manages to gobble it down fast enough." She glared at Christie. He ignored her, intent on his supper.

"Are you looking forward to going to school again?" Luke asked Martha.

"Yes, I think so, but it will seem strange to be back in a classroom after everything I've done in the last little while."

"I know what you mean," Luke said. "I found it strange, at first, when I went off to McGill after being on a farm for so long. Strange, and a little frightening. But I expect you'll find that many of your classmates are away from home for the first time, and you'll be at an advantage because you've already adapted to so many new situations."

"I hope so," Martha said. "That part of it really doesn't have me too worried."

"Then what is worrying you?" Thaddeus said.

"The examination. And then there's the actual lessons. I don't know if I'm smart enough to learn everything I'm supposed to learn."

"I'm sure you'll do just fine," he said. "And if you encounter difficulties, I'm here to help."

"As am I," Luke offered. "You have only to ask."

"And if all else fails," Christie said, "I'll have a word with this Ormiston fellow."

Martha looked appalled at this prospect.

"We'll have to make sure all else doesn't fail," Luke said in a low aside to Martha.

"What was that?" Christie said.

"I merely assured Martha that we're all here to help her in any way we can," Luke replied. Then he turned to Martha again. "I always found that the trick to taking a test was to deal with all the questions you know the answers to first. Then you can spend some time puzzling over the ones you aren't sure about."

Christie looked astonished. "Is that what you did at medical school?" he said.

"Yes," Luke replied. "I had no hope of answering absolutely everything."

"It's a good thing I didn't know that when I hired you," Christie said. "I expected to be informed about any glaring holes in your knowledge."

"It's all right," Luke said. "I picked it up as I went along. And I haven't killed anyone yet."

"That you know of," Christie replied.

"No one's complained."

"That's because they're dead already."

"Then there's nothing to worry about, is there?" Luke said with a smile.

Thaddeus was struck by how deftly Luke countered Christie's banter. A witty remark had always been the way to deflect the old doctor's eccentricities, but the remarks were flying around the table at a speed that was enough to make your head spin. Luke's self-confidence had obviously blossomed with his professional success. Thaddeus was equally impressed that Martha was so willing to jump into the fray, and Christie had been highly amused by her contributions. It looked as though they were all going to jog along together with a minimum of difficulty.

When they finished the main course, Martha jumped up and began clearing plates.

"No, no, you sit," Mrs. Dunphy said, but she looked as pleased as her dour face would let her. "I'll take them. It will be a few minutes until pudding."

"By which she means dessert," Luke explained.

"Would you truly be interested in seeing my little collection of bones?" Christie said. "We could look at it while we wait for the sweet."

"Yes, of course." She looked at Thaddeus, obviously in the expectation that he was coming with them.

"If you don't mind, I'd like a word," Luke said to his father.

"We're fine on our own, anyway. Just follow me, it's in the back room," Christie said.

Martha was wide-eyed.

"It's all right," Luke said. "It's quite fascinating. And Dr. Christie is quite harmless."

"I am, aren't I?" Christie agreed. "And alas, everyone knows it."

Luke waited until Martha and Christie disappeared into the back of the house before he spoke, and then he came straight to the point.

"I've been getting letters. The family's worried about you."

"Who? Francis?" Thaddeus said. "Don't worry, he made it clear that he's not too happy with me."

"Yes, Francis asked me to keep an eye on things. He seems to think that you and Martha together are a dangerous combination. But it's not just Francis. I've heard from Moses and Will too, and they started writing long before this latest episode."

"I'll concede that I have made some faulty decisions in the last while," Thaddeus said. "And now I suppose the chickens are coming home to roost."

"In all fairness, I have to say that their chief concern is what you're going to do with yourself. I'm told that you've declined to take another circuit."

"I've been asking myself that same question."

"Will seems to think you should settle down somewhere and sit by the fire or something."

"In other words, I'm too old to be much good for anything."

Luke shrugged. "You know, when I first came back from the Huron, I was shocked at how much you'd aged. Now that I'm older, I'm discovering that you're actually far younger than I thought."

Thaddeus had seemed old back then. He'd been carrying the weight of his wife's illness nearly as much as she was, but this was something Luke hadn't realized at the time. Since then he'd seen sickness sap the strength of whole families in their efforts to cope with it. He, himself, had been drained by the illness of a loved one.

He understood now what a load his father had been carrying. Afterwards, grief had weighed Thaddeus down for a long time. Now, though, Luke sensed that something had changed. His father seemed happier, even though, by all accounts, he'd had a miserable time in Cobourg.

"Moses thinks it would be a good thing if you married again. Preferably somebody with no children and lots of money." Luke offered this up cautiously, just to see where it took the conversation. Will had wasted no time in spreading the gossip he'd heard in London.

Thaddeus snorted. "Your brothers tried their best to find me a wife. I'm reasonably sure that every widow and spinster in Huron County was trotted past me in the brief time I was there. I didn't find any of the choices very appealing."

Luke laughed. "Yes, I remember that they did their best to marry me off as well."

And then to Luke's surprise, Thaddeus continued. "I thought, for a brief moment or two, that it might be possible. I'm not so sure now."

Luke waited in silence, wondering if Thaddeus was willing to confide anything more.

But when Thaddeus spoke again, it was of his need for work. "I intend to find some sort of employment, even if it's only short-term. Your friend Mr. Ashby was very generous. I have enough to do us for the meantime, but it won't last forever."

"Towns hasn't offered you anything else?"

"No. It's very much an as-needed sort of thing. And there's no guarantee that he'll need me at all."

"Well, the family will be relieved to hear that at any rate. They seem to blame Towns for putting you and Martha in danger."

"All Towns did was give me a job. It was me who put Martha in danger. That was one of the faulty decisions I made. And it's more or less how we ended up here, to mollify Francis."

"It's hard to imagine Francis being really angry about anything."

"He did it exceedingly well for someone who's not used to it."

"When I first saw Martha standing in the parlour, I was quite taken aback, you know. She looks almost exactly like how I remember Sarah, when I think of her."

"I know," Thaddeus said. "She looks like Betsy did too, back when she was young. Sometimes I think that's why God sent Martha, just so I won't forget."

"I can understand that, but your dependence on Martha is one of the other things that has everybody concerned. You're going to have to let her go someday. It's not fair to her otherwise."

"You don't understand anything," Thaddeus said. "It's not up to me. Martha will do what she pleases regardless of anything I might say. When it comes to getting her own way, she's exactly like her mother."

Thaddeus had described Dr. Christie's strange hobby of acquiring and reassembling the skeletons of animals, but when Martha stepped into the room she was astounded at the scope of his collection. She felt as though she had wandered into a menagerie that had been magically ossified in time and place. There were animals everywhere she looked. Or rather, the representations of animals - the flesh stripped away but the essential essence preserved in a ghostly menagerie of bones. She was enchanted.

She walked forward slowly, drinking in the wonder of what Christie had accomplished. Some of the skeletons were of commonplace animals, rabbits and mice and snakes. She found these easy to identify, as each of them had been posed in its most characteristic position – but there were others that she could only guess at.

"Is that an eagle?" she asked, of a bird skeleton that hung from the ceiling. She walked over to inspect it more closely. The wingspan was enormous, the bones spreading out over what seemed like half the room.

"Yes, it was a golden," Christie said, "and if I were you I wouldn't stand directly underneath it. I've never been able to fasten it to the ceiling securely. The hook keeps pulling out of the plaster."

Martha stepped hastily away and peered up to where Christie was pointing. She could see that the skeleton was sagging slightly to one side.

"Very finicky to put together he was," Christie went on, "and of course very delicate, and every time he falls down it's harder to put him back together again. I had the devil of a time figuring out how to make him look like he was in full flight and I'm reluctant to change the configuration. I'll just keep patching the plaster, I guess."

Martha understood what he meant by the configuration. The eagle looked as though it was about to swoop down on the small mammal that cowered below it.

"Is that a muskrat or a groundhog?" she asked.

"Hard to tell the difference to be sure, but if you look closely at the tail, you'll see it's a muskrat."

"How do you get the bones so white?" Martha had seen plenty of bones, some of them scattered along the paths she had walked, others merely what was left over after a meal. They had all been a dingy grayish colour.

Christie beamed. "Ah, that's the secret to the whole thing. You have to get them as clean as you can first, of course, and then you boil them up with magnesium carbonate. It makes them lovely and white and helps dispel any oils that are left in them. Mrs. Dunphy complains, of course, because it makes such a stink, but it really is essential for the preservation."

Next to the muskrat was a collection of smaller animals. Martha identified a salamander and what she thought must be a vole, and possibly a chipmunk.

"Come over here," Christie said. "This is my current pride and joy. A hunter brought it to me from back north."

Christie pointed at a skeleton that looked for all the world like a large cat.

"I don't know what that is," Martha said.

"A lynx!" Christie announced triumphantly. "You don't see them much this far south."

"No, I've certainly never seen one."

She walked around the lynx, fascinated. Christie had wired it together so that it was crouched, about to spring into a flying pouncing leap. She pointed to a heavy bone in its back leg.

"What is this bone called?"

"That's the femur. Come and look at the drawing and you'll be able to see it a bit better. I haven't quite finished it yet – I've been saving the head for last – but you'll be able to see how the femur fits into the joint."

She followed him to an easel, set up to catch the light from the massive window that had been set into the back wall. There on a sheet of drawing paper were the hindquarters of the skeleton on the bench. She could clearly see how the joint held the bone and how it must rotate in the socket.

"Oh, it's beautiful. I wish I could draw like that." She smiled at him. "One of the things I'm supposed to learn at the Normal School is how to draw, but I doubt I would ever be able to manage anything like this."

"I've had no formal art lessons," Christie said. "It took a great deal of trial and error on my part until I was satisfied with what I produced. I did discover a few tricks along the way, which I would be more than happy to share should you run into difficulties. He suddenly sounded quite shy. "Would you like to see some of the others I've done?"

"Oh, yes please, if they're as wonderful as this."

"You know," Christie said as he fetched a sheaf of papers from the workbench, "I've only ever shown these to a few other people, and they were nearly all Lewises."

Luke was called out just as Mrs. Dunphy served up a pound cake piled high with apricot preserves.

"Sorry," he said, "Old Mr. Pettit has taken a turn for the worse." He shrugged. "Not much I can do at this point, other than try to make him comfortable. I shouldn't be long."

Dr. Christie ate two helpings of dessert, gulped down a cup of after-dinner tea, then wandered back to his bones again. Martha helped Mrs. Dunphy clear the table, then when the housekeeper shooed her out of the kitchen, she joined Thaddeus in the front parlour.

"Well?" Thaddeus said, "What do you think?"

"Dr. Christie is a very strange man, but I think I like him."

"At heart he's a good soul."

"He's so rude! Especially to poor Uncle Luke."

"He knows he's old and not really needed anymore. Luke has taken over most of the practice. But they both pretend that Luke is young and foolish so Christie feels a little better about it. Luke thinks the world of him, and I suspect the reverse is true as well. So what did you think of the bones?"

"You told me about them, but I didn't really know what to expect. They really were… extraordinary. But I think the thing that impressed me most were the drawings he's done of them. And the fact that he knows the names of all the bones."

"He is a doctor, after all. They're supposed to know things like that."

"I know, but…" Martha struggled to find the words to say what she meant. "To spend all that time on something that only a few people will ever see seems a shame to me."

"It is," Thaddeus agreed. "On the other hand, it's a testament to learning for the sake of learning, which is perhaps the noblest form of education. It's essentially a hobby for Christie. He doesn't expect fame and fortune from it. He does it for the pure joy of the thing."

"It sounds sort of like being a preacher."

"In some respects that's correct. Christie saves bones, I saved souls."

"Do you miss it?" Martha had never really talked with her grandfather about his decision to give up the life of a saddlebag preacher, but she thought he must find it odd at times to stay in one place all the time.

Thaddeus took a few moments to answer. "I miss the idea that I was doing something good. I miss going to different places, but I don't miss the discomforts of travel. To tell the truth, there are some days when I wonder if I should have stayed home and looked after your grandmother a little better. I might have done more good there."

"I'm pretty sure that if grandma had wanted you to do that, she would have said so."

"You're probably right. I wonder all the same."

When Luke returned, he and Thaddeus carried the luggage upstairs, and Luke showed Martha the tiny room at the end of the hall that was to be hers.

"Are you sure this will be all right?" Thaddeus asked. "It's awfully small. We could always trade."

"This is fine. After school starts I won't be here a great deal of the time anyway. I can always sit at the dining room table if I need to spread my papers out. I know you're sometimes up in the middle of the night, so it makes more sense for you to have a good chair in your room, so you can sit and read without disturbing anyone else."

Truth be told, she was delighted with her little room. At some point someone had papered it with a rose pattern, and although the blossoms had faded with time, it was homey and pretty. There was room for little more than the small quilt-covered bed, a washstand and her trunk, but there were hooks on one wall for her dresses, a mirror on the back of the door, and a small window that looked out into the back garden. She would feel cozy and protected here.

And now that she had seen the bed, she realized that she was very tired. It had been a long day, and she could tell that her grandfather was weary as well. He made no objection when she suggested that it was time to retire.

And although she drifted off right away, it was a restless sleep. She would never had admitted it to anyone, but she wasn't "perfectly recovered" as Dr. Christie put it when he asked about her kidnapping. That night she had the disturbing dream again. She never saw her abductor's face in these nightmares – he would remain just out of sight – but within the dream she would know that she was helpless in the face of his power. She struggled against the bonds that held her and awoke covered in sweat, knowing that if it hadn't been for Thaddeus, she would never have got free. It was a dream she'd had a number of times before, but in this version her grandfather seemed to have magically grown younger and looked exactly like her Uncle Luke.

In spite of the fact that he was exhausted from their travelling, Thaddeus too found only a disturbed sleep that night. Finally, tired of tossing and turning, he gave up and got out of bed. Mindful of the fact that the floors creaked, he tiptoed to the chair by the big window that looked out from the front of the house. Here he could see into the street, deserted this late at night, and look at nothing while he considered his situation. His physical course seemed set, at least in the short term; as far as he was able, he would steer Martha through the coming months. After that she would have the means to look after herself, if necessary. He had been aware, right from the start, that the proposal for her further education might well take her away from him, and he felt a deep sympathy for Francis. It must seem to him that Martha had spun away before he'd even got to know her. And now there was every chance that she would spin away from Thaddeus too. And when it happened, he, like Francis, would have to stand aside and let her go.

Thaddeus knew that he'd lost his way badly after his wife's death and in many ways he was still lost, but he couldn't expect Martha to continue to provide him with purpose. She was a young woman, about to embark on a career and make a life of her own. She would no doubt marry at some point and then her husband and her family would occupy her attention and concern, not an ageing grandfather who, if Francis was to be believed, had a unique ability to cause havoc. Thaddeus had no idea what he would do, when all this came to pass.

If only Betsy hadn't died. He'd have been content with a quiet old age with her by his side. He'd have watched happily while Martha transformed from the little girl who held his hand to a mature woman with little ones of her own. It was wrong to want to hang on to her forever. But at this moment, just as she was about to take the first step on a journey that had an unseen destination, he wanted to call her back and keep things as they were, lest he grow too lonely without her.

His state of mind was troubling to him. It was ironic that so often in the past he had advised others to give their troubles up to the Lord, and yet Thaddeus had somehow lost the knack. He knew why – he was still angry because God had let Betsy die. He hadn't realized it until Clementine Elliott challenged him. He'd denied it at the time, but she was right. Irreverent, opportunistic, duplicitous

Clementine had told him a truth he didn't want to tell himself. Sometimes he wished she was still around so she could tell him what he should do next.

Chapter 5

The next day was a Sunday. Although there was no Methodist Episcopal chapel close by, Thaddeus knew that there was a meeting at Mr. Miller's house on the northern edge of the city. Or at least there had been when last he'd been in Toronto. His optimism was rewarded when he and Martha arrived at the door and Mr. Miller welcomed them in.

"Mr. Lewis! What a pleasant surprise! I had no idea you were back in Toronto. Come in! Come in!"

Thaddeus was relieved at Miller's reception. Apparently news of his adventures had not made his presence unwelcome here, if the news had reached this meeting at all – he'd always found that the Methodists in the larger centres were the last to hear gossip. They tended to see each other only at meeting, otherwise they were busy with jobs and families and lived less in each others' pockets.

There were only one or two people he didn't know. The meeting had not grown much in a year. But one of the people he had been hoping to see, a small, weedy man, jumped up out of his seat and strode toward Thaddeus, his hand out in greeting, a broad smile on his face.

"Thaddeus! Are you back in Toronto now?"

"Morgan Spicer! I was hoping I'd meet you here!"

"Sally! See who it is!" A raw-boned woman with carroty hair smiled at Thaddeus, and four nearly identical faces sitting beside her beamed. Spicer and his wife Sally had two sets of twins – boys and girls – about a year apart and, except for the differences in their clothing, they were like peas in a pod.

"Morgan, this is my granddaughter Martha Renwell," Thaddeus said.

Martha had been hanging back until then, but now she stepped forward.

"I'm so pleased to meet you. I've heard so much about you, Mr. Spicer. My grandfather holds you in very high regard."

"We've been through some adventures together, that's the truth." It was Spicer who had helped Thaddeus find his daughter's murderer, and together he and Spicer had investigated strange goings-on at the Toronto Strangers' Burying Ground, where Spicer was the sexton.

There was no time for further conversation, however. The meeting was about to start. Mr. Miller was the lay preacher who usually led the meeting, but now he looked a question at Thaddeus.

Thaddeus shook his head. He would not lead this meeting, nor any other.

"Perhaps you'll drop around afterwards," Spicer said. "I'm sure Sally could be persuaded to make us a pot of tea."

"I was hoping you'd offer." Thaddeus looked forward to resuming his acquaintance with the Spicers, and to sitting in their tiny kitchen catching up with the news. Morgan had been his protégé once, but was never able to wrangle the English language into the ground far enough to realize his dream of becoming a preacher. He had long since become resigned to his role as a keeper of dead bodies instead, his disappointment tempered by adoration of his wife Sally and their extraordinary offspring. Thaddeus had spent many hours reading to the Spicer children, and Morgan was grateful when they attained a proficiency that he, himself, had never managed. They probably didn't need to be read to any more – they could do it for themselves now – but to Thaddeus, tea was still a pleasant prospect.

And then they all took their seats and Thaddeus gave himself up to the simple pleasure of hearing someone else's worship service.

After the meeting Thaddeus and Martha walked with the Spicers toward the tiny Keeper's House that guarded the Toronto

Strangers' Burying Ground. The twins clustered around Thaddeus, and then one of the girls shyly slipped her hand into his. He gave it a small squeeze.

"So are you here for long or is this just a visit?" Morgan asked.

"For a year. If all goes well in the next few days, Martha will be attending the Normal School. Luke – well, Dr. Christie, I suppose – graciously offered to put us up."

Morgan's face broke into a grin. "It will be just like old times! Maybe I can find us another puzzle to solve."

"I hope not," Sally Spicer said to Martha. "The last puzzle nearly did them in." Her freckled face was screwed up in a disapproving glare.

Martha wanted to ask what she meant, but the girl twins began chattering at Thaddeus while the boys raced ahead, then turned around and raced back again.

"Your children certainly are energetic," Martha remarked.

"Yes, they've been a handful, but they're old enough now not to take much looking after. The boys are good about picking up odd jobs here and there. It keeps them out of trouble and they always bring their pay home, which is a help as well. They're good children, really, just rambunctious."

"That's one of the things I'm going to have to learn," Martha said, "how to deal with rambunctious children."

"Are you looking forward to being a teacher?"

Martha took a moment to answer. "I think so. At the very least, it's an easy way to keep the peace for now."

"It seems like a fine thing to me," Sally said. "I never got much schooling. Not that I was much good at it, anyway, but I'd like to do better by the twins. Your grandfather's been a help, what with reading to them and all. Morgan and I are very grateful to him."

"From what he's said to me, I think he enjoyed it just as much as they did."

"And that's makes it all the better, doesn't it? That they all liked it."

"That's the best of all," Martha agreed.

"And now here we are," Sally said. They had reached the graveyard, with its regimented rows of stones.

When they entered the Keeper's cottage, Sally tried to shoo them into the parlour.

"Can't we sit in the kitchen Sally?" Thaddeus asked. "That's where we always sat before."

"I thought perhaps, with your granddaughter here, it would be nicer in the parlour," she said.

"The kitchen is fine with me," Martha said. "Please don't go to any special trouble."

Thaddeus made straight for the kitchen table and took the chair that he was obviously used to sitting in.

"All right", Sally said, "but the twins are a nuisance in so small a space." She turned to them. "Go play outside. I'll call you when tea is ready."

They obligingly went running out the door.

"I know it's Sunday and we're all supposed to be quiet and everything," she said to Thaddeus, "but I can't keep them still for very long. It's just not in their nature."

"That's all right," he said. "I can't imagine that God would ever be upset by happy children."

Martha felt this was a far cry from his attitude when she had been small. She had spent many an excruciating Sunday afternoon being told to do nothing. She didn't make any comment though. Her grandfather looked so happy she hated to spoil the mood. Instead, she handed her cloak to Sally, who hung it on a peg in the hall, then busied herself making their tea.

"They haven't closed the Burying Ground yet, I take it?" Thaddeus asked.

The Burying Ground was smack in the middle of Yorkville, a fact the villagers found most annoying. They would like it moved, but were reluctant to pay anything towards the removal. Instead, the trustees were attempting to get families of the deceased to take care of the matter, without quite having realized that the deceased, by and large, had no families. It was why they had been buried at the Strangers' Ground in the first place.

"Things slowed right down after the first half dozen removals," Spicer said. "There's really been nothing done since then."

"So your job is safe for the moment?"

"The Board of Trustees keeps me on to cut the grass and watch over things for the time being, but there are no burials any more, what with them wanting to move the graves to the Necropolis. I fill in over there now and again. They keep paying me the same, and we're still in the house, small as it is. And they don't seem shy about setting me to other tasks. One of the trustees also sits on the board at the House of Industry. He's supposed to be a Visitor but he doesn't like doing it, so he sends me instead."

"What's a Visitor?" Martha asked.

"Someone who goes out into the community to see who needs help," Spicer replied. "Only the most dire cases are admitted to the House. Most of the poor are given outdoor relief, but someone has to recommend that they need it. It's supposed to be looked after by the gentlemen of the city, but in my case it's been delegated." He shrugged. "I don't mind. It gives me the opportunity to do something for the living while I'm still looking after the dead. I go on Tuesday afternoons usually. You wouldn't care to come along, would you Thaddeus?"

"I'd be honoured to help. I won't have much to do while Martha is in school. It would be good to keep busy."

"I'd be happy with that," Sally said. "I hate it when he goes off alone. It's a rough old part of town he covers."

"Yes, it's a shame the poor don't live in a better neighbourhood," Morgan said, and Thaddeus laughed.

Sally looked a little shamefaced. "You know what I mean," she said.

"Don't worry," Morgan said, "I'm careful. But it will be better with two of us."

And then the conversation turned to what had happened in Yorkville since Thaddeus had been gone.

"The village has grown quite a bit just in the last year," Morgan said. "And now there's talk of building a reservoir so water doesn't have to be hauled up from Toronto Harbour."

"If they can't persuade the people of Yorkville to pay to move a graveyard, how will anybody get them to pay for a reservoir?" Thaddeus asked. "They should just give it up and annex themselves to the city. It's going to happen sooner or later anyway."

"I hope it's later," Morgan said. "We don't need to get tangled up in Toronto politics."

"Do you think Hincks and Bowes will be held to account?" The legalities of the sale of railway stock by the Premier of the Province of Canada and the Mayor of Toronto had been called into question, and now scandal was looming, but Thaddeus wasn't sure that any of the mud would stick. "I can tell you a thing or two about railways and shady deals. There was enough of it going on in Cobourg. I doubt it's different anywhere else."

"Enough politics," Sally said. "There's nothing any of us can do about it anyway."

The conversation returned to village gossip, and when they had exhausted that topic, Thaddeus gulped down what remained of his tea and rose to leave.

"Luke will be wondering where we've got to," he said.

When Sally retrieved Martha's coat, she leaned close and said, "If you ever need anything, please let me know." She blushed a little. "Not that somebody like me could be much help with what you're doing, but just so you know – if there's anything I can do."

Martha smiled. "Thank you. My grandfather already told me I could count on the Spicers."

Thaddeus called for Morgan just after dinnertime on Tuesday.

"I know I'm a little early," Thaddeus said, but I have a couple of errands to see to before we do your rounds, if that's all right with you."

"Of course. We have to take the bus into Toronto anyway. It makes sense to do as many things as you can while you're there."

They boarded the omnibus that was waiting in front of The Red Lion Tavern and began the rattling ride down Yonge Street. The city seemed much nearer than it had when Thaddeus had last stayed in Yorkville. Toronto continued to grow at a blistering pace and everywhere Thaddeus looked new buildings filled the empty fields he remembered. It wouldn't be long before Toronto swallowed up places like Yorkville, whether the citizens of Yorkville were in favour of it or not. Who knew how many miles the sprawl would cover as time went on? He could imagine that it might someday reach as far as Davisville or Eglington, as improbable as that had once seemed.

They rode down into the city's centre, past shops and factories of every description – dry goods, hardware, books and stationery were all on offer. Pianos and stoves and saddles and buggies. Everything you could think of was being made in Toronto, and the jobs and money this provided fueled the growth that spilled northward.

Thaddeus had no difficulty finding Towns Ashby's office. He knew the address from their previous correspondence and when he arrived at the building on Adelaide Street, conveniently near the courthouse, he found the entrance marked by a handsome brass sign.

The office was occupied by a harried young man and piles of paper.

"Could I help you with something?" the young man asked, but he didn't look up when he said it.

"I'm wondering if Mr. Ashby is in," Thaddeus said.

The young man frowned. "Did you have an appointment?"

"No. I'm not a client, I'm an acquaintance." Thaddeus thought "friend" might be too strong a word for his relationship with Ashby, and "former employee" would open the door to too much explanation. "I find myself in the city unexpectedly, and I thought I would drop by to make my presence known."

The young man finally looked up. "Oh," he said. "I'm sorry. Mr. Ashby is out of town and won't be back for some time. Would you like to leave a message?"

"Yes, please. Could you tell him that Thaddeus Lewis called."

The man scribbled the name and the Yorkville address on a piece of paper. He misspelled the name, but Thaddeus didn't think it would make any difference, as he was reasonably sure that the piece of paper would soon be lost in the mess of other papers that littered the office. He tipped his hat and left.

So much for asking Ashby's advice. Or for leaving Clementine's money in his safekeeping. Thaddeus wasn't sure what to do now. He didn't like the idea of carrying so much cash around with him, especially since he and Morgan were headed for the poorest section of town.

And then, as they walked along the street, they passed The Bank of Upper Canada building. He could open an account and leave the money there. He would have to do it in his own name, he decided. She wouldn't have any documentation to prove that she was Clementine Elliott and he had no idea what her real name was. It would have to do.

He filled out the bank's forms and handed over the money. The teller frowned a little.

"Is there a problem?" Thaddeus asked.

"No – it's just that notes drawn on American banks are a bit of a nuisance to redeem," the teller said. "But that's not your problem, it's ours." And then he smiled and gave Thaddeus a passbook that recorded the details of the transaction. "Thank you for your business, Mr. Lewis. We hope to see you again soon."

It was the amount of money he had deposited that made the teller so friendly. Not that anyone at a bank had ever been rude to him, but neither had they shown the deference that was usually afforded to the well-heeled. It was the first time that this had ever happened to Thaddeus, and he was amused by it.

And then, just to provide a stark contrast to the day, he and Morgan set off in search of poor, indigent souls in St. John's Ward.

The worst part of it, Macaulaytown, had grown on what were supposed to have been spacious park lots for those with the means to build mansions. Too many of the owners had been unable to resist partitioning the lots and selling them off, and now weather-beaten wooden buildings huddled under the imposing shadow of Osgoode Hall, the seat of all things legal in Canada West. It was a neighbourhood of shacks and sheds and dilapidated tenements that had over the years acquired both a permanent look and an air of imminent collapse.

"A lot of the people living here now work at the breweries and the brickworks and the new factories," Morgan said, "but there are a lot who fan out to the farms in the spring and come back here when the harvest is over. Sometimes they don't have enough to make it through the winter and find themselves in dire straits."

"Are you just looking for the people who need to go to the House of Industry, or for the ones who need outdoor relief as well?" Thaddeus asked.

"Both. Generally speaking the House of Industry takes only those who have no hope of finding work. The sick, the injured, the elderly, the orphans. Our job is to figure out who should go in and who just needs a little help."

"Are there many of them?" Thaddeus asked.

"Enough. Some of them are new immigrants, but most of them are just people who have fallen on hard times. The African community tends to look after its own and so do the Catholics - the Catholic Church is talking about building their own poorhouse, mainly because of the numbers of Irish needing it, I guess. But we don't ask about religion, we just try to look after whoever we find."

In Thaddeus's opinion nearly everyone they saw needed help. Too many people were crammed into buildings never meant to accommodate so many. Some of them were never meant to accommodate people at all, but had been converted from chicken houses and pigsties, tucked away in back yards next to overflowing, stinking privies. There were children everywhere, swarming to beg a penny, years of accumulated dirt on their underfed bodies.

Spicer shooed all but one of them away. "Do you have anybody for me today Bucky?"

"There's a lady in the back room over there," the boy said, pointing off to his right. "At the end of the hall. She's in a sad state with little ones. Nobody knows who she is. Hunkered down there last week."

Spicer handed over a coin. "Thanks. Keep your eyes peeled, will you?"

The boy nodded and scurried off, clutching his money.

"I hate to send so many away with nothing," Spicer said, "but generally speaking the ones that are healthy enough to beg aren't the ones that need the most help. There's only so much relief to go around." His face was grim. "Bucky's pretty reliable. The rest of them would tell me anything for a penny."

They walked over to a two story wooden house that looked as though it could fall over in the next gust of wind. One end of the foundation had sunk, and the roof beams were twisted as a result. The cladding was weathered and grey and split in places. And to Thaddeus's astonishment, the front door and all of the windows had either been removed or never installed in the first place.

"Is this building derelict?" he asked. "There can't be anybody living here, can there?"

"All sorts of people live here," Spicer said. "It's regularly rented out."

"But there are no windows."

"No. Apparently the landlord removed them. I don't know why."

The front door led to a narrow, evil-smelling hallway, with rooms on either side. There were no doors here, either. Nor were there any people, although there were plenty of signs of habitation – bits of rag scattered here and there, ashes piled up in make-shift grates, a grubby torn corset, a shoe with a hole in the bottom of it. Nothing of value was left behind while those who lived here worked, or looked for work, or simply fled out on to the street, only to return at night to huddle against the cold.

Morgan walked down to the end of the hall, and stopped at the last doorway on the right. He knocked on the jamb. A woman and three small children squatted together in the corner of a tiny room, no more than a closet, really.

"I'm from the House of Industry," Morgan said. "I'm here to see if you need any help."

It was evident that she did. Her cheeks were hollow, her face was dirty and her hair hung down in greasy hanks. The children were filthy and skeletal.

"The poorhouse?" the woman said.

"Well, yes," Morgan replied. "But you don't have to go there to get help."

The woman sighed and pulled the smallest child closer. "The children would be better off in the poorhouse. Can you take them there?"

Thaddeus was surprised at how well-spoken she was, and that

she spoke with a Canadian accent. He had expected to hear the tones of some foreign land.

Morgan hunkered down so he was at eye level with her. "I don't think so," he said. "They're not orphans or anything. Do you have any work?"

The woman shook her head. "I don't know where to look. And even if I found work, who would see to the children? I can't leave them here all day."

She was right. Even when he took their half-starved condition into consideration, Thaddeus judged that the oldest was no more than four.

"What happened to you?" Morgan asked her softly.

She began to weep, the tears making tracks down her dirty face.

"I don't know where my husband is," she said in a low voice. "He just left. I haven't heard from him in weeks. I don't know what to do."

"Do you have any family who could help you?" Morgan asked.

She shook her head. "They're all gone. And Amos is gone too. I don't know where to turn."

"I don't think the House of Industry can take you," Morgan said. "It might be a better plan to provide you with a meal ticket. That way at least you'll have some food, and then maybe you can figure out how to get some work."

He wrote the details in the book he carried, then handed her a printed ticket. "Do you know where the House of Industry is?"

She nodded.

"You go there tomorrow, round to the back, not to the front door, and they'll give you some bread. And they can arrange to give you some coal as well. All right?"

She nodded again.

He stood up. "Do you know if there's anybody else in this building who needs some help?"

"I don't know. I don't know anybody here."

Thaddeus fingered a couple of coins in his pocket. He couldn't afford to do much, but he could certainly spare a couple of pennies. It would be enough to see them through the day, and they could go to the poorhouse tomorrow. He handed them over.

"Bless you sir," the woman sniffled. "Thank you."

"You can't do that with them all, you know," Morgan said as they walked back out to the street. "There's a neverending supply. You'd soon use up all your money."

"I know," Thaddeus said. "But I have to do what I can." Especially since he had just deposited a large sum of money into a bank account that had his name on it. The money wasn't his, but he felt guilty about it all the same.

Spicer led the way along the filthy street and deeper into the warren, following paths that snaked though what once were back gardens. No one here had bothered to clear the snow away, and Thaddeus's trousers soon became sodden as they waded through drifts that had piled up between the buildings. They passed an old woman who sat on the ground in front of a fire that smoldered beside a small shed.

"Are you from the poorhouse?" she asked as they walked by. "There's a man should go there. He's only got one foot, and the end of the one that ain't there stinks to high heaven."

"Where?" Spicer asked.

"Over on the next street, just by the corner. In the house that's got the hole in the roof."

"Thank you. And are you all right yourself, ma'am?"

"I'll bide. Jake's got work at the foundry."

Spicer nodded and they made their way to the next street, to where, as the woman had indicated, there was a weathered single-story house with a hole in the roof. It was quite a large hole. Thaddeus couldn't begin to guess what had caused it, but he could see that no attempt had been made to repair it.

They were about to enter when the door suddenly flew open, nearly knocking Spicer to the ground. He staggered a little and Thaddeus quickly grasped his arm to keep him from falling.

A burly man burst out the door and snarled at them. Thaddeus was about to remonstrate when he realized that the man had a face that was only too familiar. It was an ugly, misshapen face, with welts and sunken scars that had healed badly. Cuddy Nelson, once the henchman of a notorious crime boss, and Thaddeus knew exactly what had happened to his face. Cuddy had once chased

Luke and Thaddeus and an Irish girl across the streets of Toronto and Luke had set a vicious dog on him so that they could get away.

Thaddeus quickly lowered his head, as though in concern for his companion, and hoped that the brim of his hat was enough to cover his face. Cuddy stopped and looked at them for a moment, but evidently he found nothing to concern him, so he went on his way.

"Are you all right?" Thaddeus asked Spicer.

"Yes, I'm fine. Did you see who it was, who nearly knocked me over?"

"Yes. I'm hoping he didn't see us."

The incident with the dog hadn't been the only interaction with Cuddy. Thaddeus and Morgan and Luke had all been present when Cuddy accidentally shot his boss during an altercation at the Strangers' Burying Ground. Thaddeus had testified at the trial. He had taken great care to stress the accidental part of the incident and there had been no repercussions for Cuddy at the time, but there was still the business with the dog. Thaddeus didn't really know if the thug still bore any ill will or not , but he was just as happy not to take a chance on it.

"I often see him down around here," Spicer said. "I think he works for one of the landlords. It was probably him who took all the windows and doors out of that building."

"Does he ever bother you?"

"Not so far. I'm not sure he realizes who I am."

Not surprising, as Spicer would be easy enough to overlook on his own, but Thaddeus was afraid that the two of them together might jog Cuddy's memory. Maybe visiting the poor hadn't been such a good idea after all. There was no help for it on this day, however, and Thaddeus followed Spicer into the building. At least this one had doors and windows.

But no hallway that Thaddeus could see. Instead, rooms opened on rooms, in a long progression through to the back. Small children regarded them solemnly as they passed, and two women who were lying on pallets on the floor raised their heads. Whores, he suspected, sleeping away the day until it was time to ply their nighttime trade on the streets of the city.

It wasn't until they reached the fourth room that anyone asked their business.

"We're looking for a man with one foot," Spicer said, and a bearded man directed them through what appeared to be a closet to a tiny room on the other side of the house.

"Hello?" Spicer called, and was answered with a feeble "Here!"

They followed the voice to a corner where lay a sorry-looking man with a filthy bandage where his right foot should have been. A sickly smell permeated the room, rising above the usual smells of urine and worse.

"Can you stand at all?" Spicer asked.

"I can if someone helps me up first," the man said. "Then I can jump along, like, with my stick." He held up what was little more than a branch from a tree, picked up off the ground after a windstorm.

"Has anybody seen to your foot?"

"Not since I chopped it off. Somebody looked at it then, and wrapped it up. Don't know if he was a doctor or not. Shoulda been more careful with the axe, I guess."

"Do you have anyone to look after you?"

"Just the boys in the next room. They'll fetch me water and food if I give them a coin. I don't have much coin left, though, so I don't know how long they'll keep on doing it."

Spicer made a note of the details of the injury, and the man's name, in the book he carried.

"Will you go to the House of Industry if I fill out the ticket?" he asked.

"The poorhouse?" The man looked worried.

"They'll look after your foot and feed you. If you get well enough that you can work again, you can always leave."

"I don't know about taking charity," the man said. "It's not our way."

"It's only for a little while. You can't work right now, and you've no money left. If you stay here, you're going to die, and then charity will have to bury you."

Thaddeus thought this statement was a little harsh, but it seemed to get results.

"I suppose you're right," the man said.

"I'll put your name in, and somebody will come and get you tomorrow. All right?"

In spite of his protest that he didn't want charity, the man looked relieved.

"That foot has gone putrid," Thaddeus said when they reached the street again. "I could smell it."

"I know," Spicer said. "He'll lose more of his leg before he's done, but there's maybe a chance he'll survive it. And if he dies, at least he'll die in a bed."

They worked their way along Spicer's route, and by the end of the afternoon he had given out four more meal tickets, but had not found anyone else in such dire straits that they needed a recommendation for admission.

Thaddeus was of the opinion that everyone they saw was in dire straits, but he supposed Spicer knew what he was doing.

They had one last call to make before they could catch a bus for home.

"I need to drop my recommendations off at the House of Industry," he said. "It's just up here on Elm St."

It was an imposing building with tall narrow windows and doors, a steep roof and large chimneys. It would be daunting to approach its door and ask for help.

"What happens to the people who are taken in?" Thaddeus asked.

"They're given what they need," Spicer replied. "Food, medicine, a bed. They're expected to help out with the chores if they can, but it's not a workhouse. Sometimes children will be sent out as indentured servants, or adopted. It's not ideal, but it's better than leaving them on the streets."

"I suppose," Thaddeus said. "But I hope I'd never be so desperate."

"You saw the truly desperate today. I'm not sure what else they can do. And the House of Industry is not so bad. Most of the rooms are dormitories, but there are sitting rooms as well, and a garden to walk in for those who are able. And some of them don't stay very long – they just need a little help to get back on their feet."

Spicer handed over the notes he had made, and then their duties were completed. As they rode toward Yorkville, Thaddeus couldn't help but give thanks for the hot meal and cozy bed that awaited him.

Thaddeus kept a sharp eye out for Cuddy Nelson as he showed Martha around the city. They walked for miles, Martha marveling at the church spires that thrust into the sky, the substantial brick buildings that crowded the streets, people walking, riding, shouting. She soon learned the omnibus routes, where the different stalls were set up at St. Lawrence Market, the best shops along King Street. Thaddeus was surprised that she was content with window shopping. He thought that she might want to spend a little of her money on something new to match her new adventure, but as much as she exclaimed over a handsome hat or a pretty piece of cloth, she admired it and walked on without buying herself so much as a new hair ribbon.

Occasionally as they walked Thaddeus would get the uncomfortable feeling that he was being watched, and would look around quickly in the hope of catching the culprit in the act, but he surprised no one out of the ordinary, just housewives, businessmen and workers intent, like themselves, on making their way along the crowded street.

Chapter 6

All too soon it was time for Martha to present herself at the Provincial Normal School, housed in an odd-looking brick building of two stories and occupying an eight acre block known as St. James Square.

The entrance to the school was imposing, with pilasters reaching up to the full height of the building, topped rather awkwardly by an open cupola. The site was elegant enough – or would be someday – situated at the end of a curving drive, and with a fine view of the city and the lake beyond, but the grounds had a raw, newly-planted look, as if the school had been plunked down in the middle of a meadow, and the meadow was not yet willing to surrender its hold. But with time, the orchards would grow, the gardens would be established and then, Thaddeus thought, it would be a very pleasant place indeed.

He escorted Martha through the massive front door and found an office to one side of the hall. Thaddeus stood back while she announced her business.

"This is your enterprise," he said. "You make the arrangements."

The clerk, who according to the small plaque on his desk was a Mr. A. Sorbie, recorded her details – name, age, previous education, home address – and then asked where she was staying while in Toronto.

Martha gave Dr. Christie's address.

Sorbie frowned. "That's not an approved boarding-house," he

said. "If you aren't living with family, we require you to stay at an establishment that has been vetted for suitability."

"I am living with family," Martha said. "My grandfather and I are boarding with my uncle's employer, and will be throughout my time here."

The clerk looked at Thaddeus dubiously. "It's a little irregular."

Thaddeus held out his hand. "Reverend Thaddeus Lewis," he said. "I wrote to the headmaster in the first place. We'll be staying with my son during our time here."

"Oh," the man said and blinked. "Yes, of course. Reverend, you say?"

"Methodist. Like your Superintendant. I'm retired, though. I'm pleased that I now have time to supervise my granddaughter's education."

"I see. Well, I'm sure it's all right. Just a little irregular. I'll make a note in Miss Renwell's file and pass it on to the headmaster."

Thaddeus couldn't fault the man for his caution. After all, the school accepted students who had never been in the city before, in some cases had never been further than the nearest village. Parents would need to be reassured that their children were adequately supervised while they were here. But he wondered what the man's reaction would have been had he not been dealing with an ordained minister.

"You should be here no later than nine o'clock tomorrow, and in the lecture hall by nine-thirty," Sorbie told Martha. "The morning consists primarily of orientation – we'll show you where everything is and give you some idea of what will be expected of you. In the afternoon we test your academic abilities, and from there we'll decide where you should be placed," here he looked at Martha sternly, "or whether, indeed, you should be placed at all."

Martha smiled at the man. "Thank you," she said. "That's exactly what I had been led to expect."

Thaddeus had to admire her self-possession and refusal to be intimidated.

Mr. Sorbie apparently admired it as well. His expression didn't give much away, but his lips twitched a little. "In the meantime, you're welcome to have a look through the grounds if you like."

"Well, what did you think?" Thaddeus asked as they left.

"Too soon to tell. I'll have a better idea after Monday. If I'm still here, of course. The building certainly is impressive."

The gardens were less so. They might achieve some degree of lushness in the spring, but at the moment everything was bare and brown or covered in snow. After a few minutes both Thaddeus and Martha decided that they had seen enough, and they headed back to Yorkville.

When they arrived back at the Christie house, Thaddeus discovered another package that Francis had sent on from Wellington. This one was bigger than the first one had been, and oddly heavy.

"What is it?" Martha asked.

"Just a book."

"What book? May I read it when you're finished?"

Thaddeus had not said a word to her about the Bible Clementine sent him. He'd promised Francis not to involve Martha in any escapades, and it was sure to be an escapade if Clementine Elliott had anything to do with it. It was better if Martha had no knowledge of it.

"Of course you may read it, if you have time," he replied in what he hoped was a casual tone. "But you may be a little busy from now on."

"You're probably right."

Thaddeus took the package to his room. He was certain of what he would find when he opened it.

Even so, he was surprised. Again it was an old Bible, the leather cracked off the spine and the boards scuffed. He opened it, expecting banknotes. Instead he found gold. Ten gold eagles worth twenty dollars each.

He checked the flyleaf.

!sknahT .evas ot tool eroM More loot to save. Thanks!

Clementine had hollowed out holes in the inside of the book and pasted the coins in place. No wonder the package had been so heavy. Again he checked the brown paper wrapping. Richmond, Virginia, the postmark said. It was clear that she was on the run from something. Thaddeus wished he knew what, exactly, but in the absence of any particular instruction, he couldn't think of anything to do with the money except put it in the bank with the rest she had sent.

Male and female students were to be strictly separated, Martha learned the next morning. She followed the other prospective students into a large lecture theatre, and was directed to take a seat on one side with the rest of the girls. Separation was a practice that would be strictly enforced, she was told. She didn't mind this so much – she was there to learn, not to flirt. She was surprised that there were so many older men in the male ranks. She had expected them all to be boys her own age. The females seemed generally younger, all neatly dressed, but only a few of them sported much finery in the way of lace or ribbon, and most of them dressed their hair modestly, in a style that was a little out of date. Farmers' and shopkeepers' daughters and ministers' children, like herself, eager to take advantage of the opportunity to better their lot in life.

The girl standing to Martha's left appeared very nervous, her hands shaking a little.

"Hi, I'm Martha."

"I'm Bernice," the girl whispered back. "Are you as scared as I am?"

Martha just shook her head and returned her attention to the introductions that were being made. The headmaster, Mr. Robertson, was a tall, dark-haired man with quite an alarming set of bushy eyebrows. Martha had to strain to understand him – he had recently arrived from the Dublin Teachers' Training School and spoke with quite a pronounced Irish accent. The second master was Mr. Ormiston. Martha fought a fit of the giggles as she struggled with a mental image of Dr. Christie asking the stern-faced Ormiston if he, in fact, knew how to read. She wrenched her attention back to the introductions of the other instructors - Mr. Hind, the drawing master, Mr. Rock and Mr. Sorbie, whom Martha recognized as the bespectacled clerk who had taken her particulars the day before. Mr. Sorbie's areas of expertise were apparently bookkeeping and physical education.

She paid closer attention to the teachers of the Girls' School, assuming that these were the people with whom she would have the most interaction, and who would have the most impact on her time at the Normal School. The Headmistress, Miss Clark, was a small, rather pretty woman – or she would have been had her hair not been done in quite so severe a fashion. Her assistants were Miss Shenick and Miss Cory. Miss Shenick was heavy-set and stern-faced and taught music, amongst other things. It was a subject that Martha was dreading. She already knew that she was virtually tone-deaf, and no amount of coaching was ever going to change that fact.

After the introductions, Mr. Robertson outlined the rules of the school. There appeared to be a myriad of them, and as each new regulation was announced, Bernice shook a little more. Martha reached out and squeezed her hand.

"Don't worry, it'll be all right," she said, and Bernice responded with a timid smile.

During their tour of the school, it became clear how rigid the gender segregation would be. A great deal of the ground floor was taken up by Department of Education offices and the lecture theatre, with the majority of the classrooms on the second floor. Each side of the building had its own cloakrooms, retiring rooms and entrances designated male or female. Even access to shared spaces like the lecture hall and the education museum were organized so that at no point would the two genders have an opportunity to interact. This resulted in a confusing arrangement of halls and passages.

The model schools, where they would be given actual classroom experience, were at the rear of the main building.

"I'll never find my way around," Bernice said. "It's too big."

"Yes you will," Martha said. "Whenever you go to a new place, it seems overwhelming at first, because you don't know where everything is, but it doesn't take long to learn. You'll be fine."

"I've never been anywhere new before."

Martha had already suspected this. "Where are you from?" she asked.

"St. Thomas. In the western part of the province."

"Is that near London?"

Bernice beamed. "Yes. Are you from London?"

"No, but I just recently visited there with my grandfather. I'm from Wellington, originally."

Bernice nodded, and it was clear that she had no idea where Wellington might be, but was unwilling to admit to the fact. Martha hoped that Bernice wouldn't stick too close. It was one thing to help someone over her first-day nerves, quite another to be stuck with them for the rest of the year. Martha was quite willing to be polite to all, but she had no interest in becoming anyone's crutch. She was beginning to suspect that she couldn't afford to.

At the dinner break most of the students went back to their boarding houses for their noon meal. Martha hadn't been sure that she would have time to go back and forth to Yorkville, so she had packed a lunch, but she didn't know where she should go to eat it until Miss Clark directed her to a room on the first floor. There were only two other girls there. She nodded at them, quickly ate her bread and cheese, retrieved her coat and went out into the gardens. She wanted some fresh air so she could clear her head before the examination that afternoon. A light snow had begun to fall and the grounds were deserted, except for one person at the far end of the garden who appeared to be studying the spindly orchard trees. Martha might never have noticed her except that she was wearing an Indian paisley shawl that looked identical to the one Martha owned.

She was about to walk down the path toward the woman when she was treated to the extraordinary sight of a coatless man running through the garden with what appeared to be great purpose. As he drew closer, she realized that it was Mr. Sorbie, the master who also functioned as the recording clerk for the school. As he went past her he nodded without breaking stride, maintaining a steady jog until he disappeared around the corner of the Model School.

By then the woman had started walking in Martha's direction. Then she stopped, peered off into the distance for a moment, and veered down a side path.

"Hello!" Martha turned at the hail. One of the other girls who had stayed at the school had come out into the garden as well.

"Are you ready for this afternoon?" the student said.

"No, I'm not at all looking forward to it. I'm Martha Renwell, by the way."

"Nice to meet you. Clara Parker."

"Are you ready?"

Clara shrugged. "I suppose. It doesn't really matter anyway. I'm not too happy to be here in the first place. My father has this mad idea that I need to be educated,"

"You don't want to be a teacher?"

She laughed. "Heavens, no. But Normal School is free, you see. Ladies' Academies cost money."

"But…" Martha was slightly outraged. The whole point of the Normal School was to train teachers, not merely to provide higher education to those unwilling to pay for it themselves.

"What will you do then? When you graduate?"

"I doubt I'll last that long. I have a number of suitors already. It's just a matter of deciding which one I like the best." She said this smugly. "What about you?"

"I have none," Martha said, which she wasn't quite sure was true. "And I'd like to earn my own living, at least for a little while."

"Better you than me," Clara replied. "I can't think of anything more dreary than trudging off to work every day. I don't know how men put up with it. But I'm glad they do, because it will keep me in dresses."

"But don't we have to promise to teach?"

"I promise all sorts of things when it's convenient."

Martha decided then and there that Clara Parker was unlikely to become her friend.

"I'm cold," she announced. "Good luck on the test." She turned and walked away, leaving Clara standing alone in the garden.

Martha told herself to calm down as she took her seat that afternoon. As it turned out, her nerves were entirely warranted – the test was far more difficult than she had anticipated. The mathematical questions posed no problem – Thaddeus had seen to it that she had a good enough grounding in the fundamentals to piece through the questions and answer them, as far as she could tell, correctly. The same was true of the English proficiency section. Again, the review work she had done paid off and she had no difficulty parsing the sentences that were presented. History was more difficult. She knew the answers to some of the questions, but Thaddeus had been unable to predict what, exactly, she might be asked, and she had no idea about some of the events that were referenced. As she fumed over it, she wondered why on earth any Canadian child needed to know about the battles that had taken place during the Wars of the Roses. It was nothing to do with Canada. Bearing Luke's advice in mind, however, she completed the questions that she was confident about, then turned to the ones that puzzled her.

She found the section on geography devilish, since it was an area Thaddeus had not covered extensively, and it was a subject that had been noticeably absent from the curriculum at the village school in Wellington. She could only fall back on the knowledge she had gleaned from reading novels and newspapers. She knew, for example, that Florence was in Italy and Alexandria in Egypt, but she had never run across a mention of the Atlas Mountains and had no clue where they might be found. She kept working doggedly, making educated guesses at some of the questions, speculating wildly at others.

She happened to glance at Bernice across the aisle from her. The poor girl was red in the face and obviously distraught at her inability to furnish the information she was being asked to provide. Martha felt a little better then. Others were having as much difficulty as she was.

Too soon, time was called and they were directed to hand their papers to the supervising master.

Bernice was in tears. "I know I'm going to get sent home," she said. "I don't know what I'll do then. Pa's counting on me to be a teacher. We're all girls in our family, and it makes it hard to work the farm, you see, so we thought this would be a good plan, so I can earn some money and help out."

"Are you the oldest?" Martha asked.

"Yes, I have five little sisters."

84

"I'm sure it will be fine. I had trouble with a lot of the questions too, and my grandfather did all sorts of review before I came here. I think the exam was really hard, but it was hard for everybody. They can't fail us all."

"Do you really think so?"

"Yes, I do." Martha managed to sound confident, but truth to tell, she was feeling almost as apprehensive as Bernice. She too, didn't know what she would do if she failed. Thaddeus really had no option but to trot her back to Wellington if that happened. He had already gone out on a limb to get her here in the first place, and in spite of all her brave words to her father, she wasn't at all sure where else she could go. And if she were to be sent home, Thaddeus would have wasted money he could ill afford.

"I guess we'll find out how we did tomorrow, won't we?" Bernice said. "Just one more day of worry."

Martha agreed, but she had a suspicion that even if she passed the exam, Bernice would continue to worry for the entire year.

After Martha left for school, Thaddeus made his bed, then walked down the hall to Martha's room, but she had already tidied it. He went downstairs and brought two buckets of coal up from the cellar for Mrs. Dunphy and tidied the piles of newspaper on the dining room table. By the time he finished, it was still only nine o'clock. Then he wondered what he was going to do with himself for the rest of the day. He'd been spending all his time with Martha, and had grown too used to having company. He needed to take stock of his current situation and figure out how he was going to proceed. Finding some employment was the first order of business, he decided, not only to augment his finances, but to fill his time.

Anything that required heavy physical labour was out of the question. It had been all he could do to ride the last circuit he had ministered to and he hadn't grown any younger in the meantime. He had worked as a clerk of sorts when he was in Wellington, handling correspondence for a local businessman. He could certainly do something like that again, if only he could find some businessman who needed his services, but he couldn't think of any off-hand. He ruled out working in a shop. He had seen several *Help Wanted* signs in windows as he and Martha explored the city, but manning a counter would require long hours on his feet, and would occupy too much of the little time he would have with Martha. He had been a schoolteacher once, but that had been back in the day when anyone with a rudimentary education could take a country classroom, and as long as order was kept, no one inquired too closely as to how much actual education was being imparted. Standards were higher now, teachers more professional. And soon it would be impossible to take a position without a certificate from the Normal School, something Thaddeus found rather ironic, given the path his granddaughter was taking.

But this train of thought led him to a possible solution. Perhaps he could be a tutor. There were plenty of rich men in Toronto whose offspring needed help to get into a preparatory school or a university course. Plenty of well-to-do families who preferred that their daughters be educated at home. Thaddeus would be at a bit of a disadvantage as he could offer no help with classical studies, but he could provide a solid grounding in things like mathematics and English, and the fact that he was an ordained minister would make him acceptable in any household. He would place a small notice in the paper and see what turned up.

He was just about to ask Dr. Christie for the loan of a pen and paper so he could craft his advertisement when Sally Spicer walked through the back door.

"I'm here for the laundry," she said with a smile. "The heaviest wash is a little beyond Mrs. Dunphy these days, so Dr. Luke asked if I'd do it. I just gather it up and throw it in with my own. Except for the things that are blood-stained," she added. "That takes a little more doing."

"Is there a lot of that?" Thaddeus asked.

"No, not a huge amount. Dr. Luke is very considerate about having the patients bleed on their own sheets. The nastiest items are Dr. Christie's aprons. I have no idea what that man gets up to, to make them so filthy."

Having imparted this extraordinary information, Sally grabbed a basket and prepared to head out the door.

"I'll carry that for you if you like," Thaddeus said.

"That would be lovely, thank you, if you're going my way."

Suddenly the door to the back room opened and Christie burst into the kitchen. He was wearing a stained and foul apron. Thaddeus wanted to suggest that it was perhaps time to add it to Sally's basket, but then decided that it was none of his business.

"Are you by any chance headed into the city, Mr. Lewis?"

"I was thinking of it," Thaddeus replied. "Is there something you need?"

Christie waved the piece of paper he held in his hand. "Some gauze. And some catgut suture. Your feckless son is never around when you need him and we've nearly run out of both items. Can't think where he's gotten to."

Thaddeus didn't bother to point out that Luke was out seeing patients that morning. He was happy enough to run Christie's errand – it would give him an opportunity to place his notice in the paper and put Clementine's money in the bank. Best of all, it would use up most of the morning.

He walked with Sally down to the Spicer cottage and deposited the bundle of laundry inside the back door for her, then boarded the omnibus that was waiting at the intersection and rode it all the way south to King Street.

His first errand took him to the Lyman Brothers pharmaceutical supply, where Christie held an account. When Thaddeus entered the store, his nose wrinkled a little at the slightly acrid, astringent smell that permeated the air. While he waited for his order to be filled, he marveled at the medical apparatus that was heaped up everywhere, tubes and bottles and metal boxes designed to appeal to the self-medicator. The actual function of some of them defied his imagination.

He soon tucked Christie's parcel under his arm and emerged into the street, where he debated over which newspaper he should place his notice in. He finally decided on *The Globe*, mostly because the office was close by on King Street, but also because it was the paper with the largest circulation, and the one that the gentlemen whose eyes he was hoping to attract would be most likely to read.

He entered the office, stated his business and was offered a pen and a printed form to complete. He stood at the counter for some time, wondering how he should couch his words. He should have composed the notice before he left Yorkville, so he could tinker with it a bit, but it was silly not to complete the errand while he was in the city. Finally he wrote:

For hire: Tutor. Retired minister. Specialty in English, Mathematics and Theology. T. Lewis, Yorkville.

He handed it to the clerk, paid his money, and walked out hoping there would be some return on his investment. Then he made his way to the bank on Adelaide Street. He was about to walk past Ashby's office, when he decided he should see if the barrister was back yet. He really would like to reassure himself that he was doing the right thing by depositing Clementine's money. But when he entered the office, only the clerk was there, surrounded, as before, by piles of paper.

"Did you have an appointment?" the clerk asked, as before.

"No. I was passing by anyway and I just thought I'd see if Mr. Ashby had returned yet."

"He'll be gone for several more weeks. If it's an urgent matter, I can recommend another barrister."

"It isn't really," Thaddeus said. "I wanted to say hello more than anything."

"I can take your name and give him the message when he returns."

"That's all right," Thaddeus said. "I was here a little while ago and you took down the particulars. There's no need to do it again."

"And your name is…?"

"Lewis. Thaddeus Lewis."

"Ah, yes." The name seemed to have jogged the man's memory, even though Thaddeus himself hadn't. "I've put your note on his desk along with the rest of his personal correspondence. He'll be sure to see it as soon as he arrives."

"Thank you." For the time being, there was nothing he could do but put the gold coins in the bank along with the rest of the money.

The teller at the Bank of Canada was extraordinarily polite as he made the deposit, his conversation littered with "Sirs" and "Thank yous". He wondered what the teller's reaction would be if Thaddeus told him the money wasn't really his, but had arrived unannounced in the mail and was no doubt the ill-gotten gains of sharp practice, if not downright fraud. It probably wouldn't make any difference. Money was money no matter where it came from. As far as Thaddeus was aware, he was proceeding in an ethical manner, but he desperately wished Ashby would come back soon so he could give his advice on the matter.

He caught a bus back to Yorkville and just as he stepped off at the intersection with the Concession Line, he thought he saw Martha walking ahead of him. It was her paisley wrap that first caught his attention. He was puzzled to see her on the streets of Yorkville. That morning she had announced her intention of staying at the school over dinnertime, but maybe she'd decided to come home after all. And then a dreadful thought hit him – maybe she had been found wanting in some way and had been asked to leave the school.

He called her name, but the figure ahead of him increased her pace. It was difficult to keep her in sight through the blowing snow, and Thaddeus was almost running in an effort to catch up with her. Suddenly the figure darted into one of the lanes that led from Yonge Street down into the ravine. Then she disappeared into a thick clump of bushes.

And stepped back out again, as though to beckon him closer.

Thaddeus was about to follow when he decided that the person ahead of him couldn't possibly be Martha. It was the shawl that had fooled him. Had Martha even been wearing it that morning? He couldn't remember, but in any event, he wasn't about to be lured into the bushes by some stranger. He turned and walked away.

By the time he reached Christie's, Mrs. Dunphy was already setting dinner on the table. After the meal, Christie disappeared into the back room again, Luke was called out to see a child with a high fever and Thaddeus was left alone in the dining room. He carried the remaining dishes through to the kitchen, but Mrs. Dunphy shooed him out when he tried to help her wash them.

He wandered into the parlour, picked a book off the shelf and spent the rest of afternoon attempting to read it, but found it hard to concentrate. He was too impatient for everyone to be finished their day's activities.

Martha arrived at Christie's just as Mrs. Dunphy was setting the table for supper.

"Apparently they intend to keep us hard at it," she said when she came in. "I might be this time or even later every day."

"I won't serve anything up until you get here," Mrs. Dunphy promised. Dr. Christie looked a little put out at this announcement.

Thaddeus was downcast, although he did his best not to show it. It looked as though Martha would be gone nearly all the time. Then he took himself to task. He needed to stop feeling sorry for himself, as he had been told more than once.

Martha chattered on about the details of her first day. "The boys and the girls are strictly separated, and we're not even allowed to speak to each other," she said. "Not even outside of school. Apparently there was some trouble a couple of years ago with boys gathering outside one of the female boarding houses."

"That sounds like boys," Thaddeus nodded.

"Some of the students are quite old," she said. "You'd think they'd know better than to be such pests."

"Boys are always pests," Dr. Christie observed. "They should all be hanged."

Martha ignored him. "Some of the girls looked scared to death," she went on. "There was a girl beside me who was shaking, she was so nervous. I held her hand, just so she wouldn't faint or something. It turns out she's never been away from her village before."

"Where is she from?" Thaddeus asked.

"From somewhere near St. Thomas. She told me the name of the village but I've forgotten what she said."

"St. Thomas is down near London, I believe," Thaddeus said, "although I've never been there."

"I thought you'd been everywhere," Luke said.

"Everywhere in the eastern part of Upper Canada just about. Not so many places in the west."

"There's so much to remember, I'm half-scared myself,"

Martha went on.

"Did you have time to eat your dinner?" Mrs. Dunphy asked.

"Yes, thank you, Mrs. Dunphy," Martha said. "Plenty of time. And then I walked in the gardens for a while. It was nice to get some fresh air. One of the teachers thought so too – except he wasn't walking, he was running." She turned to Thaddeus. "It was the clerk who took my information when I registered. Mr. Sorbie."

"Not Adam Sorbie?" Luke said.

"Yes. Do you know him?"

"I don't really know him. I've met him a couple of times at the Caer Howell Pleasure Grounds, that's all. The man is mad about running. Always trying to get up groups to chase each other across the countryside."

"What were you doing at Caer Howell?" Dr. Christie asked.

"Some of us go along to watch the cricket now and again," Luke replied. "I didn't realize Sorbie was at the Normal School. Is he just a clerk or an instructor as well?"

"He teaches bookkeeping and athletics, I believe," Martha said.

"I don't pay you to sit around and watch cricket matches" Christie grumbled.

"You don't pay me for anything on my days off," Luke pointed out. He turned back to Martha. "If he teaches athletics, he'll probably make you run up mountains and through swamps," he teased.

"I don't think the girls do athletics. They only mentioned gymnastics and callisthenics."

"What are callisthenics?" Christie asked.

"I don't know," Martha giggled. "Maybe Luke is right and it means running through swamps."

"I've done plenty of running in my time," Thaddeus said. "But only because someone was chasing me at the time. Why would anyone want to do it for no reason?"

"Like I said, the man is mad for sports," Luke replied.

"He must be, to want to run around in the snow," Martha said. "It was cold out in the garden."

"Did you stay at the school for the whole dinner hour?" Thaddeus said. "The only reason I'm asking is that I thought I saw you on the street late this morning, just as I was getting back from the city."

"No. I was there all day."

"I was fooled by the shawl, I guess. The woman was wearing one just like yours."

"I saw somebody with a shawl like mine today as well, but there are probably hundreds of them on the streets of Toronto. It's a popular fashion and an economical fabric, but I'm surprised that anyone would wear it on a day like today. It isn't really heavy enough for winter wear. Better than nothing, I suppose, but I was grateful I had my wool coat."

"That must be it. I was sure it couldn't be you. You ran away from me when I called."

But Thaddeus hadn't been sure.

Chapter 7

Only a handful of students failed to pass the entrance examination, and Martha was relieved to learn that she was not one of them. Neither was Bernice. Another handful of students were accelerated into the advanced course, but these all seemed to be the older students who already had some teaching experience. The remainder were divided into classes and given their schedules. Martha was a little annoyed to discover that Bernice had been given the same timetable. She had nothing against the girl, except that she seemed so clingy, and if the examination was anything to go by, Martha would have her hands full enough with her studies without having to deal with an insecure friend on top of it all.

The school wasted no time putting them to work. As soon as their assignments were announced, they proceeded to the first class, which was on the subject of the effective teaching of geography. After twenty minutes, Martha realized that this entailed a great deal of memory work, and resolved to develop some mnemonics, like her grandfather had used to help her remember the kings and queens of England. She was distracted from this by Bernice, who every few minutes emitted a frustrated whimper.

They were just moving on to English composition when Martha was asked to see Headmaster Robertson in his office. She couldn't imagine why she was being summoned, but could think of no reason why she should be alarmed. Perhaps he intended to interview each student who had been admitted for the first term.

She entered the book-lined room and waited silently in front of the oak desk until the headmaster finished what he was writing and looked up at her with a piercing stare. From where Martha stood she could see that he had her records open on his desk. She recognized the letter of recommendation provided by the Methodist minister in Wellington.

"Ah, Miss Renwell," Robertson said. "It has come to my attention that your current living arrangements are somewhat unusual." His Irish accent was so thick she had to concentrate closely to make sure she was hearing him correctly. She was also puzzled by his statement.

"My grandfather and I are staying with my uncle. I understood that it was acceptable for students to live with their families."

"I think you'll find that the directive is intended to apply to those students whose immediate families are resident in Toronto," he said.

"I'm sorry, sir, but in my case, my grandfather is my immediate family. I've lived with him since I was an infant."

"But he doesn't maintain a residence here."

"No, but we'll be staying with my uncle until my course is completed."

"I see." He graced her with a tight little smile. "You have to understand my caution, Miss Renwell. We take our responsibility to our students very seriously, and we insist that the highest moral standard be maintained. Your circumstances are a little odd, that's all."

She attempted a conciliatory smile. "By some people's standards they're very odd," she said. "To me they're perfectly natural. And since my grandfather is an ordained minister, I think you'll find that his moral standard is of the highest order."

"Yes. Methodist Episcopal, I understand. But not currently preaching."

"No." She wondered if the headmaster had heard about Cobourg, and knew that Thaddeus had left under a cloud. She didn't know if reports of the London murder trial had reached as far as this oaken office. She had to hope that they hadn't. And then she took a chance.

"If you find that you need confirmation of my grandfather's

good character, perhaps you could contact Dr. Christie in Yorkville. I understand that he's acquainted with one of the other masters. Mr. Ormiston, I believe." She could only hope that Christie's name would be a recommendation. He was so eccentric it was entirely possible that it would have the opposite effect. To her relief, the ploy appeared to work.

Robertson seemed surprised. "Dr. Stewart Christie? He's an acquaintance?"

"More than that. My uncle is Dr. Christie's partner, and it's actually Dr. Christie's house where we're staying. One of the advantages of my attending this school was that my uncle would be close at hand should anything happen to my grandfather."

"Well." Robertson took a long moment to once again peruse the papers in front of him. "I see no difficulty with allowing this for the present," he said finally. "But I will reserve the right to monitor your situation. I'm sorry, Miss Renwell, but you do understand that we need to be very careful in these matters."

"Of course." And then she smiled the sweetest smile she could muster.

The smile disappeared at Robertson's next words. "However, since you are, as you've acknowledged, living with family, we will not be able to offer you the usual boarding fee for out of town students."

Martha was annoyed. She knew that Thaddeus had been counting on the extra money, and that it would be a blow if it wasn't forthcoming. She wasn't about to let Robertson know this, however. She put the smile back on her face.

"I quite understand. Is that all?"

"For the present, yes. You may now rejoin your class."

She did some furious mental calculations as she left the office. She wasn't entirely sure just how much money Thaddeus had, but she knew that he was hoping to find some work to augment it, which would argue that it might not be enough to see them through the whole year. She still had a portion of some money Thaddeus had given her in Cobourg, and the entire sum that Towns Ashby had paid her for helping in the London investigation. If she spent absolutely nothing on herself over the next months, it might be enough to make up the shortfall. She could save a little more by packing a lunch every day and eating it at the school instead of riding the omnibus back and forth to Christie's for dinner. And on nice days, she could walk both to and from the school, although it would use up a considerable amount of time.

But it was only fair, after all – Thaddeus had committed whatever money he had to finance her future and Martha could certainly contribute whatever she had. Even so, she suspected that it would leave them with nothing in the way of an emergency fund until she graduated and could start earning.

Up until that moment, she had still been a little equivocal about her decision to attend this school. Now she became determined to graduate, no matter how many barriers some Irish headmaster decided to put in front of her.

Thaddeus was relieved to learn that Martha passed her entrance examination and was accepted as a teacher-in-training. His situation would have been very difficult indeed if she hadn't.

"There are still hurdles to get over," she warned him that evening. "There are tests every six weeks, and anyone who falls too far behind will be asked to withdraw."

"So what do you think of it all so far?" Thaddeus asked.

"It's hard to judge at this point," she said. "I hope they don't give us so much work every night. I have forty-nine pages to read after supper."

"I suppose they try to cram in as much stuff as they can before they send you off to a school somewhere."

"I suppose. I'm a little disappointed that I didn't do well enough on the exam to jump into the advanced class. It would have meant only five months of classes instead of ten."

"I suspect they took your age into consideration," Thaddeus said. "You must be one of the youngest students there."

"Maybe. It was mostly the men and the older boys who were advanced. It doesn't seem fair, really. Never mind, with any luck I can earn a provincial license and then we can go anywhere we like."

"Only if there's somewhere that wants to hire you," Thaddeus pointed out.

"I don't think that will be a problem. There aren't that many provincially-trained teachers that school boards can afford to pass one by. Or at least that's what they said when they were lecturing us on the importance of working hard. So at least we'll have some choices at the end of it."

Thaddeus couldn't help but be mollified by her breezy assumption that he would go wherever she did.

That evening Martha helped Mrs. Dunphy clear away the dishes, then moved a lamp to the centre of the dining room table and settled down to read the preparatory material she had been handed as the school day ended. Thaddeus stayed at the table too, in case she had any questions, but the silence stretched out as she appeared to have no need of his help. He reached for a newspaper, even though he'd already read it and there wasn't much of anything that warranted a second look. The Crimean War dragged on, with typhus and cholera killing more soldiers than the Russians; more railways were being built, in spite of the fact that catastrophic accidents were happening with alarming regularity; and the legislative assembly in Upper Canada continued to be convulsed over suspected stock manipulation by Premier Francis Hincks. It was a dispiriting collection of articles.

Thaddeus knew that he would have to get used to the fact that Martha had other claims on her time. He desperately needed to find something to keep himself occupied, at least until someone answered his notice in *The Globe*. If anyone answered at all. He wondered how long Towns Ashby was going to be away, and if, failing anything else turning up, he might have some small job that Thaddeus could fill when he returned. Something that didn't entail murder or madmen. He didn't have enough experience with the law to understand how a barrister's office might be set up, but perhaps he could fulfill the same sort of position he had held in Wellington – something clerical - correspondence or some such thing. And then he rejected the notion. He couldn't expect Ashby to rescue him again.

But one day a week tagging along after Morgan Spicer through the slums of Toronto wasn't enough. And then Thaddeus decided that since he was doing nothing more than watch Martha read he should reject idleness and do something he had always intended to do but had never really started. He would write the story of his life. He had been witness to many strange and wondrous things and he would like to leave a record of them. He wasn't sure who would want to read it – possibly only Martha - but perhaps someday, if he was fortunate, some church historian would stumble upon it and decide that it had some merit.

He could bring the notes and journals he had carted around all these years down to the dining room table and spread them out. He could work across from Martha, each of them occupied with what they were doing, but company for each other nonetheless. He went upstairs and collected his papers from the bottom of his valise.

Martha looked up, surprised, when he reappeared opposite her.

"I thought I'd start getting some of this stuff in order," he said.

"Oh good. I know it's something you've been wanting to do," she said, and then went back to her reading.

Where to begin? At the beginning he decided. Surely a future reader would want to hear something of his early days even though he was sure the greatest interest would be found in his account of the years he had spent riding circuits for the Methodist Episcopal Church. He borrowed a pen and a piece of paper from Martha and then he began:

> *My father, William Lewis and mother, Elizabeth Babcock were born near New York, at that time one of the colonies of Great Britain, it being before the Revolutionary War which broke out in the year 1774. At this time, my father, being about twenty years old joined the British standard in New York and bore arms in favour of Great Britain. Sometime during the Rebellion my father and mother were united in matrimony. My father being firmly attached to the British government, at the close of the war emigrated with his family to the wilderness of Upper Canada. He arrived at Cataraqui, the place where the city of Kingston now stands, in the summer of 1783.*
>
> *I was born on the bank of the Napanee River, five miles*

above where the town of Napanee now stands. I believe there was not a town or village in Upper Canada when I was born, but it was indeed one widespread and dense wilderness, except here and there a hut, cabin or log house with a little cleared around them, or beginning to be cleared.

Bears, wolves, deer were in great abundance and there were lynx, wild cats, beavers and foxes in every direction around us.

They were happy days as he recalled them. He and his brothers and sisters had plenty to do as they helped their father carve a farm out of the forest. But work had not claimed all their time. There were games in the fields and hunting in the woods and visits with the neighbours. It was an idyllic childhood in many ways.

So many of his early companions were gone now. Thaddeus had been fourteen years old when his oldest sister died and it seemed that her death had been but the beginning of a long list of deaths of those he held dear. He had been profoundly shaken at the time, but he had learned no lesson from it. With an arrogant belief in his own immortality, he had gone marching off to war only a few years later.

The war. He had a distaste for bringing up the memories of the dirt and the blood and the lice and most of all, the terror. And the boredom. They never tell you about the boredom. But it would be necessary to write about it all in order to explain why he had answered The Lord's call. And how he won Betsy.

"I think I'm ready for bed. Shall I leave the lamp burning?"

Martha had finished her work while Thaddeus had been lost in the past.

"No, I think I've done enough for this evening as well." He tidied his journals and papers into a neat pile and left them sitting on a corner of the table, along with a great deal of his autobiographical resolve.

It was Dr. Christie, not Thaddeus, who helped Martha out of her first difficulty.

"We're to draw some flowers in a vase," she said at the supper table later that week, "but my first attempt looks dreadful. I'm afraid I don't have any more talent in art than I do in music."

"Nonsense," Christie said. "Anyone can draw. It's just a matter of understanding perspective."

"Is that the converging lines business my teacher told me about?"

"Yes, that's part of it," Christie said.

"Then that's the part I don't understand," Martha said. "It might be helpful if there were lines running through the vase of flowers, but there aren't, and I don't understand what it has to do with the lines I drew on the paper."

"That's where you need to use your imagination. Would you like me to show you after supper?"

"Would you?" Martha said. "That would be wonderful!"

Christie beamed and Thaddeus felt a little put out, although there was no way he would ever be able to set Martha straight on this particular topic. He had no experience of drawing anything.

Martha and Christie disappeared into the back room as soon as dessert was cleared away.

Luke was in a hurry to disappear as well. He'd arranged with Christie for the evening off, and he was going into the city, he said, "to meet up with some friends."

Thaddeus wondered if this meant he was going courting, a suspicion that was reinforced when Luke returned to his room and emerged fifteen minutes later with a fresh shave and a different cravat. Luke offered no further details of his plans for the evening, however, and simply waved a goodbye. Thaddeus was left sitting in the dining room all by himself.

His journals lay accusingly on the corner of the table. After a few moments of deciding that he didn't feel like writing, he cleared away the teapot and cups and took them into the kitchen where Mrs. Dunphy was washing the supper dishes. He grabbed a tea towel and began to dry.

"You don't need to that, Mr. Lewis," the housekeeper said. "I've got this in hand."

"I don't mind at all," Thaddeus said. "I've nothing else to do right now, and I'm happy for the company."

She grunted, which Thaddeus took to be agreement. They worked in silence until, surprisingly, it was Mrs. Dunphy who broke it.

"You raised a fine family, Mr. Lewis," she said.

Thaddeus assumed she was referring to Martha. "Yes, my granddaughter is growing into quite a wonderful young woman, isn't she?"

"I won't dispute that," Mrs. Dunphy said. "She's a nice girl and we're both quite taken with her, but I was referring mostly to your son. With him around, it almost feels like I have my brother back again."

Thaddeus suddenly realized that he knew very little about Mrs. Dunphy and how she had come to keep house for her irascible cousin. Her dour and taciturn nature seldom invited inquiry.

"I don't think I knew that you had a brother," he ventured.

"He died a long time ago."

"I'm sorry." Again the silence stretched out.

"He and Stewart and I all grew up together," she said suddenly. "So we felt his loss greatly. He's the reason Stewart took a chance on Dr. Luke."

None of this made any sense to Thaddeus. He knew that Christie had written to McGill University and that Luke had simply responded to a notice posted in the hall. Any one of his fellow students could have done the same, but they had all disdained the notion of being a small-town doctor.

"Luke has always been very grateful to Dr. Christie," Thaddeus said. "He's said more than once that he doesn't know what would have happened to him otherwise."

"I'm not sure what would happen to us without him. Luke looks after us more than you would think. I hope you don't mind that we feel he's our boy too."

"Not at all," Thaddeus said. "I'm just glad that it's all worked out so well."

But the conversation gave him pause for thought. Of all his sons, he got along with Luke the best. He had always had it in the back of his mind that when he grew too old to look after himself he might find a home with Luke. But it sounded like there was already a claim on him. Two claims, in fact. He had gone from being an assistant to a partner to something that bore much more resemblance to a son. With two old folks to care for already, would he have room for a third?

Thaddeus knew that Will and Moses were both prepared to take him in – they had said as much - but the thought of finding a place in the chaotic arrangements that characterized the households of his other two sons was unappealing. It would be many years before such a consideration became necessary, of course. Thaddeus was a long way from his dotage, but it was something to think about. There was always Martha, of course – and she seemed agreeable to the notion of dragging a grandparent behind her wherever she went – but at some point she would surely tire of independence and want to settle down with a family of her own. How long would she put up with a grumpy old man who monopolized the chair by the fire?

He shook off these depressing thoughts as he finished wiping the dishes. In spite of the fact that some members of his family considered him a problem that needed to be taken care of, he knew he still had good years ahead of him. He just needed to sort himself out, that's all.

Just as he was about to leave the kitchen, Thaddeus heard a peal of laughter from the back room. He opened the door cautiously. Dr. Christie was seated at his easel, sketching while Martha looked over his shoulder.

"There now, do you see?" Christie said.

"I do, now that you've explained it," Martha said.

He eased the door shut. If Martha needed Christie to help her become a teacher, then so be it. Thaddeus would stop feeling neglected and get out of their way.

The next day Thaddeus once again collected Morgan Spicer and together they set off for St. John's Ward. In spite of the fact that their mission was to search out the city's most desperate people, Thaddeus enjoyed being an unofficial Assistant Visitor for the House of Industry. He liked being out and about with Morgan, and the work gave him a sense of purpose that was, at the moment, lacking in his life otherwise.

As soon as they reached the edge of Macaulaytown they were hailed by a boy of ten or so, whose clothes consisted more of holes than cloth.

Spicer frowned. "Where's Bucky?" he asked.

"He's workin' today. Over at the dock," came the reply. "He said to tell you there's an old couple who needs some help. They got nobody to look after 'em now that their son's been killed by a runaway horse. They're both so old they can't work no more and now they's starvin'."

The boy didn't know, however, exactly where the old couple was sheltering.

"Somewhere over in that block," he said, pointing to a particularly decrepit pile of buildings, parts of which had collapsed and parts of which had been built over and added to until their yards had nearly disappeared. "I've only ever seen them shuffling along the street looking for scraps in the garbage heaps. But I'm pretty sure they have a room there somewhere."

Morgan handed the boy a penny. "Sounds like they need to be brought in," he said to Thaddeus, "provided, of course, we can get them to agree."

Thaddeus followed Spicer into a warren of back alleys, where a multitude of doorways opened onto the narrow laneways. They were soon disoriented from the twists and turns they took. Only a feeble sunlight filtered down from the sky above and the buildings cast odd shadows that further confused the search.

Thaddeus stopped at one opening in the wall beside him. It could scarcely be called a door – there was no covering of any description.

"Hello?" he called, but no one answered.

"If you'll check the rooms along this lane, I'll go ahead and see where it comes out," Spicer said.

Thaddeus stuck his head through the door, but he couldn't see much of anything. Unless someone made a noise, or moved, it was impossible to tell if there was anyone in there at all.

He had just turned back to the alley when out of nowhere, he felt a sharp blow strike the back of his head. He staggered, regained his balance for a moment, then his vision blurred and he dropped to his knees. He was aware that he shouted, but for some reason it sounded as though it was a long way away. And then he fell into a blackness that was far deeper than any of the shadows in the alleyway.

Chapter 8

The next thing Thaddeus knew everything seemed to be a peculiar shade of green, and he could hear Spicer's voice off in the distance asking if he was all right. He opened his eyes and wondered where he was. He was lying on his side. There was a mound of frozen refuse a few inches from his nose. His right leg was damp and cold. His head hurt.

"Are you all right Thaddeus?" he heard again. Spicer was kneeling beside him, pressing a handkerchief against his head.

He tried to sit up, but his head spun and his chest felt like it was tied in a knot. He decided to lie back down again. Best to be still until the spinning stopped.

"Just rest for a minute. There's no rush."

Spicer's face seemed blurred and indistinct. Thaddeus wondered if he was going to black out again and fought against it. After a few moments, the pain in his chest eased off. He felt a little better, but he was unwilling to risk sitting up again.

"Did you see who it was?" he asked.

"Who?" Spicer said. "I didn't see anybody. I heard you yell so I came back and I found you lying here."

"Somebody hit me. I don't know what with."

"Were they trying to rob you, maybe? It happens sometimes, down here."

"I don't know." But for some reason he felt sure it was no robbery attempt.

He tried sitting up again, and the dizziness wasn't so bad. He'd sit for a minute, and then he needed to get to his feet and get out of this alley.

"We'll take it slow," Spicer promised. "When you need to stop, we'll stop."

With Spicer's help Thaddeus made it to his feet. With the support of the buildings on one side, and Spicer on the other, he stumbled out into the street. The tightness in his chest came back and he had to rest for a few minutes until it settled down again. His head was pounding.

Spicer scanned the street anxiously, but few cabs ever ventured into the poorest part of Macaulaytown, and the urchins who usually swarmed around them seemed to have disappeared. Thaddeus registered this puzzling fact with the part of his mind that wasn't preoccupied with trying to stay upright. They could have sent any one of the boys for a cab, if any of them had been handy.

"We're going to have to walk for a bit until we can find a ride." Spicer said.

Thaddeus could walk only a few feet at a time before he had to stop and rest. It seemed to take forever to reach a main thoroughfare, where Spicer flagged a ride from a passing carter who was headed north.

"We need to get to Yorkville," he said. "This man needs medical attention and his son is a doctor there."

"I can take you to where you can catch the omnibus," the carter said. "But I don't know as to how I want to go all the way to Yorkville."

"How much?" Spicer asked, and when the carter named a figure, Thaddeus couldn't remember if he had enough money in his pocket to cover it. And then he decided that he didn't care as long as he wasn't required to walk any further.

"We need to stop and get Martha," he said as they passed Gould Street.

"Martha's at school. She's fine. We need to get you seen to."

"Somebody tried to kill me. Martha could be in danger too."

"Nobody's after Martha."

"But…"

"Fine. But let's get you to Christie's first, then I'll go get Martha."

In spite of the rough ride, by the time they reached Dr. Christie's, Thaddeus was convinced that he was feeling much better – until he attempted to climb down from the wagon on his own. Again, the world spun around him, and he was forced to allow Spicer and a very concerned-looking Luke help him into the consulting room and get him out of his bloodied greatcoat and jacket.

Luke asked him some very foolish questions about what day it was and how many fingers he was holding up.

"Hurry and do what you need to do," Thaddeus said. "I have to go get Martha."

"Why?" Luke asked.

"Because whoever attacked me may go after her."

"Was this a deliberate attack?" Luke looked to Spicer for confirmation.

"I think it's more likely it was an attempted robbery," Morgan said. "We were in a rough part of the city."

"With two of you there? That's pretty bold," Luke said.

"We got separated for a few minutes. I heard Thaddeus yell, and when I ran back he was lying on the ground. Whoever hit him must have heard me coming back and ran off."

"I don't think it was a robbery," Thaddeus said. "I think it was deliberate. And whoever came after me may go after Martha."

"She's surrounded by people at the school," Luke pointed out. "No one is going to harm her there."

"If it will set your mind at rest, I'll go get her," Morgan offered.

"As long as somebody goes," Thaddeus said. "And sooner rather than later."

"Well, you're not going anywhere for a while," Luke said. "You're looking distinctly worse for wear. Morgan can go, although I'm still not sure why it's necessary. Now hold still while I clean this cut."

"On my way," Morgan said.

"Wait a minute, I'll give you the money for a cab." Thaddeus reached for his jacket, which had been flung carelessly over the chair. Another wave of dizziness hit him just as he was pulling the coins out of the pocket. They scattered across the floor, along with the small wooden box that he always carried with him. Luke stooped to pick it up.

"What's this?" he asked.

Thaddeus snatched it away from him and stuffed it back into the pocket.

"Nothing," he said. Then he turned to Morgan, who had retrieved the coins. "Go! Just take the whole lot and go. We'll sort it out later."

"Calm down and sit still so I can clean you up," Luke said. "Morgan will look after Martha." Thaddeus tried to swallow down his anxiety while Luke washed the blood away from the side of his face.

"If I had to guess, I'd say somebody whacked you with a shovel. A couple of inches nearer the temple and you might not have made it."

"It takes more than a shovel to kill a hard-headed Methodist."

"At least this time it's not me who's covered in blood. Are you having any blurred vision?"

"Not now."

"But you did?"

"Well, yes, but I'd just been hit over the head. You'd be a little wobbly too if that happened to you."

Luke grunted noncommittally. "Any chest pain?"

"Only for a minute or two. And it wasn't really a pain. It was more like a knot. Like something heavy was sitting on my chest. It always goes away."

"It's happened before?"

"Once or twice, that's all."

Luke looked at him quite sternly, Thaddeus thought, for someone who was talking to his own father.

"This is very important," he said. "When does it happen? When you're walking, or when something dramatic happens like today? Or does it happen out of the blue?"

Thaddeus had to think for a moment before he could answer. There had been only a few episodes here and there. The first time had been years before, at Belleville Gaol, when the murderer Isaac Simms revealed that he had considered killing Martha as well as her mother, but that the child had scared him away when she made so much noise. He had felt the pressure a few weeks ago when he discovered Martha tied up in a cellar in London. And once when he and Luke and the Irish girl were being chased by Cuddy Nelson through the streets of Toronto. And suddenly Thaddeus was certain as to the identity of his attacker. Cuddy Nelson. He and Spicer must have been noticed after all.

"It definitely happens when I'm agitated," Thaddeus said. "And it always goes away in a few minutes."

Luke grabbed his wrist and stood, frowning, while he counted out the beat of his pulse.

Finally, after a very long minute, he looked up at Thaddeus. "Between your heart and your head, it's a wonder you survived at all."

"My heart? I don't have anything wrong with my heart."

"The pain in your chest is angina. I know you like to think you're indestructible, but this is something we're going to have to talk about."

"It's not all that serious is it? A little pain in the chest?"

"Serious enough. In the meantime, you're going to sit still and stop talking. This is going to need some stitches."

"Do your worst."

"You can have a shot of brandy afterwards. It'll calm you down."

"I don't need brandy. I'm calm."

Luke just glared at him and began laying out his suturing materials.

In spite of himself, Thaddeus was impressed with the take-charge manner of his son, the doctor.

As soon as Luke finished sewing up the gash on his father's face, he walked him to the parlour, propped him up with pillows in the most comfortable chair, and moved a stool so Thaddeus could put his feet up.

"I'd like to suggest that you don't go any further than this for the rest of the day," Luke said. "Your head is going to hurt for a while from the wound, and that's normal, but I want you to tell me if you have any more blurred vision, or if you develop a really severe headache. Or if you have any more chest pain."

To his surprise, Thaddeus agreed to this. "Don't worry, I'm happy to just sit for a while. But I won't really feel better until Martha gets here."

"She should be here soon. In the meantime, I need to tidy up the mess you made in my consulting room. Then I'll see if Mrs. Dunphy can do something about the bloodstains on your clothing. I'll be surprised if she can't – given Christie's hobby, she's quite a dab hand at it."

"I'd appreciate it if she can do something with my winter coat. The frock coat is no loss. It's twenty years old and doesn't owe me much."

"We'll see what she says. I'll be right back."

Luke grabbed the instruments he had used and scooped Thaddeus's things from the chair, then walked through to the kitchen, where Mrs. Dunphy was just taking a pan of scones out of the oven.

"Is it possible to get the blood out of these?" He held out the coat and jacket.

"Never can tell 'til I try," she said. "Leave them with me."

He threw the clothing over a kitchen chair, then went to the sink where he ladled hot water into a basin, added some soap and scrubbed the bowl and suturing needle he had used. When he was finished, he rinsed them carefully and put them in a vinegar bath. Christie always snorted at this fastidiousness, claiming that it was an unnecessary waste of effort, but Luke couldn't bring himself to use something that was dirty or blood-encrusted on a fresh patient.

Mrs. Dunphy set the pan of scones on the table to cool, then rummaged through Thaddeus's pockets. She pulled a blood-stained handkerchief out of one pocket of his greatcoat. "This won't wash up. It's only good for the rag-bag." She threw it aside, then reached into the pocket of his frock coat where she found three coins and the wooden box. "And these don't need washing."

"I need to get a damp cloth. There's some blood to clean up in the surgery."

"You know where the rag-bag is." She had long since made it clear that cleaning up consulting room messes was not one of her duties.

Luke wet a rag and took it to wipe up whatever stains he could find in his office. He was about to join Thaddeus in the parlour when he hesitated, but only for a moment, before he popped open the wooden box that had been in his father's pocket. For some reason he expected to find his mother's picture there, even though as far as he knew, no daguerreotype or miniature portrait of Betsy existed. He was slightly disappointed to discover that it was a picture of a stranger, but he had to admit that the face that stared back at him was extraordinary. The woman had her head tilted slightly to one side and a half-smile lingered around her lips as she regarded the viewer with a direct and unmistakably provocative look. It seemed for all the world as though she was about to say something charmingly witty. The woman was by no means beautiful by the standard of the day, but the expression on her face animated it, and made it hugely appealing. Luke wondered if this was the woman who had caused Thaddeus so much grief in Cobourg. He wondered if he dared to ask.

He snapped the box shut again and went through to the dining room where he poured out two small glasses of brandy. He took them into the parlour and handed one to Thaddeus.

"It will do you good. And me as well. It's not every day I have to doctor my own father."

Thaddeus looked at the brandy with suspicion.

"Doctor's orders. Drink."

And then Luke reached into his pocket, pulled out the coins and the wooden box and set them on the table beside his father.

"I retrieved these before Mrs. Dunphy had a chance to wash them."

Thaddeus reached out, and without comment, picked up the box and tucked it into his waistcoat pocket.

Dr. Christie appeared in the doorway before Luke could think of anything more to say about it.

"I was lured out of the back room by the smell of fresh-baked scones," he said. "But now that I see you're drinking brandy, I do believe I'll join you."

He disappeared into the dining room and returned a few moments later with a glass that contained at least twice as much as Luke had poured.

The old doctor plunked himself down on the settee, then noticed the glass in front of Thaddeus.

"What's this Lewis? Given up your temperance principles?"

Only then did he notice the wound on Thaddeus's face.

"Good heavens, man. What happened to you?"

"Somebody hit me over the head."

"He and Spicer were down in Macaulaytown and Thaddeus was assaulted," Luke explained.

"That's outrageous!" Christie said. "Whoever did it should be hanged! Drink up your brandy, man. Best thing for a whack on the head. As your physician, I insist."

Luke didn't bother pointing out that, at the moment, he was the physician in charge.

"I must say, Lewis, life is never quite as interesting when you're not around."

"It's the kind of excitement I could do without."

"Yes, but the rest of us are quite thrilled by your adventures. It's unbearably dull without you to keep us entertained."

Christie took a happy sip of his drink, then looked around the parlour as though someone might be hiding in the small space. "And what became of Mr. Spicer? Was he attacked as well?"

"No, I sent him to get Martha," Thaddeus said.

"Good heavens, things aren't as dire as all that are they? You're not about to expire at any moment, surely?"

"He's worried about Martha's safety," Luke said. "He thinks someone tried to kill him."

"From the look of things," Christie said, "someone very nearly did. Ah well, whatever the cause it's a grand occasion for a drink, isn't it? Cheers!"

Luke heaved a sigh, ran his fingers through his hair and looked at his father.

"You're not going to like this, but I want to say something

before Martha gets here, and I'm going to speak freely."

"There's a lot of free speech floating around these days, isn't there?"

"Yes, well, someone has to do it, and since you're living with me at the moment, it appears I've been nominated."

"Is this a family matter?" Christie asked. "Should I make myself scarce?"

"No, I'm glad you're here," Luke said. "I think it might be helpful to have a consulting physician at hand to confirm what I'm about to say."

"Oh good." Christie took a sip of whisky and settled back in his chair.

"We need to have a frank discussion about your health, for starters," Luke said to Thaddeus. "You need to understand the situation. You've never taken care of yourself and your body is starting to protest that enough is enough. It's time to slow down. Stop putting yourself into danger. When you get hurt you're not going to bounce back like you once did."

"It was just a little pain in the chest," Thaddeus grumbled.

Christie shot a glance at Luke. "Angina pectoris?"

Luke nodded. "The condition isn't morbid as it stands right now," he went on, "but it's a harbinger of what's to come. And it can be triggered not only by physical insult, but by severe emotional upset as well. You need to lead a quieter life."

"Fine words from someone who's got me into more than one pickle."

"I'm serious," Luke said.

"I'm not going to sit around like an invalid," Thaddeus protested.

"I'm not saying that," Luke replied. "I'm saying you should think twice before you jump into things. Francis has a point you know – you do have an uncanny ability to land in perilous circumstances."

"I didn't jump into anything today. I was minding my own business and someone attacked me."

"No you weren't minding your own business. You were deliberately snooping around a bad part of town."

"But it was in a good cause."

"It's always in a good cause. It doesn't matter. The result is the same. It all takes a toll on you."

"He's right you know," Christie commented. "There's a clear-cut correlation between angina and stressful situations."

"Thank you," Luke said.

"There's no question that it will kill you sooner or later," Christie continued. "So that's your choice, you see. Simmer down and live longer or go out in a blaze of glory. Entirely up to you which it is. But you should at least think about what your son is saying to you, because as the consulting physician, I can only concur with his assessment."

"Well that's desperate enough news," Thaddeus said. "What else do you have to say to me?"

But at that moment, they heard the front door open and Martha ran into the room.

Martha's class was just spilling out of the lecture hall when Morgan Spicer walked through the front doors of the school. As soon as she saw him, Martha knew that something had happened to Thaddeus.

She ran over to him. "What is it?" she said. "Is Grandpa all right?"

"Yes, he's all right. He got hit over the head and knocked out, but other than a nasty cut, I don't think there's too much wrong. Dr. Luke is seeing to him right now, but he seemed to be really concerned that something might happen to you, so I came to get you."

Martha had no idea who might want to harm her, but she had been through enough adventures with Thaddeus to believe that she was wise to listen if he thought there was a threat. "I'll just get my things," she said.

"I'll be outside. I've got a cab waiting."

It did occur to her that she should tell someone at the school that she was leaving, but when she looked in the office, there was no one there. She ran upstairs and grabbed her coat and the satchel she carried her books in. When she reached the foot of the stairs again,

Bernice was waiting for her.

"Is everything all right?" she asked Martha.

"No. My grandfather's been hurt and his friend is here to take me home. Could you tell the headmistress what happened and where I've gone?"

"The headmistress?" Bernice looked alarmed.

"Or the headmaster. Or somebody. Please, Bernice. I don't have time to do it myself. I need to go right now." And without waiting for a reply, she ran out the front doors to where Morgan was waiting with the cab.

"What happened? How did he get hit over the head?" she asked as they rode north.

"We were down in St. John's Ward and got separated and he was assaulted. I think somebody tried to rob him. He doesn't think so. He thinks he was deliberately attacked. And then he got agitated because he seemed to think something might happen to you, so I said I'd come get you."

She digested this without comment. Then, after a few moments she said, "I think he may be right. It may have been deliberate."

Had the current attack been an isolated incident, Martha might have agreed with Morgan's theory that it was merely an attempted theft. After all, Thaddeus had been in one of the poorest parts of town, where only the most desperate of people lived. A man alone would have presented a tempting target, if the circumstances were right. But there was the strange episode on the steamer in Wellington, and the carriage that narrowly missed them while they were walking along the Danforth Road. The evidence pointed toward something more sinister than a simple robbery. And Martha could think of several candidates who might hold enough of a grudge to attack her grandfather.

And then she realized that she had just made the same mistake she'd made in London. Someone told her Thaddeus needed help and she'd followed without a second thought. How much did she really know about Morgan Spicer, other than what her grandfather had told her? And then she shook the thought off. She was being unduly suspicious, her nerves jangled by the report that Thaddeus was injured. And besides, even if she'd had any real reservations about Spicer, she'd have come running anyway.

When they reached Dr. Christie's house, Martha jumped down out of the cab and ran to the front door, setting aside considerations of who might be trying to hurt her grandfather in favour of concern about his condition. She wasn't sure what she expected to find – Thaddeus lying comatose in bed perhaps, or at the very least sporting a swathe of bandages – so she was surprised to discover him in the parlour drinking brandy with Dr. Christie and her uncle Luke. An ugly gash curved from his hairline across his cheekbone, accentuated by the stitches that held it closed. His face looked swollen and a vivid bruise was starting to bloom across it, but he was quite able to sit up in a chair and look relieved when he saw her.

"Martha! Is everything all right?"

"Yes. No problems."

"Good. I couldn't be sure. Sorry to drag you away from class."

"You knew I'd come as soon as I heard."

"Let me take your coat, Martha," Luke said. "I'll hang it up for you."

"Go get her some tea, will you boy?" Christie said. "And us too while you're at it. And bring a plate of those scones if you can get them away from Mrs. Dunphy."

"Of course. Are there any other errands I could run while I'm up? I really have nothing else to do." But he disappeared nonetheless.

Morgan Spicer came into the hall and hovered in the parlour doorway.

"If you're staying for tea, Spicer, you'll have to come and sit down," Christie said.

Morgan stepped forward and gave Thaddeus the coins he hadn't spent on the cab. "I should go," he said. "Sally will be wondering what happened to me. I'll stop by and see how you're doing in the morning."

"Thank you Morgan," Thaddeus said. "You're a good man to have in a crisis."

Spicer nodded at Martha, ignored Christie and departed.

Martha perched on the stool by Thaddeus's feet. "What

happened?"

"I'm not sure. Morgan and I got separated and somebody hit me. Luke thinks it might have been with a shovel."

"It's going to leave an awful scar."

"A scar will just add to my rakish appearance, won't it? Morgan thinks it was a robbery."

"I know. He told me that. I'm not so sure."

Just then Luke returned. "Tea and scones on the way."

"Who do you think might have done it?" Martha asked.

"You're convinced it was a deliberate attack?" Luke said.

"Yes," Thaddeus replied. "I am. And Martha agrees with me."

Luke looked puzzled.

"Someone attacked him in Wellington," Martha explained, "with something sharp enough to leave holes in his coat. And then a little while later, we were almost run down while we were walking along the road."

"And someone's been following me," Thaddeus added. "I've noticed it several times, but he never gets close enough for me to get a good look at him."

"My heavens you Lewises lead exciting lives," Christie commented.

Thaddeus ignored him. "I'm wondering if it's Cuddy Nelson."

"The thug who shot his boss in the graveyard a few years ago?" Luke said. "Why would he attack you?"

"When was this?" Martha said. "Nobody told me about this."

"Maybe he's holding a grudge," Thaddeus said.

"But you testified in court that it was an accident," Luke pointed out. "He might have been hanged if it weren't for that. Why would he carry a grudge over it?"

"Don't forget we sicced a dog on him. It chewed up his face. That's not an easy thing for a man to forget."

"But I did that," Luke said, "not you."

"Cuddy doesn't know for sure which one of us did it."

"But why would he take his revenge after all this time?"

"Morgan and I saw him down in St. John's Ward. I didn't think he saw us, but maybe I was mistaken. Maybe it jogged his memory that he has a score to settle."

Luke shook his head. "If Cuddy Nelson wanted you dead, you'd be dead long since. He wouldn't ambush you. He'd just order some of his mob to snatch you off a street corner in broad daylight and we'd never hear of you again."

"Really?" said Dr. Christie.

"Besides," Luke went on, "if he wanted to get back at us, he could have done it any time in the last four years. We haven't exactly been hard to find."

It was becoming clear to Martha that she wasn't the only one who had shared in Thaddeus's adventures. Things had happened with Luke as well, things no one had told her about. She wondered if Thaddeus would tell her the whole story, now that she'd heard part of it.

"Who else could it be then?" Thaddeus asked.

"There's Jeb Storms," Martha said. "He chased you through the streets of London because you accused him of lying about who killed Hazel Warner. Or somebody from the Dafoe family. They lost a lot of money because of you."

"Good grief," Christie said. "How many murders have you been involved in Lewis?"

"Or maybe it's Major Howell," Martha said in a small voice. "Maybe he's mad about his wife."

"What happened with his wife?" Christie asked, but none of the others was willing to answer. Instead the silence stretched out until finally, Luke spoke.

"Even if it was deliberate it doesn't change anything," he said. "You had a very close call today, and I'm not entirely sure you're out of the woods yet. You need to take it easy for the next few days. I'd prefer it if you didn't leave the house and it sounds like that's a good idea anyway, just in case someone really is after you."

"What is it exactly that you're worried about?" Thaddeus said. "It's only a bump on the head."

"Sometimes a bump can lead to swelling of the brain, usually some time after the event. It doesn't happen all that often, but I'd like to err on the side of caution."

"What do you do if it happens?" Martha wanted to know.

"Oh it's quite grisly, my dear," Christie said. "Trepanning is a fine art. Boring into the skull to relieve the pressure, you see."

"What?" Martha said.

"I can't stress enough that it's not likely," Luke said, glaring at Christie. "But I think we need to be prudent."

"It's all right," Thaddeus said to Martha. "It's only a hole in my head."

"And prudence is a habit you'd do well to cultivate in general," Luke added. "Not that I have any real hope that you will."

Thaddeus would never have admitted it, but he was rattled. He got little sleep that night – his head hurt and every time he turned over the stitches in his face pulled and stung. He would have moved to the chair by the window, but to his dismay, he couldn't muster enough energy to get out of bed. Instead he tried to lie as still as he could while he confronted the prospect of his own mortality.

Strangely, he found the fact that someone was actively trying to harm him far less alarming than Luke's warning. He would have dismissed the diagnosis, but for the fact that it had been delivered with the full force of professional opinion. This was different from the yammering of his family over his personal affairs. Luke spoke with the authority of an experienced physician, backed by the concurrence of his senior partner. Thaddeus would be a fool not to take his advice seriously, but it was hard to listen to your children, especially when it was the youngest talking. When Luke was small, Thaddeus had often arrived home after weeks on the road ready to bark orders and send the boys scrambling to finish their chores, leaving lists of things for them to do before he set off down the road again. He had commanded their respect and expected their obedience. Now Luke had a calling of his own and demanded respect in turn. But was Thaddeus ready to give it?

He hadn't needed Luke's words to concede that he could no longer cope with the physical demands of riding ministerial circuits. He had no inclination to preach anymore anyway. But now it seemed his horizons had contracted even further, his options limited, his opportunities practically non-existent. Not for the first time, he wondered if he'd squandered the precious time he had on this earth. He thought he'd understood the bargain he had made – he would dedicate his life to God if only he could have Betsy by his side. But then he had ridden away from her and their children to strive for a holiness he now knew he had no likelihood of ever achieving. He should have just stayed home and looked after them all.

If Grandma had wanted you to do that, she would have said so.

Was Martha right? Betsy had certainly minced no words when it came to anything else. Was it possible that she had been perfectly happy to see him ride off regularly so she could run her life the way she pleased, without – except for the brief intervals when he came barging through the door – a by-your-leave from anyone? It was a startling thought. Maybe his bargain had been less with God and more with Betsy.

It didn't matter now. It was over and done with and he couldn't change any of it.

There's no question that it will kill you sooner or later. So there's your choice, you see.

Thaddeus had never been afraid to die. He just wasn't sure he wanted to. Not yet.

But if the alternative was a doddering invalidism spent in some relative or other's house, the choice was clear.

This time he would choose family. He would find out who was threatening him and prevent them from harming any of his loved ones. And if it killed him, so be it. He would just have to trust that a merciful God would let him into Heaven after all.

The next morning, Thaddeus marched downstairs and announced that he was accompanying Martha to school.

"I don't think you should do that," Luke objected. "I really would prefer it if you stayed in for a couple of days."

"I know you would prefer that," Thaddeus said. "But if somebody's trying to harm us, my first duty is to Martha's safety. I promised Francis I would look after her."

"If you go out looking the way you do, you'll only alarm dogs and small children," Christie commented.

It was a fair point. Thaddeus's face was swollen and the deep purple bruising in no way disguised the stark row of sutures that ran across his cheekbone.

"Does it have to be you who takes her?" Luke said. "I need the sleigh this morning anyway. I could drive her down before I make my rounds. That way you can stay put."

"I suppose." But Luke thought Thaddeus looked disappointed. He seemed ready to spring into some sort of action, in spite of the warning he had received the day before.

Just as they were leaving, Morgan Spicer arrived at the door, as promised, to "see how Thaddeus is doing."

"Can you stay with him for a bit?" Luke asked. "I don't think there are any issues physically, but he's bored already. And Christie's around if you run into difficulty."

"I'll stay until you get back," Spicer said.

"Good," Thaddeus said. "I want to talk to you anyway."

"Then we're set," Luke said, but he had an uneasy feeling about what his father was up to.

Morgan waited until Luke and Martha left before he spoke. "I already know what you're going to say. I thought about it all last night, but I didn't see anybody or anything. I heard you yell and when I came back you were already lying on the ground."

"Whoever did it must have been close by. You can't have been that far away."

"I wasn't. But I didn't see anyone."

"Someone's been following me. I first noticed it in Wellington."

"Are you sure?"

"Yes. And whoever it is has made two previous attempts to harm me. Once on the steamer that took us to Wellington, and again a couple of weeks later when Martha and I were out walking."

"Do you have any idea who it might be?" Spicer asked.

"No. I thought at first it might be Cuddy Nelson, because we saw him down in Macaulaytown, but Luke says if it was Cuddy,

I'd be dead by now."

"He's probably right. Besides, even if Cuddy just happened to be aboard the same steamer that you were, why would he hang around Wellington for so long before he made another try?"

"That's the conclusion I've reached as well. Unfortunately, I haven't reached any conclusions about who else it might be."

"Is there anything I can do to help you find out?"

"Yes," Thaddeus said. "Your twins ram all over the village. Ask them to keep an eye out for strangers. Anybody they don't normally see, or who seems out of place. They don't have to do anything about it. They just have to watch, and then let us know about it."

It was a fine morning to be driving a sleigh down Yonge Street but Luke barely noticed the bright sunshine. He was worried about Thaddeus and he needed to talk to Martha about it. Like the rest of the family, Luke was bemused by the rather singular relationship that had developed between the two. In some ways, it was ideal for both of them. Thaddeus had someone to keep him company, and by tagging along behind her grandfather, Martha experienced a freedom that was seldom enjoyed by young women her age. Luke also knew that the current arrangement was a hastily put together ploy to appease Francis. But what no one else seemed to have considered was that, at the end of it all, Martha would be independent in her own right. She wouldn't need Thaddeus anymore, and Luke wasn't entirely sure how this change would affect their current dynamic.

"Have you given any thought to what happens when you finish school?" he asked as they crossed the Concession Line.

The question seemed to surprise her. "I've promised to go be a teacher," she said. "I'll find a position somewhere, I suppose, although I have no idea at the moment where that might be."

"Are you looking forward to being out on your own and away from your troublesome family?"

Luke was joking, but Martha was obviously astonished by this comment.

"But I won't be alone. Grandpa will be with me."

"So that's the plan? To have him live with you?"

"Of course."

"I'm pleased that you seem to want him, but I hope you know that you're not obliged. He can always stay with me. Or Will and Moses."

"But I want him to come with me. Just like he wanted me to go with him. We've already talked about it."

It was a relief to Luke to hear this. He enjoyed his father's company and was happy enough to have him stay for a few months while Martha went to school. Thaddeus was normally an easy guest – as a circuit rider he had spent many a night in someone else's home and knew how to slip into a household's routine with minimum disruption. But Luke was beginning to realize that having an ailing Thaddeus as a permanent fixture in the household could be another matter entirely, especially when his hands were already full with the rapidly aging Christie, an increasingly frail Mrs. Dunphy, and a busy medical practice. He would find some way to accommodate it if need be, but he was pleased that Martha was not only willing, but eager to have Thaddeus with her. Luke just wasn't entirely convinced that it would be the best thing for either of them. And he would be remiss if he didn't make the situation clear to Martha.

"There's something you need to know. Pa has a few health problems he's been ignoring. Oh, it's nothing too dire at the moment," he said in response to her look of alarm. "But he certainly will never be able to ride a circuit again – or at least he shouldn't."

"I think he's done with preaching anyway," Martha said.

"But that raises the question of what he's going to do instead. He shouldn't attempt anything too physically demanding. And these cases he got involved in with Ashby haven't done him any good either. Too much excitement can contribute to the problem."

She turned to look at him. "So I'll work and he can keep house. He already knows how to do most everything from working at the hotel and looking after Grandma. That wouldn't be too taxing for him, would it?"

"That would be fine. I'm not trying to make a case that he's incapable or anything. And he's really not that old. With a little heedfulness, he should have many good years ahead of him. I just want you to be aware that there are some limitations as to what he can and can't do."

"Or should and shouldn't do," she pointed out. "The two things are quite different, you know."

Luke laughed. "And so they are. Anyway, I thought you should be aware of the situation, so you're not unprepared when trouble comes calling – and I'm afraid it will eventually."

"Whatever it is we'll deal with it together."

"He's lucky to have you."

"No," she said. "I'm the lucky one. He's always looked after me. It's time I looked after him."

They were nearing the school when Luke decided to introduce the topic that had his brothers so fired up.

"The picture Thaddeus carries with him – is that the woman from Cobourg?"

The question startled her. She glared at him. "No. That's not Mrs. Howell."

Then she turned away, lips slightly pursed.

It must be the other woman, then. The woman everyone in London thought was Thaddeus's wife. The woman who had, unfortunately, died. Luke was beginning to wonder just what, exactly, had gone on in London, but it was clear from the set of Martha's shoulders that she was not going to be the one to tell him.

"Do you suppose he'd ever marry again?" Luke asked, hoping to chivy at least a little more information out of her.

"You'll have to ask him that yourself, but I expect he's tired of questions about matrimony." She turned to him again with a wry smile. "Just like you are."

Luke was still laughing when he jumped out of the sleigh to hand Martha down.

A number of girls were clustered around the side-door entrance, enjoying a last-minute bask in the sun before they were forced to go inside.

As she took Luke's hand to step down to the street Martha

could hear giggles and a rustle of comment.

"Someone will be here to pick you up at the end of the day," he said. "Thaddeus will stew otherwise."

She might have protested that she was fine on her own had she not had the experience of being kidnapped once. She was eager not to have it happen again. If Thaddeus thought there was a threat, she was willing to listen to him, and take whatever precautions he thought necessary.

"Thanks for the ride." She waved a goodbye as Luke drove off. When she turned to head for the door, she walked straight into a disapproving scowl from the headmistress.

"A word, Miss Renwell?"

Chapter 9

Martha wasn't particularly alarmed as she followed Miss Clark into her small office. She had expected to be questioned about her abrupt departure the day before, but she was quite taken aback when it became apparent that the headmistress had not received her message.

"Yesterday you were seen leaving through the front doors of the school with a strange man," Clark said without preamble, her mouth set in a grim line.

"Yes. My grandfather was injured yesterday. A friend of his came to take me to him."

"Well that's a pleasant story."

"I beg your pardon? I don't understand."

"This…friend…arrived at the school and you just went blithely off without a backward glance?"

"No miss." Martha wanted to say that there had been nothing blithe about her departure, but she was afraid that she would be accused of impertinence. "I was aware that I should let someone know that I was leaving and why. There was no one in the office and Mr. Spicer was waiting with a cab, so I asked another student to relay the message."

"I received no message. Who was this student?"

Martha hesitated. She didn't want to cause trouble for Bernice, but she could see no way around it. If only Bernice had done as she was asked.

"Bernice Walters."

"And the man who delivered you to the school this morning? Is he the same *friend*?"

"No, that was my uncle."

"Are you sure? His appearance caused quite a stir amongst the girls."

"Yes of course I'm sure he's my uncle. His name is Dr. Lewis. I'm sorry if his presence caused a commotion. He meant only to deliver me safely to school."

It was clear to Martha that Miss Clark thought she was lying. That she had concocted an excuse to sneak off with an admirer.

"I'm warning you, Miss Renwell, I will be corroborating this story with Miss Walters. Would you like to amend your account in any way before I do that?"

"On the contrary, miss, I welcome an investigation. It will allow me to set the record straight."

That took the headmistress aback, but only for a moment.

"I know that you have been made fully aware of our policy concerning social contact between the sexes, as well as our regulations regarding entering and exiting the school, or leaving without notice. For that reason, you should consider yourself under warning until this matter can be satisfactorily resolved."

"Yes miss." Martha was furious, but tried her best not to let it show. It would serve no purpose. She didn't see how Bernice could deny that she'd been asked to deliver a message and that should be the end of the matter, but Martha supposed that if worse came to worst, she could ask Luke to have a word with the headmaster. And Thaddeus could confirm her story as well, but considering the circumstances, she hesitated to ask either of them. This was a minor problem. She should be able to sort this out herself.

Bernice looked up when Martha joined her class, but Martha ignored her. When class let out for the dinner break, several of the girls clustered around.

"Did you do a bunk with a boy yesterday?" said one of the boldest, a girl named Harriet Jeffers.

"No, of course not."

"So who was the man who drove you to school this morning?"

"That was Dr. Luke, wasn't it?" Alice Gleeson said. Alice lived in Yorkville. She rode the same bus as Martha, but had made no particular attempt to be friendly. "He's been looking after my little brother's measles. All of the girls in Yorkville are after him, but he doesn't seem to pay any attention. How did you get him to give you a ride?"

"He's my uncle."

"Ooh," said Clara Parker. "I wish I had an uncle like that."

"Why?" Martha said. She couldn't follow Clara's reasoning at all.

"Do you think he'd give me a ride sometime?" Alice said, but she said it with a simper, so Martha knew it was less an issue of transportation than it was of an opportunity to meet Luke.

"I don't think so," Martha said. "It's not going to be a regular thing."

"You wouldn't introduce me, would you?" asked one of the others.

"No, I wouldn't. He's very busy. He doesn't have time for girls." Especially silly schoolgirls. But she didn't say it out loud. "Besides, we're not supposed to be keeping company with anybody. You could be expelled. You know that."

"I'd be willing to take a chance for him," Harriet said and they all laughed.

By the time Martha got away from her giggling classmates, Bernice was nowhere to be seen. It wasn't until after the dinner break that she finally caught up with her in the hall.

"I'm sorry," Bernice said. "I know you're mad at me."

"Why didn't you pass on my message yesterday?"

Bernice turned bright red.

"I...I tried to. I tried to tell Miss Clark, but she was on her way out and didn't see me, and then I couldn't find her again."

"Then why didn't you tell Miss Shenick? Or one of the masters?"

"I...I didn't think of it. You said 'tell the headmistress'."

Martha knew that Bernice had probably summoned up all the courage she possessed just to try to talk to Miss Clark.

"I've talked to her now," Bernice said, a tear rolling down her cheek.

"Is that where you've been?"

Bernice nodded, and blew her nose.

"I can only hope you managed to stop crying long enough to tell her what I said."

Bernice's face crumpled.

"I'm sorry, Bernice, but I'm really quite annoyed. I've been put on notice over this. Honestly, I don't know how you think you're ever going to be able to control a roomful of children if you can't even pass along a message."

It was a cruel thing to say. It was also the truth. Unless Bernice developed some backbone, she could never become a teacher.

Bernice avoided her for the rest of the day.

At the end of the last class, Miss Clark followed Martha out of the school.

"I see you've managed to find the proper door this time," she said, but her tone was not unfriendly. "I questioned your friend. Or rather, I attempted to, but as she arrived in a state and continued to weep throughout the interview, it was a most unsatisfactory encounter. However between the gasps and sobs, I did manage to ascertain that you did, in fact, ask her to let me know that you'd left the school, and why."

"Thank you, miss."

"I trust your grandfather was not severely injured?"

This took Martha by surprise. She hadn't expected any sympathy.

"It was severe enough. He took a nasty blow to the head and my uncle was quite concerned that there could be damage beyond what was apparent at the time. But it appears that all is well."

"Ah yes, your uncle the doctor."

Martha decided it was wise to be conciliatory. "I'm sorry, miss. I know I should have told you directly that I was leaving, but I was very upset and anxious to go to my grandfather. My choice of messenger was, perhaps, ill-advised and I apologize for my lack of judgment."

"Is Miss Walters a close friend?"

"No, not at all. We met for the first time here. I've been trying to help her along as best I can, but she's finding it difficult to settle in."

"I'll see what I can do to help put her more at ease, but I must say it would be a good thing if some of your self-confidence rubbed off on her."

Before Martha could reply, Luke drew up in front of the school.

"Is this the uncle again?" Miss Clark asked. Martha thought she could hear a slightly eager tone to the inquiry.

"Yes. And that's my grandfather with him. But he wasn't supposed to leave the house."

Martha walked out to the drive with Miss Clark close behind her. None of the girls who had been watching dared crowd too close with the headmistress there.

As before, Luke hopped down to assist Martha.

"I couldn't get Pa to stay home," he said with a shrug. "The best I could do was come with him."

Miss Clark hovered, obviously waiting for an introduction.

Martha obliged. "Miss Clark, this my uncle, Dr. Lewis. Miss Clark is the headmistress here at the school." She suppressed a smirk when Miss Clark's face coloured a little.

"And this is my grandfather, Mr. Lewis."

The headmistress gasped a little when she looked up into the mess that was Thaddeus's face.

"Oh my, Miss Renwell told me you were injured. How dreadful!"

"Yes it is, isn't it?" Luke said. "He's lucky to have survived it. Fortunately, he's extremely hard-headed."

"It takes more than a whack on the head to kill a preacher," Thaddeus said to Miss Clark. "It may have ruined my good looks, but it hasn't dampened my spirits."

"More's the pity," Luke replied. "Your spirits could use a little dampening."

Miss Clark didn't seem to know how to respond to the banter, but Martha was glad that the headmistress got a first-hand look at Thaddeus's injuries. There would be no more question about whether or not Martha was telling the truth.

A bundle of letters from Wellington arrived the next day. One was for Martha, from her father, judging by the handwriting, but Francis had also forwarded the mail that arrived at the hotel for Thaddeus. There was another book-shaped package, which he took up to his room before he opened it. Again, banknotes fell from the pages. Again, they amounted to a substantial amount of money. The postmark clearly read "Richmond, Va." Thaddeus tucked the notes into the bottom of his valise. He would deposit them in the bank account at the first opportunity.

There was another letter from Will, and one from Bishop Smith. Thaddeus was fairly certain that Will's would only annoy him, so he read the Bishop's first.

It began with a polite enquiry after his health, and went on to relate the news and gossip from the ministerial ranks of the Methodist Episcopal Church. Thaddeus was surprised to read that several of his contemporaries had been superannuated. It used to be that old circuit riders died in the saddle, but times were changing. There were more located ministries now that the country was so settled, and the older preachers could retire in the knowledge that their flocks had access to regular services.

James Small, who had been Thaddeus's assistant in Cobourg was now ordained, the Bishop wrote, and had married the daughter of another minister. Thaddeus must remember to tell Martha. She would be happy to know that James was now firmly attached to someone else.

The rest of the letter was full of news of mutual acquaintances and church business, which no longer concerned Thaddeus, but he was grateful that the Bishop kept him informed.

Will's letter was entirely different in tone. There was barely a salutation.

Pa,

What on earth is going on? It was unsettling enough to think that we had a stepmother who died before we had a chance to meet her, but then two men showed up at the farm this week asking about her. I could only repeat what I'd learned in London. Moses couldn't even do that, as we have heard precisely nothing from you on the matter.

This is, of course, your business, but the detectives who were here claim this Mrs. Elliott is very much alive and a fugitive from justice. They also wanted to know your whereabouts. I stated only that you had been here briefly and that I had no idea what your plans were for the future. Which is the truth, since you've neglected to tell us anything at all.

You can do what you like, but I am becoming a little weary of being blindsided by extraordinary claims about your activities.

Your increasingly perplexed son,
Will

Two men asking questions. Detectives had tracked Clementine to London. They'd heard the same gossip as Will had. And now they were looking for Thaddeus.

He hadn't written back to Will because he had no idea how to explain about Clementine, but as it turned out, it was just as well that he had procrastinated. Will had been able to state quite truthfully that he didn't know Thaddeus's plans and had been prescient enough not to mention Wellington. And if the detectives somehow made their way to Wellington, Francis knew that he was in Toronto, but would know nothing about Clementine, other than the fact that she had been in London. Neither Will nor Francis could give much away.

Sooner or later they would find him anyway, but as Thaddeus quite genuinely had no idea where Clementine was, he decided not to worry about it.

That night at supper, Martha helped Mrs. Dunphy clear away the plates from the main course and rinsed them at the kitchen pump before she stacked them beside the sink. As she passed the pine table that stood in the middle of the room, she noticed a plate of ladyfinger biscuits sitting behind the bowl of strawberry preserves set out for dessert. There was scrap of paper on top of the biscuits. *Get well soon, Thaddeus* the note said. Mrs. Dunphy must have made them as a special treat. It seemed an uncharacteristic thing for her to have done, but Martha knew that the elderly housekeeper approved of the Lewis clan in general and Thaddeus and Luke in particular. Smiling, she carried the preserves and the plate of biscuits into the dining room and set them in front of her grandfather.

"Treats from a well-wisher," she said. "It looks as though you have a secret admirer."

Mrs. Dunphy was handing around the dessert plates, but now she stopped in mid-pass and frowned. "Where did those come from?" she asked.

"They were sitting on the kitchen table. I thought you meant them for dessert," Martha said.

"No, I've got a pound cake to go with the preserves."

"You didn't make these?"

"No. And I have no idea how they ended up in my kitchen."

"Ah well, wherever they came from, they'll do to tide us over until the cake gets here," Dr. Christie said and reached for one of the ladyfingers.

He was just about to take a bite when Thaddeus leapt up from his seat, leaned across the table and swatted the biscuit out of Christie's hand. It flew across the dining room and landed on the floor, where it broke open, spilling a powdery white substance across the carpet.

"What did you do that for?" Christie said, with a look of outrage.

But Luke was already out of his seat and bending over the offending ladyfinger.

"What's this?" he said. "Something's been stuffed into this biscuit."

Gingerly, Thaddeus took a fork and flipped over one of the ladyfingers that remained on the plate. "There's a hole bored into this one. On the side, near the bottom."

Martha reached out to flip over another of them, but Luke stopped her.

"No, don't anybody touch them. Don't get that powder anywhere near your mouth or nose."

But even as he said it, they all realized that it was too late. Dr. Christie had already clapped his hand to his mouth in dismay.

Martha was amazed at how fast Luke moved. He pulled Christie up out of his chair and pushed him through to the kitchen. The rest of them crowded behind.

Luke pushed the old doctor's head down into the sink and pumped a sluice of water over his face.

"Somebody pump while I wash," he said. Martha ran to the pump and kept the water flowing while Luke grabbed the soap that Mrs. Dunphy used for dishes and slathered it around Christie's mouth. Christie sputtered and coughed.

"Now your hands," Luke said, and pushed them under the flow of water.

Thaddeus grabbed a tea towel and mopped Christie's face as well as he could with it while Luke continued to scrub.

"That should be enough," Luke finally said. Mrs. Dunphy found another towel and exchanged it for the now-sodden one Thaddeus had used.

Christie, white-faced and wet, collapsed into a chair at the kitchen table.

"My heavens, boy, but that was a close call," he wheezed.

"I don't think you could have got enough of it to do you much harm," Luke said, "but even a little is too much." Luke's sleeve and the front of his waistcoat were nearly as wet as Christie's.

"I'll go clean up the dining room," Mrs. Dunphy said.

"No, I'll do it. No one else should go near it." Luke looked at Christie. "You'll let me know if you have any symptoms?" he asked.

Christie nodded.

"And you'll let me know right away?"

Again, Christie nodded. Satisfied, Luke wet a cloth at the pump and grabbed a pair of gardening gloves from the cupboard by the back door.

In the meantime, the kettle was boiling away on the stove. Martha poured the water into the teapot.

"I think we should finish our meal in here," she said. "Everyone sit down and I'll serve it up."

"I must admit, I'm happy enough to sit," said Mrs. Dunphy. "I'm quite rattled." She turned to Dr. Christie. "You're a dreadful old man, Stewart, but I'd hate to lose you."

Although Christie was still wheezing, he was regaining his composure. "Thank you, Flora. That's music to my ears."

"Don't think it will get you any special treatment," she warned.

"The thought never crossed my mind."

Martha tried to catch her grandfather's eye. It was the sort of exchange that normally amused them both. But Thaddeus sat at the end of the table, lost in thought.

"The pound cake is in the pantry, my dear," Mrs. Dunphy said.

Martha retrieved it, and began cutting it into slices, although the preserves were still in the dining room and she didn't dare get them until Luke had finished disposing of the ladyfingers. No one said anything as she passed the plates around. Finally, Luke came back into the kitchen. He peeled off the gloves and threw them into the belly of the stove, then went to the sink to scrub his hands. Martha slipped into the dining room and returned with the bowl of preserved fruit.

"I've put the biscuits in the office," Luke said when he finally judged that he had washed away any residual powder. "I'd like to test them before I burn them."

"How will you do that?" Martha asked. She wondered if there was some chemical test Luke could do that would tell him what was in the ladyfingers.

"I'll get the Spicer boys to catch me a rat. We'll see if a biscuit kills it."

"Why are you even doing that?" asked Thaddeus. "It doesn't make any difference, does it?"

"At the very least it will tell us whether or not we've jumped to conclusions. We don't know for sure that it was poison."

"I can't think of any other reason someone would sneak into the kitchen and leave a plate of doctored biscuits with my name on it unless they meant to poison me," Thaddeus pointed out. "Especially after there have already been three previous attempts on my life."

"But we don't know for certain that's the case. The other incidents could be explained away. Maybe this one can, as well."

"Not to mention the fact that someone's been following me,"

Thaddeus muttered.

"What?" Luke and Martha said at the same time.

Thaddeus replied to Martha. "I didn't say anything before because I wasn't sure. I think someone was following me in Wellington. And someone's been following me ever since we came to Toronto."

"Do you have any idea who it is?" Martha said.

And to her surprise Thaddeus answered, "Maybe. But I'm not sure if the two things are connected."

"But why would someone be following you unless he meant to harm you?" Martha said. "I mean …why would he be following you otherwise?"

"It is, by far, the most likely explanation, given what's happened," Thaddeus agreed.

"What other explanation could there be?" Luke said. "What else have you got yourself tangled up in?"

Thaddeus sighed. "It could have something to do with Clementine Elliott."

"Oh," said Martha.

"Who is Clementine Elliott?" said Luke.

"Ah, a woman at the bottom of it," said Dr. Christie. "How interesting!"

Thaddeus ignored them both and again spoke to Martha. "She's been sending me money."

"For what?"

"Just to keep for her. She said to put it in a safe place. And every time another package arrives, it's from a different city. I don't know what trouble she's got herself into, but sooner or later she's going to show up here looking for her cash. People may be watching me in the hopes of finding her. Will says two men were at the farm asking questions."

"What men? Do you mean detectives?"

"Yes."

"But if they're looking for Clementine," Martha said, "why would they try to kill you? You can't tell them anything if you're dead."

"That's the part I can't make sense of," Thaddeus said. "I really don't know if one has anything to do with the other."

"Who is Clementine Elliott?" Luke asked again.

"She's the woman in London whom everyone mistook for my wife," Thaddeus said. "I know perfectly well that Will told you all about it."

Luke looked puzzled. "But she died, didn't she? In the train accident."

"No, she didn't. She went to great lengths to make everyone think she died, but she used the confusion of the accident to conveniently disappear. And she was in London in the first place because she was hiding from something – or somebody. I don't know who."

"And now she's sending you money?"

"Oh bravo, Mr. Lewis. A wife who sends money instead of demanding yours! How on earth did you manage that?" Christie seemed highly amused by the turn the conversation had taken.

Thaddeus ignored the comment. "I tried to talk to Ashby about it as soon as I got to Toronto, to ask him what I should do, but apparently he's away."

"Yes," Luke said. "He just got married. He's off somewhere on his honeymoon."

Martha jumped a little at the word "married", then looked around quickly to see if anyone noticed. Dr. Christie, across the table from her, was the only one who saw.

"So what did you do with the money?" Luke asked.

"I've been putting it in the bank. It's too much to leave lying around."

"In her name, or yours?"

"In mine, since I don't even know what her real name is. It certainly isn't Clementine Elliott."

"But why would she send it to you in the first place?"

Thaddeus looked a little sheepish. "Because I offered to help her."

"Help her do what?"

"I don't know what. She's awfully devious. She's the same woman who turned up in Wellington claiming to be the wife of a local man and it all turned out to be some scheme to bilk an old farmer out of his money. And then she and her son turned up again in London."

"But why would you offer to help her?" Luke persisted. "Especially if you had no idea what she would want you to do?"

"Because…it's a long story," Thaddeus said. And the part of his face that wasn't black and blue turned a bright red.

It didn't take much imagination to supply the probable cause of Thaddeus's embarrassment. Martha jumped into the conversation in an attempt to deflect attention away from his tell-tale blush.

"She helped us. She and her son helped us solve the case and then they helped find me when I was kidnapped."

"Well," Luke said, "be that as it may, I really don't see how it gets us any further toward discovering who's trying to kill your grandfather."

"Nor do I," Martha said. "But I do suggest we start locking the doors. After all, whoever it was walked right into this kitchen without a by-your-leave."

"Good point. We all need to start being more careful."

"Whoever it is should be trotted off to the gallows," Dr. Christie commented, and for once, everyone was inclined to agree with him.

Mrs. Dunphy rose from her chair and began piling dishes into the sink.

Martha jumped up. "I'll finish clearing the dining room," she said, "and then I'm afraid I've still a lot of work to get through this evening."

"Do you need help with anything?" Thaddeus asked.

She shook her head. "No, it's all reading. I never thought I could be tired of reading, but they give us so much it's hard not to be."

"And I need to change my clothes," Christie said. "My collar is dampish from the sluicing I took." He heaved himself up from his chair and toddled away.

"And I'd like a closer look at the note that came with the biscuits," Thaddeus said to Luke. "I hope you saved it."

"It's all in my office. I'll come too and have another look. Just remember not to touch anything."

Martha had her papers spread across the dining room table by the time Dr. Christie came downstairs again. She smiled at him as he walked through the dining room. "How are you feeling? No ill-effects I hope."

"No, none. Even if there had been powder on my fingers, it wouldn't have been much and I'm fairly certain I didn't ingest any. And you, my dear? Are you all right?" His air of concern surprised her.

"Yes," she said in a puzzled tone, "I'm fine."

"Ah. I thought perhaps you had a little disappointment there in the kitchen."

She didn't try to pretend she didn't understand. "About Ashby? No, not really. I was surprised to hear that he married, that's all. He never mentioned that he was engaged. And he certainly never acted like it."

"Bit of a rake, is he?"

"More than a bit, I'd say. But it's nothing to me."

Christie looked at her for a long moment before he spoke again. "Well, that's fine then isn't it? But you know where to find me if you need to talk about it, don't you?"

"Thank you," she said, both touched and bemused by his concern. "I don't have anything to talk about, but I'd gladly come and sit with you if it wouldn't bother you too much. The lamp in your studio casts a much better light than the one in here."

Christie looked at her in astonishment. "Would you like to do that? The presence of all those bones won't disturb you?"

"Not at all. And I promise I'll sit quietly and read."

Christie beamed. "I'd be delighted with the company. I don't know why I didn't think of it before."

Luke had shoved the mess from the dining room into a wad of newspapers and put them on his desk. As Thaddeus watched, he gingerly peeled the layers of newsprint back until the biscuits and the note were exposed.

"It isn't very subtle is it?" he remarked.

"No," Thaddeus agreed. "Just holes poked in the side and the powder shoved in."

"You're lucky more pains weren't taken. If it's rat poison and it had been baked into the cakes, you'd never have known it was there. Arsenic leaves no trace when it's cooked into something else."

But Thaddeus was peering at the note. "I don't recognize the handwriting."

"Is it possible that it was written by the woman from London – this Mrs. Elliott? And that she's the one who's been following you?"

"I shouldn't think so. Every package she's sent me has had a postmark from a different city. She's on the move for some reason."

"You said she had a son. What about him? Could he be mailing them to throw you off the track?'

"I suppose," Thaddeus said. "But I can't think of any reason why Mrs. Elliott would follow me in the first place."

"She doesn't have reason to feel..." Luke groped for a diplomatic way to say what he was thinking "... spurned or anything?"

"No. We parted on good terms."

"Is the son likely to have taken offence on behalf of his mother? Because you..."

Thaddeus shook his head. "I doubt it. I don't think Joe has any illusions about his mother. He's been her partner in crime since he was a boy."

"Not the sort to leap up and defend his mother's honour or anything like that?"

"She's not a woman apt to inspire much gallantry," Thaddeus pointed out. "After all her stock in trade is fraud and deceit."

"I'm not sure that's true. You're being pretty gallant." Luke was waging a desperate struggle not to laugh at the notion of his upright father lured into the clutches of a seductive huckster.

Thaddeus glared at him. "Do you find this amusing?"

"Kind of. You seem to be having a lot of trouble with women."

"Everything's gone to rot since your mother died," he grumbled.

Luke couldn't help himself. He began to laugh. "It's no wonder Will and Moses failed so miserably with all those country widows they trotted past you. You can't have found them very appealing after someone as exciting as Mrs. Elliott."

"Stop," Thaddeus said.

"She must really be something to have reeled you in so thoroughly."

"She is the most contrary woman I ever met. All she does is argue."

"Ah."

"What do you mean, "ah"?"

"That's probably what you like about her. I seem to remember that Ma was never shy about telling you what she thought."

"You can't compare the two. Your mother was lovely. Mrs. Elliott is… annoying."

"Martha seems to like her."

"She was very kind to Martha." And then Thaddeus's expression grew glum. "Do you think Martha realizes what I did? In London?"

"I'm reasonably sure Martha already knew." Luke debated with himself for a moment before he went on, uncertain if he was betraying a confidence of sorts. "I have a confession to make. I looked at that daguerreotype before I gave it back to you yesterday. I asked Martha about it. She refused to tell me anything."

Thaddeus groaned. "I don't know what she must think. I'm supposed to be an example to her. How do I explain this? Do you think I should talk to her?"

Luke was dying to hear an explanation himself, but he knew better than to press for one. "If I were you, I wouldn't say anything at all. Martha is quite prepared to interpret anything you do in the best possible light. And she may know all your secrets, but I suspect it would take a herd of wild horses to drag them out of her."

"That's more or less what Clementine…Mrs. Elliott… said too." Thaddeus's face softened with the recollection and Luke realized that, at least as far as his father was concerned, there was more to the story than a temporary lapse in judgment.

"Regardless of what Martha knows, this isn't getting us any closer to coming up with a culprit. Excluding Mrs. Elliott as a suspect, who are we left with?"

Thaddeus appeared relieved to leave the subject of Clementine behind. "I can't be positive" he said, "but the note looks to me as though it's written in a female hand."

"It does. And you may not agree with this, but the attempts on your life have been pretty clumsy. The powder in the biscuits was poorly disguised. Running someone down with a carriage is an uncertain way to murder someone."

"And whoever stabbed me didn't have the strength to push a blade through heavy clothing."

Luke nodded. "The most damage done was the blow to your head. If whatever was used had been swung a little harder it might have done the trick. Either the culprit didn't mean to kill you, or didn't have the strength to do it properly."

"Do you really think it might be a woman?"

"It's worth considering. So if it's not Mrs. Elliott, I have to ask what other females you've crossed."

"I suppose there must be some," Thaddeus admitted.

"So the question is why someone would be angry enough to want to kill you. I can't help but think that it has something to do with your previous adventures. Martha mentioned someone chasing you through the streets in London. What happened there?"

"A woman was murdered and Ashby asked me to investigate. There were any number of people who were unhappy with the outcome for various reasons, but they're all male. And I can't think that any of them would be disgruntled enough to come after me."

"What about the woman in Cobourg then?"

"There really wasn't anything to that, other than a lot of nasty gossip and it was mostly directed my way. The woman in question was entirely circumspect and has gone out of her way to avoid me since. I don't see why she would suddenly turn up angry."

"What if her husband thought there was more to it than just gossip?"

"I suppose." Then Thaddeus shook his head. "She's a very frail woman. And she walks with a slight limp. I'd have noticed if she'd been following me."

Luke's mother had walked with a slight limp, after her bouts of illness. Luke was beginning to understand what had happened to his father in Cobourg. He knew that Thaddeus had been severely depressed after his wife's death. It wasn't surprising that a woman who reminded him of Betsy would attract his attention, especially if she was in vulnerable circumstances. And there was scarcely a circumstance as vulnerable as being unjustly accused of murder. No wonder Thaddeus had galloped to her rescue, even though she was such an inappropriate object for his affections. Luke had first-hand experience with inappropriate affection and he knew that the heart seldom took notice of what the world thought suitable. Poor Thaddeus.

Luke wasn't so sure about the liaison with Mrs. Elliott. Had she found out about the events in Cobourg somehow, and used the knowledge to manipulate Thaddeus while he was still struggling with guilt and disappointment? How would she have found out, when Martha was being so close-lipped? Unless she'd heard the tale from Ashby – he was the only other person who had been in both places.

It was entirely possible, Luke supposed, that Mrs. Elliott had wormed it out of Ashby, but he couldn't for the life of him fathom what her motives might have been. She had asked Thaddeus for help, but what did that entail? Something to do with the money, no doubt, but what exactly? Mrs. Elliott's stock in trade was fraud. Was she using Thaddeus to further some scheme? Luke wished Ashby was in town, so he could discuss the legalities of what Thaddeus was doing. And so he could hear Ashby's assessment of the Elliott woman. And, he had to admit, so he could find out more about what had happened in London.

"What about the first time you met Mrs. Elliott? In Wellington?" he asked.

"Again, the only woman involved was Mrs. Elliott herself. And she was grateful that I let her get away."

"You've let her get away with a lot, haven't you? It's no wonder she's been so grateful." Luke couldn't keep the smirk off his face.

"That's enough. I'm not discussing Mrs. Elliott with you any more."

"All right, I'm sorry. But whoever is doing this must have a reason. Are there any other women from your past who might want to kill you?"

"I can think of no one – unless I've somehow crossed someone and didn't realize it, which I suppose is entirely possible. Or maybe we've got it wrong and it isn't a woman after all, but if that's the case all it does is broaden the list of suspects. Can you think of anyone who might have a bone to pick with me?"

"Not really, except for Cuddy Nelson. But as I said, if Cuddy wanted you dead, you'd be long gone. And me too, I suppose."

"Was there anyone in Kingston?"

Luke cast his mind back to his volunteer time in the fever sheds. He had uncovered murder amongst the dying Irish emigrants, and enlisted his father's aid in his pursuit of the killer. There had been victims aplenty in a sea of victims, but justice, of a sort, had been served in the end.

"I can't think of any," Luke said. "Especially not the girls. We helped them. Or at least I think we did. What about the first case? The Simms murders?"

"The women were all victims. There was no one else involved except for Simms himself."

Luke was familiar with only the broad outlines of the story. He had never asked about the details, nor had Thaddeus offered them. Luke knew only that his sister Sarah had been murdered. The loss had driven his father into a tailspin and his mother into an early grave. He didn't want to talk about the Simms murders any more than Thaddeus did.

"I don't know why anyone connected with Simms would turn up at this late date," Thaddeus said. "It's been..." he stopped to count up the time that had passed, "... thirteen years since he was hanged."

"It does seem unlikely, doesn't it? But we should both think about it some more. There must be something we've missed. For all I know, you've left a whole trail of angry women in your wake."

Thaddeus glared. Luke laughed. "All right, I'm sorry. But let's consider all the possibilities."

"Agreed. In the meantime, we don't need to tell Francis about any of this, do we?"

Luke shrugged. "You're my patient, and we're in my office. As far as I'm concerned, everything you've just told me is confidential." Thaddeus looked relieved, but Luke wasn't quite ready to let him off the hook just yet. "I do, however, reserve the right to be a little amused by all your romancing," and then he laughed again at the look on his father's face.

Chapter 10

"**H**ave you had measles?" Luke asked Thaddeus the next morning. "There's quite an outbreak in the village. I'd just as soon you didn't catch them. It's the last thing you need on top of everything else."

"Yes I have. In 1813," Thaddeus replied. "During the war. I was sick as a dog."

Luke nodded. "It seems that the older you are, the harder it hits. What about Martha?"

"She was just a little thing. Three or four, I think. I seem to recall her covered in rash and worried that it wasn't ever going to go away."

"Good. I don't have to worry about either of you then. By the way, I have to harness the mare this morning anyway, so I'll drive her down to school."

"You don't have to do that. I'm well enough to ride the omnibus with her."

"I have patients in the north end of the city I need to see," Luke said. "I can drop her off and then make my visits."

Thaddeus grumbled, but acquiesced. "I'll get you at the end of the day," he said to Martha. "Wait until I get there."

"All right," she said, "if you think I should."

"I know you think I'm being a fussbudget, but I'll feel better if I know you're safe."

She smiled. "Then that makes it worth doing, doesn't it?"

After she left and everyone else went about their business for the day, Thaddeus lingered over a second cup of tea. His abortive first attempt at writing his memoirs lay accusingly at the end of the table. He felt even less inclined to write about the horrors of the war than he had before, but maybe he should set that part of his story aside for the moment and follow up on Luke's suggestion that the attempts on his life were somehow connected to his previous involvement in bringing criminals to justice. Maybe if he wrote details down something would become clear. And he had his journals and records close at hand so he could verify things like places and dates, in case a pattern emerged that had some bearing on the current situation.

His recollection of the case in London was freshest in his mind. An arson that resulted in murder. The wrongly accused was exonerated, thanks to Thaddeus. Who would bear a grudge in the case? Not the young man who had initially been arrested for the crime. His father maybe, who had been presented with a huge legal bill for his son's defence. But he would have no reason to come after Thaddeus – it was Towns Ashby who had presented the bill. One witness lied and was called out, but there had been no consequences to his lying. Nothing in the London case seemed to fit, unless Luke was right and Clementine was trying to kill him, a notion Thaddeus continued to discount. Irrespective of anything else, the attempts were too clumsy. If Clementine ever wanted to kill him, he suspected that she would be every bit as efficient about it as Cuddy Nelson.

Cobourg. As much as he didn't want to revisit his disgrace, Thaddeus had to give some consideration to Martha's suggestion that Major Howell might have a bone to pick. Ellen Howell had conducted herself with the utmost propriety, but what if her husband was the sort of man who didn't believe his wife? Except that Howell was wanted on counterfeiting charges in Canada. He would be taking a very great risk if he came back. More likely to seek revenge were those who had lost money in the fraudulent railway scheme that Thaddeus had uncovered.

He wrote "Cobourg" on a fresh sheet of paper, then "follow the money" and put a question mark beside it. He would talk it over with Martha. She might well have some fresh insight.

"How are you feeling today?" Morgan Spicer appeared in the doorway.

"My face is sore, but other than that, there seem to be no lingering effects. Come in, sit down. I want to talk to you. Someone tried again last night."

"What? To kill you?"

"Yes." Thaddeus filled him in on the poisoning attempt of the previous evening. "Fortunately it wasn't very well done or Dr. Christie might be in a bad way. What have you found out?"

"The twins say there are an awful lot of new people in the village," Spicer said. "There are three new employees at the brickworks, two at the mill, two women who are staying at Mrs. Gleeson's boarding house, and another at Mrs. Bell's, half a dozen farm workers, a peddler who was here for two days but left again, and a new hired girl at the Armstrong farm."

"Tell them to concentrate on the women," Thaddeus said. "There was a note with the poisoned biscuits. I'm not sure, but it looked to me like a feminine hand."

"Really? Do you really think a woman would be capable of trying to murder you?"

"Women are as capable of evil as men," Thaddeus replied. "It just doesn't express itself very often in as violent a fashion."

Spicer looked dubious.

"Are you still sure you didn't see anything down in the alleyway?"

"Positive. Even if I thought it was a woman who hit you, I wouldn't be able to claim that I saw her. Or anybody else for that matter."

"I'm wondering if we weren't deliberately sent that way," Thaddeus said.

Spicer frowned. "How do you mean?"

"The boy who told us about the old couple wasn't one of your regulars, was he?

"No. Bucky is my best informant. But he was working that day."

"Was he? That's what the other boy told us, but we don't know for sure, do we?"

"No, I suppose not. I can always ask him when I go there again."

"Do you think you could find the other boy?"

Spicer shrugged. "It's hard to say. There's so much coming and going in Macaulaytown."

"I'd like to know whether or not somebody set us up. It was awfully odd that there weren't any children around when we needed them to get a cab. It's like they knew there was going to be trouble and cleared out."

"I suppose."

Thaddeus could see that Spicer wasn't convinced that the boy had anything to do with it. "Just see if you can find him and ask him about it. I can't do it. Luke will have a fit if I go down there again."

"All right," Spicer said. "But who do you think it could be?"

"Luke thinks it must be someone from my past. I've been racking my brains trying to think who." He gestured toward the paper in front of him. "I've been writing things down, trying to make some sense of it. Maybe you can help. Do you remember the night Cuddy Nelson accidentally shot his boss?"

"It's hard to forget."

"There was a woman who jumped over the Burying Ground fence that night. Do you remember anything about her?"

"I didn't see her. The twins were sitting on top of me at the time."

"Oh. That's right," Thaddeus said.

"Besides," Spicer said, "she'd have no reason that I can think of to wish you harm. She got away with whatever she took."

"That's true enough. I'll ask Luke if he remembers anything." He wrote "Burying Ground fence-jumper – Luke" on the list. He had always thought that Luke knew more than he let on about the series of events that led to that night, but he had no idea if it had any bearing on what was happening now.

"What about before. In Kingston?" Morgan said. "From what you've told me that's where the whole thing started, really."

It had. But except for Cuddy Nelson, everyone he had crossed in the course of helping Luke was either dead or had left the country. And none of the women involved had any reason to be upset with the way things turned out. Kingston was a dead end in terms of the current question.

The same was true of the strange events in Wellington. Clementine was at the centre of the attempted fraud, but had nothing to do with anything else. Thaddeus could think of no other woman who had been involved at all – unless you counted the people who were convinced she could contact the dead with her table rapping nonsense. Was it possible that any of these might be disgruntled because Thaddeus had exposed her chicanery? Reluctantly, he put Wellington on the list.

And that brought him to the case he didn't want to think about. The first time he had tracked a killer, spurred on by the death of his daughter.

In spite of his personal loss, Thaddeus had always had a certain amount of compassion for the murderer. Isaac Simms had been a man under enormous stress who desperately sought relief from the pressure that weighed him down. Thaddeus had found pity for his weakness, even as he condemned his actions. He had tried, many times, to forgive sincerely and whole-heartedly, but in spite of his best intentions, he couldn't. Martha would say something, or move in a certain way and Thaddeus would be painfully reminded once again that his daughter was gone, solely because she bore a passing resemblance to her killer's sister, and her killer had taken her because she reminded him of his sin.

The sister. Complicit in her brother's crime, she had shown no remorse, only fury that he had been stopped.

"What do you remember of the Simms business?" he said to Morgan.

"I remember that we chased half-way across the province before you would even tell me what was going on."

"That's because I didn't know who to trust back then. I'm wiser now."

Spicer appeared mollified by this. "I don't recall any woman except the one that was killed. Oh, and the one that was almost killed. And the sisters, I suppose."

"Do you remember where the Simms family went? After Isaac

was hanged?"

"No, but I'll ask Sally, if you think it might help."

"Ask her what she remembers about the youngest sister, starting with her name, which for the life of me I can't remember. I seem to recall that Sally didn't have much use for her."

Sally Spicer had been working for the Simms family at the time. She had been instrumental in helping Thaddeus and Morgan track the killer. It was, in fact, how she met Morgan in the first place.

"No, she didn't like the youngest sister," Spicer said. "Sally didn't have a good opinion of any of them, except for Isaac, and he's the one who turned out to be a murderer. Just goes to show that you never can tell. But I'll ask her about it, if you think it would help."

"It might," Thaddeus said. "I don't know how, but it might. And anything else either of you can recall. About anything, because at this point I don't really know what to think."

Martha wasn't surprised to see Miss Clark waiting by the door along with a group of students, in spite of the fact that it was nearly time for classes to start. She suspected they were all anxious for a glimpse of Luke. Martha had no idea how on earth any of them thought they could attract his attention, not even Miss Clark, who was pretty enough, but in kind of an unremarkable way. A couple of the students were better-looking by far, but only a few of them were stylish, and all of them would seem downright dowdy next to her urbane uncle. Not that any of the girls were serious, she supposed. They were just starved of male companionship, and Luke made a convenient focus for their frustrations. Martha wasn't sure the same was true of the headmistress.

As Luke drove away, the knot of students separated and headed for the school entrance. Except for one, who walked away toward the street. That wasn't unusual; the girls who had family in Toronto were often accompanied - a sister or a brother or an aunt would walk with them to school on their way to other errands. But there was something about the figure that stirred Martha's memory. She was sure she had seen the woman before, but not with other students.

Then she shrugged the notion off, and continued into the school.

She was to practice teach in the model school for the first time that afternoon, and she was dreading it. Classmates who had already taken their first class reported that the pupils were well aware that the teacher was judged on how well he or she could control the classroom, and that they would take advantage of anyone who appeared less than confident.

She went upstairs to deposit her coat. Several girls standing in the upper hall watched her for a moment, then turned quickly away, stifling giggles. Martha ignored them. Many of the girls had formed into little cliques, almost from the beginning of the term. These groups gossiped a great deal and Martha had frequently overheard comments about others' hair and dress and whether or not some boy was sweet on someone. Martha kept herself aloof from these groups. She was there to get a teaching certificate, not to gossip, but she was aware that this made her a target, and that occasionally the comments were about her.

Lately, though, it seemed that more of the attention was directed Martha's way. And it happened again when she walked into the lecture hall. A group of girls noted her arrival with covert glances and then whispered together while she took her seat. It gave her an odd feeling, but she shrugged it off and concentrated on what the master was saying about the importance of the Norman Conquest.

As usual, she ate her lunch by herself. She wanted to walk out to the garden to stretch her legs, but when she looked out the window, she realized that a sleety snow was falling. It was then that she remembered where she had seen the woman from that morning. Martha was positive that it had been the same woman she'd seen in the garden on her first day of classes. The woman who had worn a wrap almost exactly like Martha's. The woman who had briskly walked away as soon as someone else joined her in the garden.

She tried to remember who had been standing outside this morning. Alice Gleeson for one. Clara Powell. Nettie Winston, who had expressed a great deal of interest in Luke, and had seemed put out when Martha declined to introduce her. Harriet Jeffers. And three or four other girls who had attached themselves to Alice and Clara, and who were nearly always found in their company. But what was the connection with the strange woman? Martha knew better than to ask directly. It would be seized upon as a golden opportunity to tease, and Martha would be told all sorts of things, in the hope that she would somehow embarrass herself by repeating them. She wasn't sure why she should ask at all, except that she was curious.

But her first teaching experience loomed, and Martha would be better served by setting her curiosity aside and concentrating on what she needed to do that afternoon.

Fortunately, she had been assigned a girls' class and the subject was arithmetic, something she was extremely comfortable with. There were about twenty children in the room, eight and nine year olds drawn from the surrounding neighbourhood. Their regular teacher sat at the back of the room to supervise – and to judge.

Martha knew she needed to take charge from the outset.

Be like Thaddeus. Her grandfather stood very straight when he took the pulpit, and always took a moment or two to look across the faces in the congregation before he began to speak.

She took her place at the front of the classroom. She looked around the room for a moment, taking note of each expectant face. Expectant but for one - a little red-haired girl who sat halfway down the room and who was looking out the window. She needed to be brought to attention.

Martha resisted the urge to clear her throat before she spoke. *Be like Thaddeus.*

"Good morning children." To her relief, the words came out clear and strong, and she was pleased to see that the window-gazer's head snapped around. "My name is Miss Renwell."

She went to the blackboard and wrote her name at the top, on the left-hand side.

"Let's begin with a review of the seven times table," she said. "One times seven is…"

"Seven," came the chorus of voices as the pupils answered.

"Two times seven is…"

"Fourteen," came the answer.

The little girl was looking out the window again. Martha could see that the teacher at the back had noticed the inattention. *Control the room. Be like Thaddeus.*

"Three times seven…"

She casually walked down the aisle, as if she were merely listening to the responses.

"Four times seven…"

"Five times seven…"

She worked her way around the back of the room and along the side until she was right behind the girl, who was lost in the view and didn't notice.

Martha leaned over very close to the girl, and in a loud voice said "Six times seven…"

The girl jumped, looked around and blushed. As Martha turned away, she had the satisfaction of seeing a look of approval on the supervising teacher's face.

She continued the times table to twelve, then wrote multiplication problems on the blackboard for the pupils to solve. She had the girl's full attention the whole time.

She would be fine.

Luke was nowhere around when it came time to fetch Martha from school. He'd come in at dinnertime, wolfed down his food and disappeared again.

"I've got several children who have come down with pneumonia on top of their measles," he said, "and one of them I'm particularly concerned about. He'll reach a crisis at some point today, I figure, so I need to be close at hand."

"I'll hold the fort should anything turn up," Christie said. He was happy enough to have Luke do most of the work, but could still be counted upon to pitch in during the periods when various epidemics swept through the village and their practice needed more than one doctor.

Thaddeus had been ordered to stay put for the day, but as the minutes ticked by, he decided he was certainly well enough to ride a bus the few blocks to the school and back again. Besides the day was nearly over, so he wasn't exactly disobeying doctor's orders.

He grabbed his hat, poked his head into the kitchen to tell Mrs.

Dunphy where he was going, and stepped out through the back door, just as a woman came out of the driveshed at the back of the garden.

"Hey what are you doing!" Thaddeus shouted.

The woman regarded him for a moment and then, seeming in no hurry, sauntered down the street, occasionally glancing back at him.

Mrs. Dunphy appeared at the back door.

"What is it?" she asked. "Why did you shout?"

"I surprised someone in the shed. A woman. I'd have chased her except that I don't think I'm up to running very far just now."

Mrs. Dunphy looked worried. "Maybe we should be a little more careful about locking the shed, too. Dr. Luke leaves it open when he's out, since the thing that's most likely to be stolen is the horse."

"I think locking up would be a good idea," Thaddeus said, "at least until we discover what's going on."

"Are you sure you're all right going off alone?" She peered at Thaddeus anxiously.

"I'm fine. There will be all sorts of other people on the bus. And Martha will be with me coming back."

She nodded and disappeared back into the kitchen.

As Thaddeus predicted there were several other people on the bus, including a couple of women, but none of them looked liked the figure he had seen skulking around Christie's drive shed.

Martha was waiting by the student entrance, standing slightly apart from a group of girls. Miss Clark waited with her. They all looked disappointed when they saw Thaddeus. The girls whispered amongst themselves and then the group broke up.

"Good afternoon, Miss Clark," Thaddeus said and tipped his hat to the headmistress as he walked up to Martha.

"Good afternoon, Mr. Lewis. I trust you're feeling better?"

"Yes, thank you, although my son remains unconvinced that I'm well enough to be out on my own. But if my granddaughter is ready to go, she can see me home safely."

Once again Miss Clark didn't seem to know how to respond to banter. She merely looked confused, nodded a goodbye and reentered the school.

"How are you feeling?" Martha asked as they walked along the drive.

"A little sore. A little headachy. And more than a little alarmed. There was someone snooping around the driveshed this afternoon. A woman."

"Did you recognize her?"

"I don't know. I've seen her somewhere before. But I can't quite put my finger on where."

"I had the same problem today."

"What do you mean?"

"There was a woman waiting with a group of girls this morning. I knew I'd seen her before, but I couldn't figure out where until later. She was in the garden on my first day at school, but walked away when one of the other girls came along."

"That's worrisome." Thaddeus had been right to protect Martha as much as he had, even though no one else had seen the need for it.

"Who do you think she is?" Martha asked.

"Someone from my past, I'll warrant. It remains to be seen who."

"Speaking of the past – why didn't you tell me that Clementine was sending money?"

"Because I don't know the why of that, either. And because I promised your father I'd keep you out of things. It looks like I haven't been very successful."

"No, you only promised that you wouldn't involve me in anything to do with Ashby," Martha pointed out. "Since he's currently out of the country, I don't see how Francis could claim that I'm involved in any of his business."

Thaddeus looked at her sternly. "That's not what he meant and you know it."

"But none of this is happening because of anything you've done. It's just happening. How could you be expected to keep me out of it?"

"By sending you back to Wellington, maybe."

"There's no guarantee that I'd be any safer there," she said. "If someone wanted to come after me, it would be easier to get at me in Wellington than it is here. Here I'm surrounded by people all the time."

"I suppose," Thaddeus said, "although I'm not sure Francis would see it that way. And, if I might make a small observation, having a conversation with you is starting to feel like talking to Mrs. Elliott. You're twisting everything to your advantage."

"I'll take that as a compliment. It was one of the things I admired about her."

Thaddeus hesitated. Luke had suggested that he say nothing to Martha about Clementine, but it felt awkward not to, given that it was now out in the open anyway. He wanted to point out that what he had done was wrong. That he had sinned. That he had tried to set it right. That he had prayed for forgiveness.

Martha didn't give him the chance.

"Do you think she'll come looking for her money some day?"

"I don't think there's any question of that. It's just a matter of when."

"What will you do?"

"I'll give her the money, of course. It's not mine."

"No, I don't mean that," Martha said. "I mean what will you *do*?"

Luke was right. She'd known all along.

"I would have been sorely disappointed if you'd taken up with any of those women Will and Moses introduced you to," she went on.

"None of them were very interesting, were they?"

"They agreed with every word you said. You could have told them that fish can fly and they would have nodded and said, "Oh, you're so clever, Mr. Lewis!""

It was exactly what Thaddeus thought about them, and he couldn't help but laugh at Martha's mimicry. "Agreeing with me was certainly never an issue with Mrs. Elliott, was it? She'd challenge me just for the fun of it."

"Sometimes she got a little carried away. But mostly it was fun." And then as the omnibus clattered to a halt in front of them, she added, "Well that's my opinion. You can make of it what you will."

The next afternoon, Martha discovered why the whispered conversations about her had become more frequent. She walked past a group of girls who were huddled in the hallway and overheard one word that made everything crystal clear.

Kidnapped.

Chapter 11

Martha didn't care particularly, that news of her adventure in London had somehow reached the Toronto Normal School. But she did wonder how her classmates had found out. There had been reports in the newspapers, but she doubted that many of the girls read the papers, or that they retained anything they read even if they did. She wondered if Bernice had anything to do with it – she was from St. Thomas, not far from London – and people there would be far more aware of such a dramatic event, as it happened so close to home. Had Bernice written to her family and mentioned Martha's name, and the name jogged someone's memory about the girl who had been snatched off the streets by a mad murderer? Martha could think of no other explanation. She was a little annoyed that Bernice had chosen to spread gossip, but otherwise she was quite prepared to ignore the whole thing.

There were more whispers and titters during her physical education class, which mercifully died down when Martha's classmates realized that Mr. Sorbie would be joining them that day.

Miss Shenick had already guided them through a series of exercises she called "rhythmic gymnastics". These consisted of waving lengths of ribbon in the air while running, or balancing clubs or balls while performing a prescribed set of movements. The idea, Miss Shenick said, was to improve posture and develop grace through exercise. It was, she said, "like dancing without music". Martha wasn't sure what Thaddeus would make of this.

Methodists were against dancing in any form, whether there was music or not. Whatever he might think, she found the whole thing extremely tedious. If this is what dancing was, she wondered that so much of the world seemed fascinated by it. Nevertheless, she neglected to mention the exercises to Thaddeus, in case he suddenly turned Methodist-stubborn and demanded that she be excused from the class or something. She needed to complete the physical training course to get her teaching certificate, and she wasn't going to take any chances that might jeopardize her goal.

With the appearance of Mr. Sorbie, it became clear that the routine, at least for that day, would change, and as far as Martha was concerned, it was not a change for the better. Sorbie was, as Luke put it, "mad about running". The girls had occasionally been treated to the sight of the male students, coats off, running through the gardens. They were made to clear small garden walls, weave their way through the saplings and jump over the small creek that ran through the property.

The girls made great fun of this, pointing and laughing when one of the boys fell behind or misjudged his jump and landed in the creek bed. Surely the girls weren't about to be subject to a similar torment?

"Mr. Sorbie has agreed to join us today to introduce you to the art of callisthenics," Miss Shenik said. Maybe Luke was right – callisthenics was nothing more than running through swamps and up mountainsides.

"I'll let him explain to you what this entails." Miss Shenik stepped aside and Sorbie stepped forward.

"The word callisthenics comes from the ancient Greek words "kallos" which means beautiful, and "sthenos", which means strength," he said. "And that is the essence of what callisthenics is about. A strong body is a beautiful body."

He went on to describe at length some of the callisthenic exercises, such as push-ups and kneebends. None of it sounded very appealing. Surely they wouldn't be required to lie on the ground and flail their arms and legs around? But as he warmed to his subject, his earnest face grew enthusiastic, and the girls began to listen more closely.

"Physical education is most important in the schools," he said. "A healthy body leads to a healthy mind, and children need an outlet for their natural energy and high spirits." And then, as Luke might have predicted, Sorbie advised running as the most healthful exercise of all.

"Even the smallest of schoolyards can be utilized for running," he went on, and then demonstrated how markers could be set out about thirty feet apart.

"The idea is to run from one to the other, turn sharply and run back again as fast as possible. This builds both stamina and agility."

Martha thought that, in terms of providing exercise for children, a rousing game of tag or hide and seek would do as well and be more fun, but she kept her opinions to herself. She couldn't help but snicker, though, when Clara Parker pointed out that the girls would be at a disadvantage in this exercise because of their long skirts, not to mention the older girls who were in stays.

Sorbie blushed and muttered something about getting them to do it "as well as they can, regardless".

He was just launching into a description of how to set up a cross-country running course when Miss Clark tapped Martha on the shoulder.

"The headmaster would like to see you in his office," she said in a low voice.

Martha was puzzled, but even an interview with the headmaster was preferable to hearing anything more about how to get children to run.

"Do you know what it's about?" Martha asked as she followed Miss Clark down the hall.

But the headmistress was tight-lipped. "That's not for me to say." She knocked on the door of Mr. Robertson's office and ushered Martha into the room.

"Ah, Miss Renwell," he said, looking up as they entered. And then he paused, as though he was uncertain how to begin.

Martha stood beside Miss Clark and waited until he collected himself.

"You certainly seem to have a talent for finding yourself in unusual circumstances," he began.

Surely this couldn't be about her living arrangements again. And since Robertson had already decided that the school wasn't paying anything toward her board, Martha didn't see how it would concern the headmaster anyway.

She was annoyed, and threw caution to the wind. "My circumstances have always been unusual, sir, and nothing has changed in recent days. I must admit I'm perplexed as to why I've been called here."

And then she noticed that he had a crumpled piece of newsprint in front of him.

"There seems to be a great deal of talk about you in the school," he said.

"Yes sir, I'm aware of that."

"I dislike gossip."

"As do I, and I pay no attention to it."

Again, she sensed an uncertainty in his manner. He seemed lost in thought for a few moments before he spoke again.

"We have all been aware of the talk," he said finally, "but weren't sure how much credence to give it. And then this morning, Miss Shenick intercepted this news article as it was being passed around. It contains a great deal of information about some unfortunate events that you experienced this past fall."

"Yes sir." Martha was mystified. She couldn't see what any of this had to do with the Normal School.

"I find myself forced to investigate the matter. The Superintendant of Education would expect nothing less."

"I'm afraid I don't understand."

"The Province invests a great deal of money in the students at this school," Robertson went on., "with the expectation that their investment will be rewarded by the superior calibre of its teachers. This assumes, of course, that each student will proceed to a teaching position when he or she graduates."

"I thought that was established when we were first enrolled. We declared our intentions then."

"It's not your intention that I'm questioning Miss Renwell. My question is whether or not your experiences will affect your employability."

"I'm sorry, sir, I don't understand what the two have to do with each other."

Robertson sighed. "There are some people who maintain that a respectable young woman should see her name in the newspapers precisely twice in her life – once when she's married and once when she's buried."

"With due respect, I fail to see how I can be held accountable for what appears in the newspaper."

"According to these reports you were snatched off the street and held prisoner for some time."

"It was only for a short time. My grandfather rescued me very quickly."

"Ah yes. The famous grandfather. He does seem to lead an exciting life, doesn't he?"

Apparently news of Thaddeus's adventures was circulating through the school as well.

"The difficulty here, Miss Renwell, is that there are some who would question how you managed to get yourself into such a position."

Martha's anger was growing. "Are you implying that what happened was somehow my fault?"

"I'm not implying anything. I'm telling you how some people might interpret the matter. They might well ask what you were doing on the street in the first place."

Martha was convinced that this was her final interview with Headmaster Robertson. She was furious and she didn't care if he knew it or not.

"I have done nothing to discredit either myself or the school, sir. I was on the street that evening because I received a message that my grandfather needed me. And in all honesty, I have to say that should someone come into the room this very minute to inform me that my grandfather needed my help, I wouldn't hesitate for a moment to go running to wherever he is." She glared at him.

"Yes, you've made that abundantly clear."

She shrugged and turned toward the door.

"Where are you going?"

"To fetch my things. I'm being asked to leave, am I not?"

"You shouldn't be so impetuous, Miss Renwell. I see no reason to ask for your withdrawal."

"But…"

"I was obliged to ask about this. I've asked. You've answered in a satisfactory manner. As far as I'm concerned the matter is closed. You should be aware, however, that it may prove troublesome in the future, that's all."

"Oh. I see. Thank you sir."

She turned again to go, relieved beyond words.

"Just one more thing, Miss Renwell – I should like, at some point, to meet this grandfather of yours."

"I'm sure he'd be happy to meet you as well, sir. I'll ask him when I get home."

And as she and Miss Clark left the study, Martha thought she detected a look of approval on the headmistresses' face.

There was still Bernice to deal with.

Martha finally cornered her in the cloakroom at the end of the day.

"What do you mean by spreading gossip about me?"

As was usual whenever someone spoke sharply to her, Bernice's face crumpled. "Wha..what do you mean?"

"You know what I mean. You're from St. Thomas. Who else would have a clipping from a London newspaper?"

"That wasn't me." Bernice began to sniffle.

"Then who was it?"

"I don't know. All the girls were talking about it. They said…" Martha had to listen closely through the sniffles to understand what she was saying. "They said the reason you signed up to be a teacher is because no one would ever want to marry you now."

"What?"

"And… and that… you weren't really kidnapped. You made it all up because you'd gone off with a man. And that Dr. Lewis drives you to school because you can't be trusted not to do it again."

Martha was so angry she couldn't speak. Instead, she spun on her heel and marched out the door.

"Martha! Wait!" Bernice wailed.

She stopped only when she reached the exit and saw that, as usual, there was a group of girls loitering by the door. These girls knew that she had been called to the headmaster's office. No doubt more rumours were flying, the most likely being that Martha had been sent home.

She would not give them the satisfaction of seeing her upset in any way. She would hold her head high, walk out the door and let them speculate as much as they wished.

The girls parted to let her through, and the whispers followed her. She had expected to see Luke waiting with the sleigh and was surprised when she spotted Thaddeus standing with the headmaster. Luke must have decided that he was well enough to be let out on his own.

"Yes, I know Egerton Ryerson," she heard him say as she walked up to him. "However, Mr. Ryerson and I agreed to disagree many years ago."

Martha knew that Thaddeus despised Egerton Ryerson, holding him responsible for the deep schism that afflicted the Methodist Church. She hoped he wouldn't go on at length about it. Ryerson was also the Superintendant of Education for the province and Headmaster Robertson's boss and Martha felt that the ice she was currently skating on was thin enough as it was.

To her relief, Robertson turned to her as she reached them.

"Ah, Miss Renwell, I've managed to meet your grandfather all by myself. I was told there was a regular deputation by the girls' door for all your arrivals and departures."

Martha was about to point out that she didn't think the girls were there for Thaddeus, but just then the true object of interest arrived in the sleigh.

"Why didn't you wait for me?" Luke said to his father.

"I didn't know whether or not you were coming. I figured the measles were keeping you busy."

"They are. But not so busy as they were." He smiled a hello at the headmaster.

"Mr. Robertson, this is my son Dr. Luke Lewis."

Robertson's glance darted over to the group of girls, then back to Luke again. Then he bowed slightly. "Your practice is in Yorkville, I've been told."

"Yes. I'm in partnership with Stewart Christie."

While Thaddeus, Luke and the headmaster discussed whether or not the measles posed any threat to the Normal School students, Martha felt the last bit of anger seeping out of her. She shouldn't have jumped to conclusions about who had started all the gossip. She would have to seek Bernice out the next day and apologize. After all, the kidnapping wasn't exactly a secret. There had been reports in many papers, and Martha supposed anyone could have seen them. Someone had been nasty enough to deliberately bring it to the attention of the student body at the school, but she had no idea who it might be. She couldn't think of anyone she had crossed, particularly. She kept to herself, mostly, and hadn't aligned herself with any of the groups of girls. Maybe that was the problem.

"I trust you'll continue to mend," the headmaster was saying to Thaddeus. "Perhaps when you're fully recovered, you might join me for tea some afternoon. I'd be very interested to hear about the early church history of the province."

"I would be honoured to tell you about it if you'd care to listen," Thaddeus said. "And now, my granddaughter awaits."

They all climbed into the sleigh and Luke flicked the reins. The mare, eager to get home to her feed, started off at a brisk trot and they soon reached Yorkville.

Just as they rounded the corner to turn into Christie's drive shed the sleigh skewed sharply sideways, Luke shouted and Martha was thrown against the side. The mare stumbled as she tried to keep her balance.

"Whoa! Whoa!" Luke yelled.

The horse took a few more steps, then came to a stop.

Thaddeus leapt out and ran forward to grab the mare's head. "There now, girl, you're all right! That's it. Good girl," he said in a soothing tone.

Luke and Martha scrambled down as well.

"Well isn't this just fine!" Luke said. "A trace broke the other day. I asked the saddler to repair it, but he can't have done it properly."

"When was this?" Thaddeus asked.

"Two days ago. Fortunately I wasn't in the middle of nowhere when it happened and I was able to patch it up well enough to get home again. At least this time I can just lead the horse into the shed."

"Give her a moment to settle down," Thaddeus said. "She's still a little spooked."

Thaddeus continued to stroke the mare's neck. When she began to look less wild-eyed, Luke began to unhitch her.

"It wasn't the trace after all, it was the girth that parted," Luke said. "See?" He held out the offending piece of harness.

"That's been deliberately cut," Thaddeus said, "but only part way through so it wouldn't come apart until you were already on the road. You can see that only half of it is ragged."

Luke's face was grim. "If this had happened on a hill, we could have been seriously injured."

"It's a wonder we weren't injured just now. It's a good thing your horse is so steady."

"Are you sure this was cut?" Luke asked.

"Looks like it to me. And there was a woman in the shed yesterday. I surprised her when I was on my way to fetch Martha. I expect that's when it happened."

"So this was this meant for you? But how could anyone be sure that you'd be in the sleigh at the right time?"

"As you pointed out, all of the attempts on my life have been clumsy. It might have been done on the off-chance that I'd be with you. Or maybe it's just meant to wreak havoc."

"That's worrisome. It means none of us is safe," Luke said.

"None of us ever were," Martha said. "Grandpa was nearly run down by a carriage – but so was I. Any one of us could have eaten a poisoned biscuit. And I've seen a strange woman at the school on a couple of occasions. She hasn't done anything so far, but she hasn't been able to get very close to me either."

"You have no idea who it is?" Luke asked.

"No. It's no one I know."

"Well that puts paid to my theory that it's Mrs. Elliott," Luke said.

"Mrs. Elliott?" Martha was mystified. "Why would Mrs. Elliott want to hurt grandpa?"

"You keep saying that. It was just a thought, that's all."

"But…" suddenly Martha didn't know how to say what she meant without causing Thaddeus more embarrassment. "No," she said firmly. "It's not Mrs. Elliott."

"Well I, for one, am getting tired of this." Thaddeus said. "We need to figure out who it is."

Luke missed breakfast the next morning. He had been called out first thing to see to an old woman who was almost certainly dying, Dr. Christie said, but was "doing her best to stave it off as long as possible. Just when you think the end is near, she rallies again."

"That's how I intend to go," Mrs. Dunphy said as she deposited a bowl of porridge on the table. "I see no reason to rush into the thing. And by the way Mr. Lewis, Mrs. Spicer is here for the laundry, but she'd like a word with you if you're free."

"Of course," Thaddeus said, "please ask her to come through."

"I'm sorry to bother you at breakfast," Sally said as she hovered in the doorway, "but I just put a huge great rat on your back step. The twins wanted to leave it in my kitchen but I put my foot down."

"Why did they want to leave it in your kitchen?" Thaddeus asked.

"They want to watch it die."

"Well that's bloodthirsty. Please, sit down with us. Would you like a cup of tea?"

"No, thank you, I should get on my way, but the twins said to tell you that one of the ladies who was staying at Mrs. Gleeson's moved out, but they don't know where she went. And the hired girl at the Anderson's didn't work out, so she went back home and now Anderson's don't have anybody."

"Interesting," Thaddeus said. "Did Morgan happen to ask you about the Simms family?"

"Yes. I think maybe they went to Kingston after they sold their house, but I don't know for sure. I'd been let go by then."

"Do you recall the name of the youngest sister? I can't remember."

"Her name was Esther." Sally's face clearly showed her contempt. "Do you think it's Esther doing all this?"

"I don't know. She's on the list of possibilities."

"I wouldn't put it past her. She was a nasty piece of work. Not that I thought much of the others either."

"I know she resented me because I brought her brother to justice," Thaddeus said, "but I can't figure out why she would wait all this time to get back at me. It's been thirteen years. And I've been a lot harder to find in recent times. It would have been easy enough when I was living in Wellington, but I've been on the move since then."

Sally thought about this for a moment and then she said, "Maybe the old woman finally died."

"What old woman?" Martha wanted to know. "You never told me about an old woman."

"Esther was the youngest daughter," Thaddeus explained. "She was pretty, and received a number of marriage proposals. Her two older sisters were quite homely and had no beaus at all, but the old mother refused to let Esther marry out of turn. She insisted that the youngest wait until the older daughters found husbands, but as that was unlikely to happen…"

"Esther was out of luck unless she went against her mother's wishes," Sally interjected. "And none of them was willing to cross the old lady."

"Really?" Martha said. "I heard about the murders, but I didn't hear any of this."

"It's a nasty tale," Thaddeus said. There was no need for Martha to know the sordid details of Esther Simms' unnatural liaison with her own brother. "Keep your eyes peeled Sally. You're one of the few who would recognize her. If it is her. And be careful - she might recognize you in turn."

Sally snorted. "I doubt that. People like Esther Simms don't take any notice of the help. Even if she saw me, she probably wouldn't remember that I ever worked for her."

"Be careful all the same. Whoever is doing this is getting desperate."

"She doesn't want to come anywhere near me or mine. But don't worry, I'll keep an eye out. And now I'll get the laundry and be on my way." She made to go then turned back again. "If I do see her, what should I do?"

"Just let me know. It's just a possibility at this point. I have no evidence of anything."

"Maybe I should see if I can find the family," Thaddeus said when Sally had gone. "Find out if Esther's still there. It would only take me a couple of days to go to Kingston."

Dr. Christie had been busy gobbling his porridge until then, but at this point he stopped in mid-spoonful and fixed Thaddeus with a glare. "Your son may have something to say about that."

"I only want to ask some questions."

"Do you remember what he said about not putting yourself in danger?"

"I wouldn't be."

"It's seems clear to me that someone is watching your movements very closely," Christie said. "The last thing you want to do is go off by yourself. All you'd be doing is setting yourself up as a target."

"I suppose," Thaddeus said grudgingly.

"Has it occurred to you, dear man, that you could simply write a letter? Surely you must know someone in Kingston who would be willing to find out what you need to know."

"Oh," Thaddeus said. "Yes, I suppose you're right."

"Good. And now that we've averted the wrath of your ill-tempered son, could you perhaps pass that plate of bacon?"

"Whatever anybody else is going to do, I need to leave for school," Martha said. "I'm going to be late if I don't get going."

"I'll ride down with you," Thaddeus said. "Then I'll go to the saddler's. Luke will be wanting the sleigh later today."

Thaddeus escorted Martha safely to the school door and then collected the damaged pieces of harness and walked to the local tack shop.

"You'll need a new girth," the saddler said. "To tell the truth, that harness is so old it probably all needs to be replaced." He peered at the piece of leather again. "It's odd that it would have broken like that, though. It almost looks like somebody cut it."

"That's what I thought too," Thaddeus said. "Oh well, I'll take the piece I need now, and I'll tell Luke to drop by and talk to you about the rest of it when he has time."

Thaddeus peered closely at everyone he passed as he walked back to Christie's. He saw no one who looked suspicious, but it would be helpful, he reflected, if he was sure who he was looking for.

Martha was scheduled for a second stint of practice teaching that morning. This time she was given a class full of the oldest pupils in the Model School – rowdy eleven and twelve year old boys who, had they lived in the country, might well have been pulled out of school to work full time on their father's farm by now. She would have to work hard to establish order and maintain control of the class.

The subject was botany. She drew the outline of a simple flower on the chalkboard at the front of the room. She hoped it looked like a petunia, but it didn't really matter as long as the parts were all in the right place.

"Can you identify this part of the plant?" she asked.

One boy shot up his hand. "The pistil," he said.

"That's correct."

As they went along, she labeled each part on the drawing, but though the class gave their responses at the appropriate time, she could sense that her pupils were restless.

Finally, one of them shot up his hand. "Is it true, Miss, that you was kidnapped."

"That you *were* kidnapped," she corrected. "And that's no concern of yours."

The rest of the boys were wide-eyed, anxious to hear her answer. Martha could see the regular teacher, Mr. Barnes, frowning at the back of the room. She needed to take control of this immediately, before the class strayed too far from the subject at hand.

"It's true then?" the boy said. "How did you get away?"

"Once again, that is no concern of yours," she said, "but I'll tell you anyway." She walked down the aisle toward the boy. When she reached him she leaned over close and said, "I bit his ear off." As she said it, she grabbed his ear lobe and pinched it. He yelped, and the class dissolved in laughter.

Mr. Barnes' frown grew deeper.

"Now," she said walking back to the front of the room. "Can someone please define the term "pollination"? You." She pointed at a boy in the front row. He jumped.

"It's when a bee carries pollen from one plant to another," he said in a voice that was barely above a whisper.

"Very good. And what are some of the other ways a plant can be pollinated?"

It was enough to re-establish order and to her relief she completed the rest of the lesson without any further disruption. At the end of the class, the students filed out of the room, but, she noticed, they gave her a wide berth as they left.

"You have a very unorthodox style, Miss Renwell," Mr. Barnes said, "but all in all I think you handled the situation well."

"Thank you."

He looked slightly conspiratorial. "I hope you don't mind me asking this – were you really kidnapped?"

Martha sighed. "Yes. For a very short period of time. And no, I didn't bite his ear off. My grandfather found me before I could come to any harm."

"My goodness," he said. "Well. I assume then, that a classroom full of unruly children holds no terror for you?"

"None whatsoever," she said firmly. "Good day Mr. Barnes."

To Martha's surprise, Bernice sought her out at the end of the day. Martha knew she needed to make amends, and immediately offered an apology.

"Listen, Bernice, I'm sorry I jumped to conclusions. I was very upset, but that's no excuse for what I did. I shouldn't have accused you of spreading gossip."

"That's all right", Bernice said with a triumphant smile. "I know who it was! Or at least I found out who brought the newspaper clipping to school. It was Alice Gleeson." Bernice turned quite red, heady with achievement.

"How do you know?" Martha asked.

"I confronted them. Alice and Clara and the others."

"Did you just walk up to them and demand that they tell you?"

"Oh no!" Bernice crowed. "I was cleverer than that. They were talking about you again when they came back after the dinner break. They said some really ugly things. I told them I didn't believe it for a minute, and asked them what proof they had. And Alice said that she knew it for a fact because one of her mother's boarders told her all about the kidnapping. She even had a newspaper with the story in it."

Alice Gleeson. Martha hadn't known that Alice's mother ran a boarding house. Alice lived in Yorkville. She knew Luke. She had asked Martha if she could arrange a ride with him. The woman who had been in the garden on her first day of school was the same woman she had seen again with the group of girls who clustered around the side entrance every morning. And Thaddeus had seen a strange woman in Christie's driveshed in Yorkville. It couldn't possibly be a coincidence. If Martha could find out the identity of the boarder, there was a very good chance that it would prove to be the same person who was trying to kill Thaddeus.

Bernice's face was shining with what she had accomplished.

"Bernice, you're brilliant!" Martha said, and Bernice's smile grew even wider. "Did Alice happen to mention the boarder's name?"

"No. But I think I've seen her a couple of times, talking with Alice and Clara and that group of girls who wait around the door so they can look at your uncle."

"Yes, I've seen her too. She has a paisley shawl just like mine."

"Yes, that's right. I think that's her."

She was watching them all. Thaddeus and Martha and Luke, too. She meant to hurt Thaddeus any way she could.

"You have no idea how important this is, Bernice. I don't know how to thank you."

"Could we maybe be friends again?" Bernice said shyly.

"I don't deserve you, but yes we can be friends again. And the next time I say something unkind, you should remind me about today."

Bernice began to sniffle, something she seemed to do in nearly every circumstance, and something that Martha supposed she was going to have to get used to if Bernice was going to be her friend. Never mind, she'd more than proved her worth, and Martha was grateful.

"I have to go now," Martha said. "My ride will be waiting – but I'll bring an extra sandwich tomorrow and if it's a nice day we can walk together in the garden. And I promise, just as soon as I can, I'll explain what a wonderful thing you've done." And then she went flying out the door.

It was Luke who was waiting for her. "I had calls to make down this way as soon as the harness was mended, so I said I'd get you," he explained.

Martha waited only until the horse kicked into a trot before she blurted out, "I know who's trying to kill Thaddeus. And she's doing her best to harm us any way she can."

Briefly, she outlined what had happened – the woman in the garden, and with the group of girls. The gossip, the newspaper clipping, and Bernice's extraordinary effort to get to the bottom of it.

Luke's face grew worried as she filled him in. "That's dreadful. Are you all right?"

"Yes, it's been a little unsettling, but nothing I couldn't take care of myself."

"I wish you'd told me before."

"There really wasn't anything you could have done."

"I could have listened."

Martha decided then and there that Luke was by far her favourite uncle. "I didn't say anything because I didn't realize it had any bearing on anybody but me. The only wrinkle in all this is that the Spicer twins say one of Mrs. Gleeson's boarders moved out this week. We'll just have to hope it wasn't the one we want to find."

"If she's no longer there, it's going to be hard to find her until she tries again. But at least you'll know her when you see her.

That's got to help. But I must admit it's worrisome that you've become a target."

"What do you think we should do now?"

"I'll talk to Mrs. Gleeson," Luke said. "I looked after her youngest son's measles. Fortunately he recovered without complication, so she's inclined to trust me. Whether or not she has any useful information to impart remains to be seen."

Chapter 12

"**S**he's moved out," Mrs. Gleeson reported when Luke dropped around to see her the next day. "When she came here she said she had taken a position as a seamstress with one of the dressmakers in the north end of the city. She seemed like a perfect boarder – nice manners and everything. I thought she probably came from a good family that had fallen on hard times or something."

"Did something happen to change your mind?" Luke asked.

"She had a nasty temper to be sure. Didn't like the lamp in her room, said the bed wasn't comfortable, things like that. Complained about the food. I found her in my kitchen one day, but I chased her right out of there. Nobody messes around in my kitchen."

If Martha was right, that would explain why the woman had simply shoved the rat poison into the biscuits, rather than baking it in. She hadn't had access to cooking facilities.

Mrs. Gleeson shrugged. "You put up with all sorts when you run a boarding house, so I didn't think anything of it, and she was good about seeing my daughter Alice down to the Normal School near every day. But then Alice tells me that she hangs around the school a lot, when I would have thought she was supposed to be at work. She wasn't keeping the hours of any seamstress I ever knew. And then I started asking myself just what it was she was working at, if you know what I mean."

"It does sound odd, doesn't it?"

"I'm telling you, if she hadn't announced she was leaving, I was going to ask her to go anyway. I run a respectable house here."

"Yes, I know you do," Luke said.

"So what's your interest in her?" Mrs. Gleeson asked.

"My father saw her hanging around our driveshed the other day. I wondered who she was and what she was up to."

"Well, like I said, I don't really know what she was up to, but I expect it was no good. And as for who she is, she gave her name as Polly Wilson, but now I'm wondering if even that was true."

"Yes, one has to wonder. You don't happen to know where she went from here?"

"No, I don't. She just announced that she was leaving, and I was relieved so I didn't ask."

"Thank you. You've been most helpful Mrs. Gleeson. I just have one more question – do you remember when exactly she left?"

"Four days ago."

"The same day she left the ladyfingers in the kitchen," Thaddeus said when Luke reported the conversation.

"She must have figured they could be traced back to Mrs. Gleeson's somehow. Or maybe she just decided there was a risk if she stayed there any longer."

"Whoever 'she' is. I doubt very much that her name is really Polly Wilson. And we don't really know if it's the woman we're looking for. I admit the coincidences are piling up, but I've been caught in that trap before."

"At least it's given us something to focus on," Luke said. "Up until now we've been working in the dark."

"I agree. But I'm not going to discount other possibilities until we're certain. By the way, I've been meaning to ask you about that night at the Burying Ground. There was a woman who hopped over the fence and grabbed whatever it was that Cuddy Nelson and his boss dug up out of the grave. I asked Morgan about it, but he says he didn't see her. Did you?"

"Yes," Luke replied. "I saw her. She's not the woman we're looking for."

"How do you know?"

"Well, for one thing, she was an African."

"Oh. The woman I saw come out of the driveshed wasn't."

"I'm sure Martha would have remarked on it as well."

"Yes, I suppose she would have, wouldn't she? Oh well, it was worth considering. I really can't come up with the names of very many people who would be carrying that big a grudge."

"Unless someone was really angry with you and you didn't notice."

"It wouldn't be the first time," Thaddeus said glumly. "In the meantime, we all need to be extra cautious. Someone is intent on hurting me in any way possible. And that means that both you and Martha are at risk."

Yorkville's measles epidemic had finally run its course. Luke reported that the majority of his patients had fully recovered, with only one new case coming to his attention in the last few days.

"I've still got a couple who developed pneumonia and three or four with conjunctivitis, otherwise they all seem to be on the mend," he said. "And since I now have a little more time on my hands, I'm happy to keep driving Martha to and from school. I think it would be wise."

"I'll come with you," Thaddeus said. "If the woman's still following me, maybe I can spot her on the street. Besides, it's better if we stick together."

"You're not coming with me to see patients," Luke said. "I draw the line there."

"I can always wait outside."

"No."

"Oh well, all right," Thaddeus grumbled, "but make sure you look the harness over before you drive off. And lock the shed behind you."

Every day Thaddeus and Martha scanned the streets for Mrs. Gleeson's boarder as they went back and forth from the school, but after ten days there was still no sign of her. Nor was there any answer to the note Thaddeus had dashed off to Caleb Webster, a fellow itinerant whom Bishop Smith had told him was ministering in the Kingston area. They had been ordained at the same time, and although they had seldom seen each other since then, Thaddeus was sure he could prevail upon Webster to make a few general inquiries about the Simms family. In the meantime, he was puzzled that there were no further incidents.

"Maybe she's given up," Luke said one day as they were sitting down for their noontime dinner. "Maybe she's realized it's a lost cause."

Thaddeus dismissed this idea. "She'll try again. Either she's biding her time until we let our guard down, or she's gone off somewhere to find a more efficient method of doing me in. I think we should remain vigilant."

"Oh don't worry, I will. The rat died rather horribly when I fed it a biscuit. I don't fancy going that way myself."

"How do you fancy going?" Dr. Christie asked.

"Asleep in my bed at a ripe old age, of course," Luke replied. "By the way, I've decided not to go into the city tonight. I'd be more comfortable staying here until the situation is resolved."

Christie nodded. "Yes, under the circumstances I think that's wise. Pass the potatoes this way, will you boy?"

Luke plunked a mound of potatoes on his own plate before he passed the bowl down the table, but before he could take his first bite, someone knocked at the front door.

"I'll get it," Luke said. "It's probably for me anyway."

"Astounding how patients have an uncanny ability to fall ill at the most inconvenient times," Christie noted.

Luke opened the door to a woman who appeared startled at the sight of him.

"Oh," she said. And then she recovered herself. "I'm sorry to bother you, but I'm looking for Mr. Thaddeus Lewis. I can only assume I have the right address, given your resemblance to him."

Luke knew who she was immediately. Her face was thinner than it had been when the daguerreotype was taken, but she had the same direct gaze, the same wry smile on her lips.

"Yes," he said. "I'm Luke Lewis, by the way. Please come in and I'll fetch my father."

She looked furtively around before she stepped into the hall.

Luke took her cloak, then showed her into the parlour. "Please have a seat," he said. "I'll get him."

He returned to the dining room.

"It's for you," he said to Thaddeus. "I do believe it's Mrs. Elliott."

Thaddeus made no move to get up. Luke couldn't tell what his reaction was from the expression on his face.

"She's in the parlour," Luke said.

"My goodness, boy, where are your manners?" Christie said. "Show her in so we can all meet her."

"No," Luke said. "I think the parlour is preferable."

He'd give his father his privacy, but from the dining room he would be able overhear the conversation well enough to detect if there was trouble. Thaddeus and Martha had dismissed his suspicions of Mrs. Elliott, but Luke wasn't prepared to take any chances. He would stick close.

"What?" said Christie. "But I..."

"The parlour," Luke said in a firm tone of voice.

"Oh well, all right," Christie grumbled. "But it seems rude to me."

Thaddeus still hadn't moved, nor had his expression changed. Luke sat down again and began eating his dinner. No one said a word as Thaddeus finally got up out of his chair and walked out of the dining room.

"Is that the lady?" Christie whispered as soon as Thaddeus was out of sight. "The one who's been sending money?"

"Yes, I believe so," Luke said.

"What's she like? I must admit I'm mortally curious."

"It's hard to say. We didn't have much of a conversation. I realized who she was right away and just said I'd get my father."

"What do you think he'll do?"

"I don't think he knows that himself," Luke replied. "But I think it's best if we stay out of the way while he sorts it out."

Thaddeus stopped in the doorway of the parlour. Clementine was standing at the window with her back to him. She had twitched one corner of the curtain aside and was peering out at the street. He leaned against the jamb and folded his arms.

"Looking for someone?" he said.

She turned at the sound of his voice. "Yes, I'm looking for you." Her eyes darted over the scar that crossed his cheekbone. "What on earth have you done to your face?"

"Someone tried to kill me."

"I'm not surprised. You can be awfully annoying at times." She tilted her head as she studied him. "I like it. It makes you look piratical."

"How did you find me?"

"I went to Ashby's office. I figured he'd know where you were. Ashby himself wasn't there, but a rather pleasant young man managed to find a note you'd left with your address on it. He didn't want to tell me at first, but I was able to persuade him." Thaddeus could tell from her smile that she'd accomplished this by means of some subterfuge or other. "I must say it was pleasant to discover that you're so close by. I was afraid I might have to risk a visit to Wellington."

"I missed you after you left."

"Did you really?"

"Yes. I've had no one to argue with since you've been gone."

She laughed. He'd forgotten what a pleasant sound it was when it was genuine.

"We had some fun didn't we?"

"You look tired. What have you been up to?"

"Oh, I've been here and there. And everywhere. It's been quite a trying time."

"I was pretty cut up when I thought you were dead."

She frowned. "You got Joe's telegram though, didn't you?"

"Telling us that Clementine Elliott died in the accident? Yes. But we didn't realize what it meant until Ashby went to view the body and discovered it wasn't you."

"Ashby went?"

"I wanted to, but he persuaded me that he was in a better position to deal with the authorities. Don't worry, he didn't give anything away."

"I'm not sure it would have mattered anyway." She sighed. "I made a mistake, Thaddeus."

"Got yourself into a jam? The proverbial big pickle?"

"Barrel-sized. Joe and I quarreled all the way to Chicago. I knew he wanted to go off on his own, but I hoped he'd stick around long enough to help me dispose of some property. I didn't know anyone in Chicago, and when he left, I had no one to… make advance inquiries for me. I didn't know who to trust. So I went to New York where I still have some contacts."

"And someone who was looking for you saw you there?" Thaddeus guessed.

"Yes."

"And now they're chasing you."

"Yes. Actually two sets of somebodies are chasing me. So far I've managed to give them both the slip."

"Are you sure about that? I'm being followed, although I don't know if it has anything to do with you. Is there any reason either of your somebodies would want to kill me?"

"I doubt it. Their only interest in you would be to get to me. Any attempts on your life must be on account of something you did, not me."

"Well that's a relief. I'll have nobody to blame but myself then."

It was a typical Clementine conversation, twisting and turning and taking off in unexpected directions. He had often fantasized about what he might say to her when they met again, but he realized now that it had been a wasted exercise. There was no predicting how it might go.

"What are you going to do now?" he asked.

"Did you get the money I sent you?"

"Yes. I put it in the bank."

"In whose name?"

"In mine. I could hardly put it in yours since I don't know what it is. We can get it this afternoon if you need it."

"It's not for me."

Thaddeus had assumed all along that the money was her emergency fund, a bankroll set aside for easy retrieval. Surely she hadn't meant it for him. "I want no part of it," he said. "I don't know how you came by it."

"I know. That's why I sent it to you in the first place. I knew you'd never touch a penny of it, and that's more than I can say about anybody else I know. It's for Joe. In spite of the fact that my trip to New York proved so unwise, I at least managed to complete my errand. I have more than enough for myself, and Joe is entitled to some of it but I don't know where he is. I was hoping he'd been in touch with Martha."

"I don't think she's heard from him. She hasn't said anything, anyway."

"No?" Clementine looked puzzled. "That's odd. Is she here in Toronto with you? Could I ask her about it?"

"Yes, she's in school here. She'll be home late this afternoon."

"Not until then?" Clementine looked disappointed. "That's too bad. I'd like to have seen her again."

"You're not leaving right away are you?"

"Yes. I'm catching a train out of here this afternoon." She reached into a pocket and pulled out a bundle wrapped in brown paper. "I have some more to add to Joe's share." She held it out to him, and when he failed to take it, she set it on the table under the window. "Can you put it in the bank and take care of it until he turns up?"

"I will if you tell me one thing."

"What?" There was a wary look on her face.

"Why did you come here?"

"To tell you what to do with the money, of course."

"You could have done that in a letter. You didn't need to show up in person."

"And to see if you know where Joe is."

"Try again."

She looked away from him and stared at the floor. "And to say goodbye. I'm going to Europe and I don't know for how long. I couldn't bear the thought of not seeing you one last time." She glared up at him, daring him to make light of what she had just confessed. "Did you ever think I could be so sentimental?"

Thaddeus did what he had been wanting to do ever since he'd arrived in the parlour doorway. He stepped forward, stroked her cheek gently, then leaned in to kiss her. She moved into his embrace and returned the kiss. A small waft of her scent swirled over him. He felt he could stand in it forever.

And then, before he really knew what he was doing, he said, "Don't go. Stay here. Stay with me."

She pulled away to study his face. "You really mean it this time, don't you?"

"Yes."

"This isn't Methodist guilt talking again?"

"No."

Her reaction took him by surprise. She balled her hand up into a fist and whacked his arm, hard. "Damn you, Thaddeus!"

"Ouch! What?"

"Why did you have to ask me now, just when things are at their most impossible?"

"Whatever it is we can sort it out."

"No we can't. It would be hard enough under the best of circumstances. It's completely out of the question now."

"We can talk to Ashby. I don't know what you've done, but surely he can clear it up. That's what barristers are for."

She looked at him sadly. "You don't know what kind of people I'm dealing with. They don't take any notice of the law. If they find me, they'll do whatever it takes to get what they want."

"We'll go somewhere out of the way where they can't find you."

She shook her head. "My best chance of getting out of this in one piece is to disappear across the ocean. I need to travel fast and I need to travel far. I can't stay here and you can't come with me Thaddeus. You'd only slow me down."

He felt mildly offended by this remark. He was, after all, a famous tracker of murderers. He had been in a tight spot or two in his time and had handled himself to good account.

"The problem with you," she went on, "is that you have a conscience. It makes you dangerous to be with."

"But…" But what? What could he say that might change her mind? She seemed convinced that her only reasonable course of action was to run as fast as she could and based on the little he knew, Thaddeus was willing to concede that she might be right. Contrary to what she believed, he had, in fact, had experience with the sort of people she was talking about. They made their own rules.

"Will you ever come back?" he asked helplessly.

"I don't know, Thaddeus. I just don't know."

He sighed and drew her back into his arms. "Would you say yes if things were otherwise?"

She took a moment to answer. "I might. Who knows, I might even try to behave myself."

"So I'm not being ridiculous?"

"No. You're not. But can things ever be otherwise enough? That's the problem, isn't it, between you and me?" Then she adopted a lighter tone. "There is one thing I should point out though. If you're going to go around making proposals, you really need to practice a bit. That's twice now you've asked me, and both times have been pretty uninspiring."

"There's no point now. I don't intend to ask anyone else."

"Not even the woman in Cobourg?" she teased.

"No, not even. Why do you have to be so aggravating?"

"Because you like it."

He did. And he proved it by kissing her again with the full knowledge that he might never get to do it again.

"I need to go now," she said after a few minutes.

"Could I at least take you to the station? I can borrow my son's sleigh and drive you there."

"Yes, you can go that far. But I think it's better if we take a cab. Less noticeable. Is there a back door to this place?" But she made no attempt to disengage from him, so he kissed her again.

Finally she pulled herself away. "Damn you. Let's go."

Even though they had long since finished dinner, no one had moved from the dining room. Three heads swiveled to watch as Thaddeus ushered Clementine into the room.

Thaddeus made a brief introduction. "Mrs. Elliott, this is Mrs. Dunphy, Dr. Christie, and my son Luke."

They all nodded, but still no one said a word.

Thaddeus turned to Luke. "I'm taking Mrs. Elliott to her train. Do you think you could flag a cab and have it meet us at the back garden gate?"

"But…" said Luke. Then he looked first at Clementine, then at his father, and back again. "Of course. Nice to meet you ma'am." He went loping out to the front door.

Christie finally found his voice. "I don't know why you've kept this lovely lady a secret for such a long time, Lewis."

Clementine dazzled him with her best smile. "Mr. Lewis is so reticent," she said. "Sometimes it's like trying to get information out of a stone. He certainly never mentioned how distinguished you are."

Mrs. Dunphy snorted.

But Christie was clearly flattered. "Are you really leaving us so soon, Mrs. Elliott? We would be charmed to have you stay a little longer."

"I'm afraid I must go. My train is leaving soon."

No one seemed to know what to say after that. Thaddeus retrieved his coat and helped Clementine into her cloak, then they waited awkwardly until Luke returned. They nodded their farewells and made their way through to the garden. Luke followed them.

"Are you sure it's wise to be going off by yourself?" Luke asked.

"No. But I'm going anyway," Thaddeus replied.

"But…are you coming back?" he asked as his father climbed into the cab after Clementine.

"Yes. Don't worry. I'm coming back."

After he saw them off, Luke walked back into the dining room, to be met by the expectant faces of Dr. Christie and Mrs. Dunphy.

Luke shrugged. "Pa said he'd be back. That's all I know."

"I hope he's marched her off to a parson," Christie said. "That's what I'd do with a woman like that."

"You wouldn't have any idea what to do with a woman like that," Mrs. Dunphy said.

"You're probably right, my dear," Christie said sadly.

"I think it's more complicated than that," Luke said.

To his surprise, it was Mrs. Dunphy who replied. "How complicated can it be? He likes her, she likes him. He's not getting any younger. What's he waiting for? You don't get so many chances in life that you can afford to waste them, you know."

"I know. But I don't really know what's going on."

"Ah well, nothing to be done but wait and see I suppose." Christie heaved himself to his feet and disappeared into the back of the house.

Mrs. Dunphy began clearing dirty dishes from the table. "When I've done these, I'll be upstairs mending your socks if you need anything," she said.

Luke knew that this was a euphemism for having a nap, something the housekeeper had taken to doing more and more in the afternoons.

He had only a couple of calls to make that afternoon, and he supposed he might just as well make them right away. Maybe by the time he was finished, his father would be back. Whether or not Thaddeus would then vouchsafe any details remained to be seen.

The house was quiet when he returned. Dr. Christie was still in his studio. Mrs. Dunphy was still upstairs. And there was no sign of his father. Luke was puzzled. Thaddeus had seemed to indicate that he was merely escorting Mrs. Elliott to the station, and that he intended to come back right away, but maybe Luke had mistaken his intentions. Or maybe the train was late. Or Mrs. Elliott had changed her mind about leaving.

He should have gone with them. Thaddeus and Martha both insisted that Mrs. Elliott was no threat, but Luke had never been able to put his suspicions entirely aside. Maybe she had come to the door because it was the only way she could think of to get Thaddeus off by himself.

They had both been flushed and unhappy looking when they finally emerged from the parlour. Whatever had been discussed had not reached a happy conclusion, that much was clear. But what had been the topic? Try as he might, he had not been able to pick up much of their conversation. Only once or twice did their voices rise to a level that indicated disagreement and he would be about to rise from his chair to intervene when they would fall back to a low murmur followed by intervals of silence. Even if Mrs. Elliott was innocent of any intent to harm Thaddeus, it was clear that they had talked about far more than the simple matter of retrieving money. But if that was the case, why had she insisted on leaving so soon? And why hadn't Thaddeus returned by now?

As the minutes ticked by, Luke fought his growing anxiety. Why hadn't he gone with them to the station? Even if Thaddeus had been annoyed by the intrusion and refused to let him into the cab, Luke could have followed at a discreet distance.

He had just about made up his mind to harness the mare and go looking when there was a knock at the door. When Luke answered, there was a scruffy-looking man in shabby clothing standing on the step.

"Are you Dr. Lewis?" he said. "Cuddy Nelson sent me to get you. Your father's been shot."

Chapter 13

Clementine's suggestion of a public horse cab was a good one. Not only was it less likely to attract attention, but it afforded Thaddeus the opportunity to reach over and clasp her hand as they rode.

"Your son looks like you," she said as the cab turned down Yonge Street

"Yes, Luke favours me, but nature took the opportunity to correct a few mistakes on the second go round."

"I like what it did the first time. I even like your scar. What really happened to your face?"

"Somebody bashed me in the head with a shovel."

"And you really are being followed?"

"As far as I can tell. But I don't know if it has anything to do with you. You'd have to give me a little more information before I could make that assessment."

"Do you remember the detective who died in Wellington?"

"Yes. He was working for an old man in New York that you bilked some money out of." And then the import of what she was saying struck home. He groaned. "I wrote to him to ask for information."

"Yes."

"And he hasn't given up."

"No. And he may have joined forces with some other people."

The detectives hadn't traced Clementine to London. They'd gone there looking for Thaddeus, whose name had been splashed all over the newspapers. They'd been told about his stylish wife and her tragic death. Even if they'd bought the story, they would still want to talk to him. Clementine had risked a great deal to come and say goodbye.

"Who are the other people?"

"Just some people who don't like something I did," she said. "But if it will set your pesky conscience to rest, I was perfectly justified in doing it."

"I know I may regret this later, but right now I'm willing to take your word for it." He kept his tone light. It was the only way he was going to get through this farewell.

She must have decided the same thing.

"So what were you going to do with me, if it had really been me in the train wreck?" she asked. "It's not something I've ever really thought about before – what will happen to my body when I die."

"I was going to take you to Wellington. So you could rest beside your husband."

"Joe would have liked that. That was really very thoughtful of you Thaddeus."

"I couldn't think of anything else to do. But I had to do something because I felt so guilty."

That surprised her. "Why would you feel guilty – other than the fact that it seems to be your usual state of mind?"

"Because if I'd talked you into marrying me you wouldn't have been on the train."

"Do you Methodists torture yourselves over everything?" she said, but she squeezed his hand when she said it.

"Yes," he replied. "We do. You know, when I found out the truth I was angry with you. But only for a moment or two. And then I was relieved. And then I laughed. You really are a remarkable woman, you know. Bothersome, but remarkable."

"I know, I am, aren't I?"

The drive down Yonge Street was happening far too fast for Thaddeus. They were already well into the city. He wanted to tell the driver to slow down, because he wanted to keep talking to this woman for as long as he could.

"What are you doing now?" she asked. "Are you still working

for Ashby?"

"No. I haven't heard from him since he discovered that you aren't dead. Martha's father was extremely upset about what happened to her in London. He threatened to make her stay home. She dug in her heels. The compromise we reached was that she would attend teachers' college here."

"So she's going to be a school marm?"

"That's the plan."

"Good. I'm glad to hear she'll have a way to be independent. She's a wonderful girl."

"You seemed surprised that Joe hadn't written to her."

"I don't think Joe really knows what he wants right now, but I was sure he'd be in touch with Martha. I thought he was quite smitten. That would be ironic, wouldn't it? If you and I ended up as in-laws."

"Family gatherings might be awkward. Or entertaining. Or both."

She laughed. "Yes, they might. And Joe better make up his mind soon or Ashby will get in there first."

"No he won't. Ashby married just recently. That's why he wasn't in his office."

"Married? After the way he was carrying on in London? What a skunk."

"I don't think Martha likes him anyway."

"I wouldn't be so sure about that."

"Maybe you're right. That's the sort of thing I never pick up on," he said.

"I know. That's why you're so much fun to tease."

They had already passed King Street when Thaddeus suddenly remembered the daguerreotype. He dug into his pocket and pulled out the wooden box that held it.

"I should give you this. The daguerreotypist brought it to the hotel in London for you, but you'd already gone."

She took it and studied the picture for a moment. "Have you been carrying this around in your pocket this whole time?"

"Yes."

"Do you take it out and look at it sometimes?"

"Yes."

"Every day?" she teased.

"Stop." But he smiled at her as he said it.

She put it back in his hand and folded his fingers over it. "I want you to keep it. So you'll have something to remember me by."

"You're hard to forget. But thank you, yes, I would like to keep it."

And then, all too soon they arrived at the station.

Thaddeus waited outside the low wooden station building while Clementine confirmed that her baggage had been loaded. When she came out, he didn't ask her where she was going. He guessed Niagara Falls, where she could make connections that would take her to some port on the eastern seaboard of the United States. New York would be the easiest to reach, but he didn't know if she dared go back there. He didn't want to know, because then he was in no danger of giving her away.

There was a bustle on the platform as passengers began lining up to board.

"Will you write?" Thaddeus asked. "After you get to Europe?"

"Only if you want me to."

"I would like it. If for no other reason than to know you're safe at the time of writing."

"I will if I can. That's all I can promise. And now it looks as though people are boarding."

Thaddeus looked around with dismay. Surely it was too soon. But she was correct. The first of the people in line were already on the train.

"You should go," Clementine said.

"I can wait to see you off."

"I won't crane out the window and wave goodbye, you know. I'll find a seat in an out-of-the-way corner and keep my head down."

"I..."

"Please, Thaddeus. Don't make it any harder than it is."

"I guess this is goodbye, then."

She nodded. "I guess it is." Her lips were pursed, her mouth held in a tight line. He could see tears shimmering in her eyes. "I wish things could be different."

"I know," Thaddeus said. "But I don't know how to change them."

And then she marched up to the train and climbed aboard without looking back at him. He walked to the side of the station and slid around the corner of it to where he could still see the train, but where no one looking out of the windows could see him.

"Last call," shouted the porter. "Last call. Departing now for Port Credit, Burlington, Hamilton and destinations west, with connections to London, Niagara Falls and Sarnia. Last call."

Thaddeus stood by the side of the building as the train pulled away. He remained standing there until it disappeared from view and only the plume of smoke from its stack was still visible in the distance.

And then he began to walk aimlessly. He wandered beyond the quay and into the shipyard, through boats in dry-dock and past factories that manufactured he-knew-not-what.

He'd been surprised by his reaction when he saw Clementine standing in the parlour. He'd been so certain in London that she was manipulating him for her own ends. He'd been relieved when she turned down his half-hearted proposal and gone on her way. And then, when he thought she was dead, he had wished her back again. And he had continued wishing it, every time he opened the carved wooden box and looked at the picture inside. But until that afternoon, he had had no clear notion of what he would do when he saw her again. And no sooner had he decided than she was gone again.

Would you say yes, if things were otherwise?

Can things ever be otherwise enough? That's the problem between you and me, isn't it?

What would he have done if her answer had been different? There was no getting around the fact that she was a crook and he was a preacher; he had no money and she had no scruples. Everything about Clementine was a problem except for the way he felt when he held her.

Long ago, when he was courting Betsy, he had declared that he wished he was a better man. She smiled and said, "Then become one." And he had. He changed for her. It was the cornerstone of their union and the foundation upon which he had built the rest of his life.

How could he bend his principles for Clementine without making a mockery of everything he'd done for Betsy? But it didn't matter, anyway, did it? She was gone again, and there was little prospect of her ever coming back.

His face was wet. He wiped the moisture away, but the tears welled up and spilled down his cheeks again. He walked on, and let them fall.

He turned around only when he realized that he had no idea where he was. He would have to walk back in the direction he had come and hope that at some point he would cross Yonge Street. From there he could catch a bus back to Yorkville.

He reached one of the mainly industrial areas and had just passed a squat brick foundry building when a black-clad woman stepped in front of him. He was about to walk around her when he suddenly realized that he knew who she was. And only then did he notice that she was holding a brace of small pistols and that they were pointed in his direction.

"Miss Simms?" he said, trying not to stare at the guns she held.

"I hope you're prepared to die Lewis," she snarled. Thaddeus wrenched his gaze away from the guns and looked into a face that no longer reminded him of his dead daughter. This woman's mouth was twisted with malice, her eyes full of hate and anger. If she still bore any resemblance at all to Sarah, it was a Sarah grown old and mad with bitterness.

"I am prepared to die," he replied, "but not today. This is what? – the sixth time you've tried to kill me and you haven't succeeded yet."

"I'll do it this time."

She waved one of the guns at him. "I really wanted to kill your granddaughter first, so you could know what it's like to lose the one thing you hold most precious. Her and your pretty son. I wanted you to carry the guilt to your grave. But I'll settle for you."

"Did you never wonder why I rode so hard after your brother?"

She blinked and her grip on the gun wavered slightly. There was a sheen of sweat on her face.

"One of the women he killed was my daughter," he said. "You can teach me nothing about loss."

"Your daughter? I didn't know that." She began to laugh, but it turned into a wheezing cough.

Thaddeus took a step forward, but she halted him with a wave of a pistol.

Now that he was closer he could see the fading rose-red rash that covered her face and hands, the crusty matter that coated her eyelashes. Esther Simms had arrived in Yorkville sick in mind and now she was sick in body, one of the last victims in the village to succumb to measles.

"Give me the guns."

"Not before I shoot you, Lewis."

"That won't bring Isaac back."

"Because you killed him!" The words came out in a wheeze, and she coughed again, the sweat running down her face.

The sun was low in the western sky, but still shone with a winter brightness. Thaddeus turned slightly to his right.

"Isaac was a murderer," he said. "He had to be stopped."

"No one would ever have known if it wasn't for you!"

He shifted again and took a half-step, forcing Simms to move to her left. They were now at right angles to the setting sun.

"Isaac knew. It tormented him."

"That's not true!"

He took another half-step. She countered his move and waved the pistol at him again, squinting against the glare of the light.

He moved again. The sun was directly in her eyes now, her sore, infected, pustular eyes. They began to run.

"He was trying to get away from you."

"Isaac loved me!"

"He hated you at the end."

It was enough. She howled and extended her arm to take aim and Thaddeus leapt. He grabbed her right hand and swept his left arm sideways, hoping to knock the second gun out of her grasp.

He wasn't fast enough. One of the guns went off and suddenly he was aware of an excruciating pain and the smell of gunpowder. He staggered, lost his balance and fell to the ground. He tried to get up again, but he couldn't seem to get his feet under him. He was helpless to do anything but look up into the barrel of the gun pointed at his head. He closed his eyes and prayed that she would end him quickly.

He heard a click. Howls of outrage and a paroxysm of coughing filled the air. He opened his eyes again.

The gun had misfired. She threw it aside, her hands shaking as she took out a small bag and tried to pour black powder down the barrel of the first pistol. A great deal of it spilled harmlessly to the ground. Even so, she loaded, aimed and pulled the trigger.

Nothing happened. She needed to remove the spent cap before the gun would fire again, but she either didn't know this, or had forgotten it. Thaddeus hoped that by the time she figured it out, someone close by would have heard the commotion and come running.

But by then he was fighting a new pain. His chest felt as though it was in a vice, the pressure tightening until he was sure all the air would be forced from his lungs. He attempted to roll over so he could catch his breath, but that only served to intensify the pain that gripped his shoulder and neck. He felt dizzy and nauseated, and then everything went grey and slowly faded to black.

And then slowly rose to light again. All the pain was gone and he could see a bright, white light that shimmered in the distance. It grew in magnitude and through its filmy haze he saw the figure of a woman. The light became more diffuse and then he could see that the woman was Betsy, and just behind her was Sarah with the little ones, all his little lost daughters, playing around her skirts.

He knew then where he was. Was it really possible that the Lord in his infinite mercy would allow him through the gates of heaven after all, in spite of his failures, in spite of his sins? That his loved ones were there to welcome him in exactly the way he had always hoped? He was filled with joy and took a step toward them.

And then a voice spoke from somewhere behind him.

"Oh, don't be ridiculous, Thaddeus. You can't go yet. You need to look after Martha."

It was Clementine at her most annoying, telling him the truth about something he already knew but didn't want to admit. What was she doing here? She'd run away, hadn't she?

And then he took a step back.

The light grew opaque and faded and he was jerked back into a world of pain. With a breath that threatened to tear the lungs out of him, he opened his eyes and looked straight into the ugly, pock-marked face of Cuddy Nelson.

"So you're not dead after all," Cuddy said. "More's the pity, preacher, since I already sent for the coroner. He should be here in a minute, so if you feel like dying in the meantime, go right ahead. He'll be vexed if he comes for nothing."

Thaddeus tried to reply, but no words would come.

"Shot? Where?"

"He's at the iron works down by the harbour," the man in the shabby clothes said. "There's a doctor been fetched, but Cuddy said I'd better find you, 'cause it don't look too good. I've got a wagon here to take you."

"I..." there were a million questions Luke wanted to ask, but he could ask them on the way.

"I'll just get my bag," he said. He walked into the office and grabbed his coat and his medical case. And then he walked straight through to the back room.

"Pa's been shot. Will you come?"

And Dr. Christie, who never went anywhere if he could help it, didn't hesitate for a moment. "Of course. I'll get my coat."

"What happened?" Luke asked as they trundled toward the city. "Who shot him?"

The man, who said his name was Jimmy, shrugged. "Some woman, Cuddy says. He heard a shot and went to see what was up. She'd got him once and was trying to reload so she could finish him off, but she ran away when she saw Cuddy. Or that's what he says, anyways."

A woman? Luke could kick himself for allowing his father to go off with Clementine Elliott. He should have leapt into the cab after him, or better yet, tackled him to the ground and held him

there until the cab drove away without him. Thaddeus had been so
sure that she posed no threat, and now he was lying wounded in a
factory yard.

"Where exactly is this place?" he asked Jimmy.

"Down by the harbour."

It didn't matter where it was. It only mattered that the wagon
was moving too slowly and that Luke needed to be with his father.

Finally the driver turned off Yonge into a side street, and by a
series of complicated detours, pulled up in front of a brick
building.

"Around the back," Jimmy said, and pointed toward a small
alleyway. Luke raced down it to where a knot of people were
standing in a circle. He elbowed his way through them. Thaddeus
was lying on his side, a grey-haired man bent over him. His
clothing had been pulled back and his neck and part of his shoulder
were bare, exposing a blackened hole just under his collarbone.
Luke dropped to his knees beside his father.

"Who are you?" the man said.

Christie came wheezing up before Luke could reply.

"Dr. Baker," Christie nodded at the grey-haired man.

"What are you doing here, Stewart?"

"This is my partner," Christie said, pointing at Luke. "And
that's his father. What's your assessment?"

"Obviously there's the gunshot wound," Baker said. "The ball
struck his clavicle, but where it went from there is anybody's
guess. There's something else going on with him as well."

"He's been having angina," Luke said. His father's face was
grey, his pulse rapid, his skin cold and clammy.

"Hard to tell which is causing the most harm, then, the lead ball
or his heart," Baker said. "To be honest, I was called out to
pronounce a dead body, and I won't be a bit surprised if I do it
yet."

But this pessimistic statement seemed to evoke a response from
Thaddeus. He opened his eyes. "Martha," he said.

"Is that the name of the woman who shot him?" Dr. Baker said.
"I've sent for a constable but in the meantime we should take note
of anything the patient says."

"No," said Luke. "Martha is his granddaughter. He's been worried about her."

Dr. Christie heaved himself down to the ground on the other side of Thaddeus, his face a mask of concern.

"Can you hear me, Lewis?" He grasped Thaddeus's left hand and squeezed. "Can you feel that? Squeeze back if you can."

There was no response. Christie let go the hand and gently palpated along Thaddeus's collarbone and the back of his neck. Then he rocked back on his heels and looked at Luke. "There are signs of pressure on the spine. I don't know if it's from the bullet or a bone fragment from his clavicle, but we need to explore the wound and at the very least get rid of any blood that's pooling there."

"He needs to stabilize first," Baker objected. "His heart will fail if you operate now."

"His heart may well fail him anyway," Christie said. "But if it doesn't, the pressure on his spine will either kill him or leave him paralyzed. As far as I'm concerned, it's a Hobb's choice."

Baker shrugged. "It's your decision."

"No, it's not. It's Luke's."

Luke stared at Christie for a moment that seemed to last for years. "I think we have to try whatever we can."

"Are you sure, boy?"

"Yes. And please, will you do it? You have more dexterity than I do. And far more experience. There's no one I'd trust more." He looked at Dr. Baker. "Will you assist?"

"I might just as well," Baker grumbled. "If I leave now, I'll just have to come back again after he's dead."

"What about anaesthetic?" Luke asked.

"Now there's a rum question," Christie said. "The tiniest dose of chloroform we can get away with, I think. Just enough to keep him under for a few minutes. And I'll do it here. I don't think we dare move him." He waved toward the crowd of spectators. "Maybe we can commandeer a couple of these fine fellows to hold him down just in case we miscalculate the dose. I'll be as fast as I can."

Thaddeus opened his eyes again.

"We'll get you through this," Luke said. "Dr. Christie is going to operate." Was it just wishful thinking, or had his father's colour grown a little pinker in the last minute or so?

Thaddeus nodded slightly, then groaned.

"Sensibility to pain," Christie noted. "That's a good sign."

"Simms," Thaddeus said in a voice that was barely above a whisper.

"Later," Luke said. "Plenty of time later."

He pulled a handkerchief out of his pocket while Christie directed two burly men to hold Thaddeus by the arms and legs and the rest of the cluster of gawkers to stand back. They did so reluctantly. This was more entertainment than they had expected, and they were eager to take note of the details so that they could cash the story in for a drink or two later.

Luke willed his hands to stop shaking and dripped a tiny amount of chloroform onto the handkerchief. Then he cradled his father's head and clapped the handkerchief over his nose and mouth.

Christie gently ran his finger along Thaddeus's neck and then, at a nod from Luke, snatched up a scalpel and extended the wound. He was as fast as Luke could ever have hoped. All the years of dissecting animals and studying the relationship of muscle and nerve and bone had given the old doctor a sure knowledge of anatomy. And all the years of translating joint and skeleton to pen and paper had honed a precision that Luke could never have matched. Christie was a superb surgeon, and Luke was in awe of his skill.

"Swab," Christie called. "Look at the blood in there."

Baker balled up a wad of gauze bandaging and sopped away as much as he could.

"I can see the shot."

Christie gingerly inserted a set of forceps into the wound.

"There, you've got it," Baker said as Christie pulled out the lead shot. "It looks intact."

Christie threw it on the ground. One of the men watching scuttled forward and grabbed it. It would make a fine souvenir of the day.

"All right over there boy?"

Thaddeus moved his head slightly. Luke gripped it tight. He didn't dare administer any more chloroform. "Yes, we're all right, but hurry."

"I think I can see a bit of bone in behind," Christie said. He hesitated for only a moment, then re-inserted the forceps and pulled out a splinter of bone. "The bullet must have clipped the clavicle and chipped it off. Swab."

Baker mopped up the gush of blood that spurted out in the wake of the extraction.

"I'll give it room to drain," Christie said. "And then we wait." He closed the incision with a loose stitch, and packed a wad of gauze over it to sop up the blood that continued to ooze from it.

When he finished, Luke stole a glance at his watch. The whole procedure had been accomplished in just under four minutes. Thaddeus seemed to be breathing a little more easily, and when Luke checked his pulse it had slowed slightly.

The crowd of spectators parted as Cuddy Nelson sauntered over to them.

"Is he still alive?" Cuddy asked.

"So far," Baker said.

"He's a tough old bugger, ain't he? I was sure he was a goner."

"Did you see what happened?" Luke asked.

Cuddy shrugged. "Not really. I heard a shot and when I came out to see what was going on some woman was standing over him with a gun. She ran away as soon as she saw me." He looked at the crowd around him and grinned. "You have to wonder what the old goat's been up to, that some woman wants to take a gun to him."

The crowd laughed.

"Wonder it don't happen more often," he went on.

"Thank you for sending Jimmy," Luke said, "and for getting Dr. Baker."

Cuddy's affable manner evaporated. He fixed Luke with a cold glare. "It's like this, Doc. You and me and your old man are square now, right? I don't bear no grudge, but I don't owe you nothin' either. The next time we meet, it's on equal ground. Got it?"

"Understood."

"Let me know when you want to move him, and I'll get Jimmy to take you all home."

"Whoever did this should be trotted off to the hangman," Christie commented as Cuddy walked away.

"She probably will be," Luke replied. "But we have to catch her first."

Chapter 14

Martha was surprised when there was no one to pick her up from school at the end of the day. She joined the group of girls waiting by the side door, but one by one they gave up on catching a glimpse of Luke and set off for home until finally she was left standing alone.

Perhaps Luke had been called out for an emergency and had needed the sleigh to get there. If that were the case, she would have expected Thaddeus to come instead, but maybe he was busy with something and had forgotten, although this seemed unlikely given his general level of anxiety about her safety. She could easily catch the next bus, but then she would risk missing either of them if they were, indeed, en route. If, on the other hand, she started walking along Yonge Street, she might well meet them coming the other way. In any event, there was no point in continuing to wait at the school when nearly everyone else had gone.

She was about to set off down the drive when Mr. Sorbie went jogging by. He passed her, stopped, and turned back.

"It's Miss Renwell, isn't it? What are you still doing here?"

"Both of my escorts appear to have deserted me, I'm afraid. I'd have set off long since, but I kept expecting that my uncle or my grandfather would turn up at any moment." She peered anxiously up the drive. "It's not like my grandfather to be late. I hope nothing's wrong."

"Could I be of assistance in any way?"

"Thank you, I'm fine. I think I'll just walk over to Yonge Street and catch an omnibus."

But Sorbie didn't appear to have heard her. He was looking, eyes narrowed, at something off in the distance.

"You don't happen to know who that woman is, do you? I've seen her loitering around the school on a number of occasions recently."

Martha turned to follow his gaze. The woman she had seen with Alice Gleeson was standing at the end of the drive. She noticed them looking and immediately walked away.

"I've tried to approach her several times to ask her business here, but she scuttles away before I can get close to her. It's very odd. I'm sorry, you were saying…?"

"Actually, Mr. Sorbie, would it be a terrible imposition if I asked you to walk with me to the bus stop? I waited here too long and now I have no classmates for company."

"It would be my pleasure. And by far the most prudent course. The street is pretty deserted at this time of the day and there are strangers about."

Sorbie set a brisk pace and Martha had to walk very quickly to try to keep up with him. She soon fell several paces behind. He noticed this only when he turned to say something to her and realized that she was no longer at his side.

"I'm sorry," he laughed when she caught up. "I'll slow down. It's a good thing I turned to ask you a question, otherwise I'd have left you in the dust."

"I know what you're going to ask," Martha sighed. "Yes, I was kidnapped, but not for very long." It was the question everyone wanted to ask.

"No that isn't it. I wanted to know if you're enjoying your time at Toronto Normal - although you might be interested to hear that the entire student body at the Model School is convinced that you'll bite their ears off if they misbehave."

"Really? Oh, dear." This extraordinary conjecture could only have come from the boy whose ear she had pinched. "Do you think I should tell them I was joking?"

"I wouldn't. Having the pupils a little afraid of you isn't a bad thing when you're a teacher. Unfortunately, they'll get over it far too fast and then you'll have to think of some other way to make them behave."

"I wondered why I was having so little trouble in the classroom recently."

"Enjoy it while you can."

She laughed. In spite of her worry over what had happened to Luke and Thaddeus, Martha found she was enjoying Sorbie's company. He was very easy to talk to, unlike some of the other masters.

"In response to your intended question, I'm finding the amount of work we're expected to get through somewhat onerous. But I understand the need for it. We seem to be covering a great deal of material in a very short period of time."

He nodded. "That's quite deliberate. It sorts the wheat from the chaff, so to speak."

"All the more annoying that some of the girls spend so much time gossiping."

"Yes. You've been the victim of a great deal of that haven't you? I hope it hasn't coloured your view of the school."

"Not at all. I'm here to get my certificate and I have no intention of letting a little gossip get in the way."

This statement seemed to meet with his approval. And then they were at the bus stop. There were two people waiting already, a woman who looked as though she was a domestic, and a man who wore the shabby cloth cap of a factory hand.

"Thank you, Mr. Sorbie. I'll be fine from here," she said.

"I'll see you safely onto the bus," he said. "I don't mind at all."

But the bus was already rumbling down the road, and no further conversation seemed necessary.

As soon as Martha stepped down at the corner of Concession Road, the Spicer twins barreled toward her.

"Miss Renwell!" they called. "Martha!"

They swirled around her, their faces split into grins. One of the girls - Martha didn't know if it was Ruth or Rebecca since she could never tell them apart - shyly took her hand.

"How was school today?" she asked.

"Jerry Maxwell got whipped," said one of the boys. "He cried."

"Why did he get whipped?" Martha asked.

"Because he was late."

"It's not fair," said the twin who was holding Martha's hand. "He lives too far away."

"Why did you come on the bus?" One of the boys bounced up and down in front of her. "You never go on the bus alone."

"No one came to pick me up," she said. "I expect they're all busy."

"Maybe they're busy with the lady."

"What lady?"

"The strange lady. We saw her at Dr. Christie's on our way back to school after dinner."

Martha stopped walking abruptly, narrowly avoiding a collision with the twin who had been skipping along behind her.

"You saw her? Here in Yorkville?"

"She knocked on the door and Dr. Luke answered. He let her inside. We didn't wait to see what happened after that 'cause we didn't want to end up late for school."

"We didn't want to get whipped," said the twin who had Martha's hand – was it Rebecca?

"So maybe they're still busy with the lady."

"Yes, maybe they are," Martha said and her anxiety grew tenfold. "Thanks for telling me."

All four twins beamed at her. "You're welcome!" they chorused. And then they raced off down the street.

The back door of the Christie house was unlocked. There was no one in the kitchen. Mrs. Dunphy should have started supper long since, but there was no sign of her. Neither was there anyone in the dining room or the parlour. She tried the door to the consulting room. Luke normally kept it firmly locked, but now it swung open to reveal an empty room. She ran through to Dr. Christie's studio, but the old doctor was nowhere to be seen.

Heart pounding, she ran up the stairs.

"Hello?" she called.

The door to Mrs. Dunphy's room opened, and the housekeeper came out, rubbing her eyes and yawning. "You're home early," she said when she saw Martha.

"No, actually, I'm later than usual," Martha said. "Where is everybody?"

The housekeeper's eyes widened. "Oh my goodness, you don't mean to say I've slept the afternoon away? They'll all be sitting down there with their mouths open, waiting to have their maws filled."

She rushed past Martha and down the stairs. "I've got to get supper started."

Martha followed her. "There's no one waiting," she said. "There's no one else here."

Mrs. Dunphy stopped. "Not even Dr. Christie?"

"No. No one."

"That's odd." Her brow furrowed. "I never know where Dr. Luke is, so that's not unusual, and your grandfather went off with his lady friend, but I don't know where on earth Stewart might have got to. I hope there wasn't some emergency that required the both of them."

"A lady friend? What lady?" Had Thaddeus gone off with Mrs. Gleeson's boarder for some reason? Martha didn't think he would ever be so foolish, but she couldn't think what other woman it could be.

"It was the woman who's sent him money," Mrs. Dunphy said. "She came to the door, and Dr. Luke made us stay in the dining room while they talked, and then they both went off to catch a train."

"Mrs. Elliott? He went off on a train with Mrs. Elliott?"

"No, no, he didn't go with her on the train. He just took her to catch it. And now I've got to get supper on the go, or they'll all be unhappy. It's a good thing I made extra tatties at dinner."

Martha followed as she bustled into the kitchen. "Don't worry, I'll help you, but tell me more about Mrs. Elliott."

"I don't know anything more. She came to the house and they had a talk and then they left. They both looked unhappy about it, but there you go. Here, you set the table while I get the stove stoked up." She handed Martha a stack of dinner plates.

Martha's mind was whirling as she took the dishes through to the dining room. She wasn't entirely sure what to make of the news that Clementine had turned up. Had she come just to get the money she'd sent, or was there something more to it? If there was, Martha wasn't entirely sure what to make of that either. She liked Clementine very much, but in spite of everything that had happened, she didn't really know how her grandfather felt. Mrs. Dunphy's report would seem to indicate that nothing had come of the meeting, except that it had made them both unhappy. But if Thaddeus had escorted her into the city only to catch her train, why wasn't he back yet? Had something changed along the way? Had he boarded the train and rumbled away? But no, Martha decided, Thaddeus would never just leave without telling her. Something else had happened.

She continued to fret while she sliced some bacon for Mrs. Dunphy to fry up with her "tatties".

She was just setting out the bread and butter when the front door flew open and Luke burst in, his face grim. "Clear a path to the parlour," he barked and disappeared again.

Martha moved the newspapers and coats and boots that had accumulated in the hall and shoved a couple of footstools to one side of the parlour, then ran outside where everyone she had been waiting for was clustered around a wagon driven by a man she had never seen before, along with the unexpected addition of the entire Spicer family.

Dr. Christie climbed down out of the wagon and walked over to her.

"Your grandfather was attacked again. He was shot, but I think he'll be all right. Luckily, the Spicers saw us coming along the street and are here to help get him inside."

Luke and Morgan helped Thaddeus out of the bed of the wagon, his face nearly as pale as the white bandage that was wrapped around his neck and the sling that supported his left arm. He took a moment to steady himself, and looked around him. When he saw Martha, he smiled slightly.

"I'm fine from here," he said to Luke, who had a firm hold on his good arm, but he staggered a little as he took his first step. Luke refused to let go until they reached the parlour and Thaddeus was safely lowered into a chair. Everyone crowded in after him, the small parlour too full of people.

"Dining room!" Luke ordered. They all filed out again, but Luke waylaid Christie. "Could you stay in here with him while I tell everyone what's happened?"

"Yes, if you can bring me a sherry. And one for the patient as well. We're both quite worn out."

Martha hovered in the hallway, anxious to assure herself that her grandfather truly was all right.

"You can fuss all you like later," Luke said to her. "He needs some quiet right now."

She followed him into the dining room.

"What happened…?"

"Who was …?"

"The twins say…"

Everyone attempted to speak at once, but Luke silenced them with a wave of the hand.

"First things first," he said, and poured two glasses of sherry, which he took into the parlour.

"I'll tell you what I know," he said when he returned, "and what I think we should do." Briefly, he outlined what had happened, placing special emphasis on Dr. Christie's role in extracting the bullet. "Thaddeus says it was Isaac Simms' sister who shot him."

"We saw a woman!" one of the twins exclaimed. "We told Martha!"

"When was this?" Luke asked.

"When she was walking home."

"No, when did you see the woman?"

"At dinnertime. She was knocking on the door."

"That wasn't the Simms woman," Luke said, and the twins looked downcast. "It was Mrs. Elliott." He looked at Martha sheepishly. "At first I thought it was her who shot him. I thought it right up until he managed to tell me that it wasn't."

"Who is Mrs. Elliott?" Sally asked.

"An old friend of my grandfather's," Martha replied. "It's a complicated story, and I don't think it has anything to do with what's happened." She looked to Luke for confirmation of this

209

statement.

"No, it doesn't," he said, "other than the fact that she's the reason Thaddeus was in the city this afternoon. He saw her off on the train. The Simms woman must have been following them and found an opportunity to ambush him. And there's no question in my mind that she'll try again."

"Should we not just go to the police?" Sally asked. "Get them to arrest her?"

"I've lodged a complaint, Luke said, "but I have no great faith in them being able to do much of anything."

Sally's brow wrinkled in concern. "We can't keep watch forever."

"The fact that she used a gun in broad daylight in the middle of the city indicates to me that she's getting desperate and frustrated," Luke said. "If she attacks again, I'm fairly certain it will be soon. And since Thaddeus is in no shape to go anywhere, she'll try to get at him here."

"What kind of shape, exactly, is he in?" Martha said in a small voice.

"There's no question he had a close call, but as long as the wound heals cleanly, he's no longer in danger from the effects of the gunshot. Of more concern is the state of his heart. It took some damage today and he's going to need a long convalescence. In one respect, I suppose, that makes him a little easier to protect, since he's effectively corralled anyway."

"If she tries to get into the house, she'll come through the back," Morgan said. "There's no cover at the front."

Martha gasped. She couldn't remember if she had locked the back door behind her when she came home and found an empty house. She jumped up and ran into the kitchen. She hadn't. She slid the bolt home and returned to the dining room.

"But what if she tries poison again?" Morgan was saying as she returned to her seat.

"I think it will be more direct than that," Luke said. "Thaddeus has been lucky that her efforts have been so ineffectual up until now. But now she has a gun. I think she'll try to get into the house to finish him off."

"I can keep a watch tonight," Morgan said. When Sally began to protest, Morgan cut her off. "He watched for us once. We'll watch for him."

"You can find shelter in the driveshed," Luke said. "There's a clear view of the back door from there. Take a key with you so you can slip inside the house if you get too cold."

"If you're going to be sitting up all the night, you're going to need something inside you," Mrs. Dunphy said, rising from her chair. "Supper's been waiting all this time. We might just as well eat up what there is."

"I'll help you get it." Sally jumped up and followed her into the kitchen.

"Would you like go in to him now?" Luke said to Martha. "Just try not to get overwrought. His nerves need to settle. And send Dr. Christie in to get some food, otherwise he'll grumble."

Thaddeus was lying back with his eyes closed when Martha entered the parlour. A little colour had come back to his face, even though the sherry he had been given sat untouched on the table beside him. His feet were propped up on a footstool, but no one had thought to remove his boots.

She knelt in front of him and began unlacing them. He opened his eyes at the movement.

"I'll get rid of these for you," she said.

"Is there any sign of supper yet?" Dr. Christie asked in a hopeful tone.

"Yes, Luke said you're to go in. I'll stay here."

Christie hummed a little to himself as he left the room. Martha reminded herself that she must thank him later for his efforts on behalf of her grandfather. By all accounts, he had been magnificent.

She eased Thaddeus's boots off.

"Are you all right?" he asked. His voice was low and weak.

"Yes I'm fine, but I don't think I'm the one everyone is worried about."

"I'll survive."

"You should drink some of your sherry." She picked up the

glass and held it to his lips. He took a sip, grimaced at the taste of it, then closed his eyes again.

Martha took a seat across from him and sat silently until Sally appeared in the doorway, a plate in hand. She passed it to Martha.

"Would you like a little bit to eat?" she said to Thaddeus.

"Yes, a little," he said.

"I'll give him some of this," Martha said. Sally nodded and disappeared.

Thaddeus managed only a few mouthfuls. But the food, or maybe it was the sherry, seemed to perk him up.

"Mrs. Elliott was here," he said.

"I know. Mrs. Dunphy told me."

"The money's for Joe. She wanted to know if you've heard from him."

"No. Not a word."

"I'm supposed to hang on to it for him."

"I'll let you know if I hear anything."

Martha could think of no good way to phrase the question she wanted to ask.

"So... how is Mrs. Elliott?" she finally ventured.

"On the run again. She was sorry not to see you."

"Oh."

"You'd like her to have stayed wouldn't you?" Thaddeus said, and Martha knew he was talking about more than a social visit.

"Yes."

"So would I. But I don't know if it's possible."

"Oh." Martha wanted to say "I'm sorry", but mindful of Luke's caution not to get too emotional, she decided it was best to leave it alone.

The moment passed anyway, when Sally came back in to gather up their plates.

"Morgan's keeping watch on the house tonight," she said to Thaddeus.

Martha expected him to protest that a watch wasn't necessary, but to her surprise, he said, "Tell him to be careful."

"I will," Sally said, her face knotted up in worry.

"Tell him she's got pocket pistols. They're only good at close range."

She nodded. "I'll keep the twins away from you until tomorrow. They're desperate to ask you what it's like to be shot."

"Tell them it hurts."

Sally left and Luke came in, a glass of brandy in his hand. He seemed worn, and for once looked every bit his age.

Thaddeus frowned at the glass Luke held.

"You're enough to drive anybody to drink," Luke said. He set his glass on the table, and bent over his father to check his pulse. "How are you feeling?"

"Better, now that I'm not jouncing around in a wagon."

"Your hand feels warm. That's good. Any pain?"

"My neck and shoulder. Especially when I move."

"You should drink up the rest of that sherry. You can have a dose of laudanum later to help you sleep."

Luke slouched into a chair, leaned back wearily and took a sip of his brandy. "By the way, Cuddy Nelson had a message for us. He says we're all even now. From here on, all bets are off."

"So you were right – he knew where to find us all this time."

"He certainly knew where to send for me. He probably saved your life. He and Christie."

"I'll thank Cuddy if I ever see him again. I hope I don't. I'll thank Christie later."

"Oh, I wouldn't do that," Luke said. "It would only embarrass him. He did express the opinion that whoever shot you should be hanged, though."

Martha laughed and Thaddeus started to, but winced.

"It's going to hurt for a while, I'm afraid," Luke said. "You'll need to take it easy for a few weeks, and not just because of the gunshot wound. You know you had a heart attack, don't you?"

"I guessed as much."

"No physical activity. No excitement."

"I'll do my best," Thaddeus said. "But I can't guarantee there won't be any excitement."

Only one person was able to fall soundly asleep that night. Luke wanted to set up a bed in the parlour for Thaddeus.

"There's no way you should be climbing stairs," he said. "And it will be easier to look after you if we don't have to go running up and down."

"If it's all the same to you, I'll just stay here in the chair," Thaddeus said. "As long as I can keep my arm propped up on a pillow my neck doesn't hurt too badly. It won't be the first time I've slept sitting up."

"Fair enough, as long as you're sure. And I'll be sitting up with you, at least for tonight."

"Is that necessary?"

"Given what you've been through today, I think it's wise. I would do it for any of my patients in the same circumstances," Luke said. "And if the Simms woman tries again tonight, she'll have to get past me to get to you."

He moved the lamp over beside his chair and turned it down low, hoping it would encourage Thaddeus to drift off to sleep. He pretended to read a book, but from time to time glanced sideways at his father. Thaddeus's colour was much better and his breathing unlaboured, but Luke wasn't taking any chances. Heart attacks were tricky things, relapses frequent, especially in the first few hours after the initial onslaught.

In spite of the brandy he had downed, Luke found that his nerves were still jangled. As a physician, he dealt with a multitude of injuries and accidents in the normal course of his practice. He dealt with them coolly and competently and liked to think that he had saved more than one life. But the sight of his own father lying on the ground close to death had been enough to send his hands shaking as badly as they had when he first started doctoring.

He glanced over at his father again. Thaddeus appeared to be asleep and Luke took a moment to study the map of years reflected in his father's face – the strong features weathered by miles of hard riding, the deep lines that framed the corners of his mouth. It was the face of a man who had lived a burdensome life, but held the secrets of those burdens close. Thaddeus would probably never reveal what had been discussed with Mrs. Elliott, just as Luke, as much as he wanted to, could never bring himself to confide his own secrets to Thaddeus.

When he was a boy, Luke had been half-afraid of his father. He had always turned to his mother when he was troubled and needed advice. His father was too stern, too uncompromising, too remote and, most of all, too often absent. They'd grown closer after Betsy's death, and of all of the family, Luke was the one who most understood how lonely Thaddeus was without her.

He had always respected his father. Over time, respect had grown into affection and affection into love. Now, as he watched his father sleep, Luke realized just how sad he would be to lose him.

Thaddeus shifted in his chair from time to time, searching for a more comfortable position. In spite of the laudanum Luke had given him, he was unable to find one. He dozed fitfully and when the pain jerked him awake again, his mind went round and round the tumultuous events of the day.

There was a lot to think about - being gunned down in the street, the reluctant farewell to Clementine, what the Simms woman might do next – but most of all he thought about the strange vision he'd seen when he died. And there was no question in his mind that he had died and been called back.

That his beloved wife and daughters would be waiting to greet him was what his church had promised him if he strove toward a state of holiness. Sanctification was a prerequisite, he had been told, and there was no guarantee that anyone who failed to embrace it would be admitted to heaven. And yet, in spite of his failings, Thaddeus was convinced that the door had been open and his loved ones were beckoning him through. All he'd had to do was step forward and be received into glory.

The voice had called him back. It had reminded him that he had earthly obligations yet to fulfill. But why, of all people, had it been Clementine who called?

He had no answer for this, but there was one thing of which he was certain. Ever since, through everything that followed – his painful reentry into the world, the extraction of the bullet, the jolting wagon ride through the streets of Toronto – he'd felt a sense of tranquility that he had never before experienced. He might not be perfectly at one with the Lord, but he was in the shadow of His grace, and when the time came the Lord would welcome him home - not because he had achieved a state in which it was impossible to sin - but because he had done his best to be a better man. Apparently that was enough.

Martha tossed and turned while she fretted about what had happened to her grandfather and whether or not she could have done anything to prevent it. The only reason they were in Toronto at all was because of her. Would they have been safer if they'd stayed in Wellington? But Thaddeus had been attacked there, as well, just not to so grave an extent, so she couldn't convince herself that it would have made any difference. She felt guilty even so.

And what had happened with Clementine?

You'd like her to have stayed, wouldn't you? So would I. But I don't know if it's possible.

Martha had assumed that if and when Clementine turned up again, she and Thaddeus would more or less take up where they'd left off, but apparently that wasn't to be.

She's on the run again.

What had she done that she couldn't stay for more than a few hours? Why come so far for such a fleeting visit? It must have been to see Thaddeus again, but to what purpose?

Of more concern is his heart, Luke said. *It took some damage today.*

She knew that Luke was speaking of his father's physical condition, but she suspected that the statement could equally well apply to his emotional state. Martha could only wish that wherever she had run, Clementine might somehow, some day, run back to Thaddeus.

Mrs. Dunphy couldn't fall asleep either, but it was because she'd napped all afternoon. The floor creaked as she got out of bed, something she did often in the middle of the night when she'd dozed off during the day. It was a self-perpetuating cycle. She'd have to nap the next day too because she would be tired from being up in the night.

When Martha heard the housekeeper stirring, she decided that she might just as well get up. She'd keep Mrs. Dunphy company for a while, get something warm to drink, and maybe by the time she'd drunk it, she'd be able to sleep. She wrapped a shawl around herself and slipped into the hall.

She and Mrs. Dunphy met at the top of the stairs and together they tiptoed down them.

When they reached the kitchen, Martha stoked the stove as quietly as she could. She turned to the housekeeper and mimed drinking a cup of tea. Mrs. Dunphy nodded and sat down at the table. Martha had just turned back to slide the kettle onto the hot burner when she heard a clatter of noise from the back room.

Chapter 15

Martha froze, and listened closely, but she heard nothing more. She grabbed the iron poker from beside the stove and approached the door, treading as softly as she could, and pressed her ear against it. Nothing. She glanced at Mrs. Dunphy, who had risen from her chair and followed her with, of all things, a broom.

"Should I get Luke?" she whispered.

"Let's see who's there first," Martha whispered back. "It might just be Dr. Christie. Or a mouse or something."

But before she could open the door Morgan Spicer appeared in the kitchen.

"Someone lit a lamp in the back room a few moments ago," he said. "No one's entered the house from the rear, so I'm assuming it's someone from the household, but I thought I'd better check."

"We heard a noise," Martha answered. "I expect it's Dr. Christie. He probably couldn't sleep any better than we could."

"Let's have a look," Spicer said. He jerked the door open. In the corner by the workbench, shadowy in the glow of the shaded lamp, stood Esther Simms. At her feet lay a pile of crumpled paper.

Mrs. Dunphy screamed. "Murder! Murder!" she called. "Help!"

Morgan stepped into the room. "What are you doing here?" he said to Simms.

"Stand back!" she hissed. She grabbed up a small pistol that had been lying on the bench beside her.

Martha held the poker high and stepped in behind Morgan.

"You can't shoot us all," Morgan said. "Give me the gun."

"I don't intend to shoot all of you. Just the Lewises," Simms said. "I'll burn the rest of you."

She'd crumpled up Dr. Christie's drawings and thrown them on the floor. Dr. Christie's beautiful, elegant drawings of animal skeletons. And she was going to use them to set the house on fire.

"How dare you!" Mrs. Dunphy shouted and raised her broom. Simms grabbed the lamp with her free hand, poised to smash it into the pile of paper at her feet.

And then, suddenly, Luke was there. He grabbed the poker out of Martha's hand and pushed past Morgan.

"This won't solve anything, Miss Simms," Luke said. "It is Miss Simms, isn't it?" He took a small step closer.

"Get Lewis!" she hissed. Then she coughed, and Martha could hear her wheeze from across the room.

"He can't come. He's too ill."

"Get him anyway!" She coughed again.

"You sound sick yourself," Luke said in a soft voice. "Why don't you put the gun down and I can help you get better?"

In answer, she trained the gun on Morgan and reached into her pocket to pull out a second pistol. She pointed it directly at Luke. "Maybe I should start with you. Or the girl. And then I'll tell Lewis what I've done before I shoot him too."

"You only have two shots," Morgan said. "If you use them both now, you won't be able to reload fast enough to shoot anyone else. You're outnumbered."

Luke took another step forward.

"Put the poker down!" she screamed. Luke slowly lowered the poker to the floor, but he took another step toward her as he did it. At the same time, Martha saw Spicer slide forward to Luke's right.

The lamp cast strange shadows around the room as it flickered through the bones of the animals that Christie had hung from the ceiling. It was difficult to see the woman clearly, and all the more difficult to judge her movements. But, Martha reasoned, it was just as difficult for her to see them. She slid further into the shadow beside Luke as he held his hands out in a conciliatory gesture. "Let's everyone stay calm," he said. "There's no need for anyone to get hurt."

"There is every reason. I want to make Lewis suffer."

"Then do your worst," came a voice from the kitchen doorway.

It was Thaddeus, swaying slightly, sweaty and pale from effort. He reached out with his good arm and steadied himself against the jamb.

Esther Simms howled with triumph and pointed both guns at him.

"You'll never hit me from there," Thaddeus said. "You'll have to come closer."

Wary, the woman moved a few inches forward.

"Did you figure out yet that you have to remove the percussion cap?" Thaddeus said. "That's why you couldn't fire a second time."

Simms didn't answer, but took another step forward. She was now directly underneath the eagle, the great magnificent eagle whose outspread wings spanned half the room, and which sagged on one side because the hook was pulling free of the plaster ceiling.

Simms held both guns at arm's length, pointing them directly at Thaddeus.

"You're still not close enough," he said. "Those pistols don't have much range, you know. You'll miss me if you fire now."

Luke took another half-step toward her. She swung one of the guns around to point it at him.

"I won't miss him."

Spicer tried to shift a little closer. She swung the other gun around. "Or him."

Martha slowly reached down to grab the poker, hoping the shadow was enough to mask the movement.

"Leave them alone. It's me you want," Thaddeus said.

"Then you'll have to come over here."

Thaddeus let go his hold on the doorjamb and took an unsteady step forward.

"Closer," Simms said. "I want to look into your eyes as you die."

Thaddeus took another step, swaying as he struggled to remain upright.

"Closer."

He stood looking at her for a moment, then suddenly lurched to his right and crashed to the floor.

Simms trained both guns on him, but before she could fire, Martha raised the poker high and swung it as hard as she could into the eagle that loomed overhead. The hook pulled free and the bones came crashing down.

One of the guns went off as Simms threw up her hands to protect her head from the falling bones. There was a bang and a flash and a pistol went clattering across the floor. Simms screamed and staggered backwards and both Luke and Spicer leapt at her, but she dodged them and crashed into the bench. A shot from the second pistol flew harmlessly off into the ceiling.

Luke wrested the gun out of her hand, then Spicer pulled both of her arms behind her. Even in the poor light Martha could see that the lower part of Esther Simms' face was scorched and blackened, one side of her mouth raw, a piece of her nostril blasted away, bits of metal embedded in her cheek. Tears and pus streamed down her face, leaving tracks in the residue of black powder.

Spicer tore off his cravat and used it to bind her hands.

"Get some cold cloths," Luke directed Mrs. Dunphy. Then he went to his father, still lying where he had fallen.

"I'm all right," Thaddeus said, to Martha's great relief. "But I think I'd like to lie here for a little while longer."

Luke checked his pulse. "Any chest pain?"

"No. But I jarred my neck when I landed."

Luke peeled the bandages back, seemed satisfied with what he saw, and rewrapped them.

Luke looked up at Martha. "Stay with him, while I see to the woman."

She knelt beside Thaddeus, folded her shawl into a pillow and tucked it under his head. He smiled at her weakly.

"My eagle!" It was Christie, standing in the doorway, his hair tousled, his face aghast. The only member of the household who had been able to fall sound asleep that night had finally been roused by the commotion in the studio. He looked around the room, open-mouthed with dismay. "What are you doing on the floor, Lewis?"

"Having a rest," Thaddeus replied.

"My drawings!" Christie rushed over to the pile of crumpled papers, and picked up the topmost. "Oh dear!"

"Stop moaning about your drawings and make yourself useful." Mrs. Dunphy had returned with a basin of cloths in cold water. She set it down beside Luke. Only then did Christie seem to notice Luke and Spicer and the whimpering woman they held down.

"Oh," Christie said. "My goodness. What happened here?"

"The gun exploded when she tried to fire it," Luke said. "It's scorched half her face."

"And her hand," Spicer added.

Christie lowered himself to the ground, prepared to help Luke, but Simms was having none of it. She spewed a stream of garbled, foul-mouthed invective and writhed and twisted in an attempt to avoid Luke's touch.

He finally threw up his hands in defeat. "I can't help her if she won't let me." He turned to Christie. "Can you keep an eye on Pa while I fetch the constable? He'll come faster if I go."

"That was a very dangerous thing you did," Martha said to Thaddeus while they waited for Luke to return.

"No, not really. Those small pistols aren't very reliable."

"She got you the first time," Martha pointed out.

"It was point blank range. She was lucky."

The sleepy constable took one look at the shambles in the studio, and quickly replaced Spicer's cravat with a stout set of handcuffs. Simms cursed and continued to scream threats against Thaddeus, Luke, Martha and the constable himself.

"A word, sir?" he said to Dr. Christie and while they were huddled in conversation Martha overheard the words "quite mad" and "Provincial Lunatic Asylum". Christie nodded and the constable walked over to where Thaddeus had, with Morgan's help, heaved himself up into a sitting position.

"It's like this, sir," the constable said. "I'll take her to the gaol for tonight, and if you want to lodge a complaint, I can keep her there until she comes up in front of a magistrate. Dr. Christie has suggested that the asylum might be a better choice, but it's up to you what happens."

"It's clear to me that she's insane," Thaddeus said. "It would serve no purpose to put her in gaol. Perhaps the doctors at the asylum can help her."

"In that case, we can run her over there tomorrow and get the doctors at the madhouse...er...the asylum to sign all the papers. And don't you worry, she'll be kept locked away tight. You don't have to worry anymore."

"Take her first thing in the morning, if you can" Luke said. "She also needs physical treatment, and not only for the burns. She's got conjunctivitis and incipient pneumonia as complications of a case of measles."

Simms offered little resistance as Spicer and the constable hauled her to her feet, but she took one last parting shot at Thaddeus. Just as she went past him she turned her head and attempted to spit at him, but she was hampered by her mangled mouth and the drool spilled harmlessly down the front of her dress.

The kettle was boiling furiously away on the stove, so Martha went ahead and made tea while Luke and Dr. Christie helped Thaddeus back to the parlour. Mrs. Dunphy would want a cup. They all would. She guessed that it might be some time before anyone would want to go back to bed, if they went at all.

Luke came in as the tea was steeping. "I'll take a cup when it's ready," he said. "And one for Pa."

"How is he?"

"His wound opened up a little when he fell, but I don't think he did any lasting damage. More than anything he just needs to rest. And I think he'll be able to now that he's not so worried."

"What will happen to her? The Simms woman?"

"She'll be kept at the asylum for a good long time. Maybe for the rest of her life.

"Oh." For some reason this made Martha feel sad.

"I wouldn't waste any tears on her," Luke said. "Isaac Simms broke our family once. His sister tried to break it again. It's hard to feel sorry for either of them."

But Martha did anyway.

To her surprise, she began to feel sleepy before she'd even finished her tea, and when Mrs. Dunphy and Dr. Christie finally announced that they were off to bed, she went upstairs and got her pillow and quilt. She tiptoed into the parlour where both Luke and Thaddeus had fallen into a doze, their even breathing interrupted now and then by a soft snore, Thaddeus in the leather armchair, Luke sprawled across the sofa. She wrapped herself in the quilt, curled herself up on the floor by her grandfather's feet and there she stayed in a dreamless sleep until morning.

Luke was surprised when Martha appeared at the breakfast table dressed for school.

"I was sure you'd take the day off," he said.

"I have things I need to do today. And if I stay here I'll just fuss over grandpa when what he needs to do is rest."

"I think that's wise. He's still asleep and I'll be happy if he sleeps all day."

"Will he really be all right?"

"It will be a few days before I can answer honestly," Luke said. "The wound needs to heal."

"And his heart?"

"Once damaged, there's no fixing it. He needs to slow down."

"But he didn't suffer another attack last night? When he collapsed?"

"As far as I can tell, no, he didn't. I don't know why. It was about as stressful a situation as anyone could be in, and yet he seems to have come through it relatively unscathed. Sometimes that happens, especially when the patient is tough as nails to begin with. It's like they're too stubborn to give in. And if you're determined to go to school, at least let me drive you there. I need the sleigh this morning anyway."

He looked in on Thaddeus again before they left. He was still sound asleep, his breathing deep and even, and his face had lost the pasty pallor of the night before. Best to leave him alone and let him sleep the day away.

"What about you?" Luke asked as he turned the sleigh down Yonge Street. "How are you doing?"

The question seemed to surprise her. "Me? Oh, I'm fine. Just tired."

"You showed some quick thinking last night. What's the phrase my father uses? 'You're a good man to have in a tight spot.'"

She laughed. "I didn't do much of anything. Dr. Christie told me the eagle bones were in danger of falling. I could see that you and Mr. Spicer were getting ready to make a move, so I just helped them along a bit."

They trotted along in silence for a few minutes. Luke cast a sidelong look at his niece. Her face was troubled.

"If you don't want to tell me, that's fine," he said, "but I know there's something bothering you."

"I don't see how you can keep the news from the rest of the family," Martha said. "About Thaddeus being shot I mean."

Luke had to agree. "I think they have a right to know."

"I don't know how Francis is going to react, that's all."

This hadn't occurred to Luke, but now that Martha said it, he could see why she would be concerned. Francis was sure to be angry if he thought that Thaddeus had put Martha in danger again. He would be more than likely to demand that she leave school and return home.

"What happened last night is sure to be all over Yorkville by this evening," he said. "And sooner or later the newspapers will pick it up too, although I don't know how big a story it will be. There's no trial for them to report on, so it should die quickly. I have an obligation to let Will and Moses know before they hear it somewhere else, but I don't see why your name needs to brought into any of it. And I don't communicate with Francis all that often anyway, so it won't seem odd if I don't write to him."

"Thank you."

"You will, however, have to explain to Dr. Christie why you wrecked his eagle. I won't do that for you."

She turned to him, wide-eyed, then realized that he was teasing. "I'll help him put it back together again. Maybe he'll forgive me then."

"There's one thing I can't figure out though," Luke went on. "How did the Simms woman get into the house? I was at the front and Spicer was watching the back door."

"That may be my fault." She hesitated for a moment and Luke could see that she was debating what to tell him. "When I got home from school yesterday, the back door was unlocked," she said finally, "and Mrs. Dunphy was still asleep upstairs. Everyone else was gone. And then there was all the confusion with Thaddeus and I didn't think to lock it until later. She must have slipped in when we were all busy and hid in the back room until she figured we were all asleep."

"And then she was going to set the place on fire and pick us off as we tried to get out of the house." He sighed. "I'm going to have to find some more help for Mrs. Dunphy. It's getting to be too much for her. She spends most afternoons napping. Most of the time it doesn't matter so I've been ignoring it."

"I'm sure Sally Spicer would be happy to have more work," Martha said. "And the girls are old enough to help too."

"Sally is already doing the laundry and the heavy cleaning and she's got her own family to look after. What it really requires is someone to live in – to do the meals and so forth."

He happened to glance over at Martha and caught the expression on her face. He began to laugh.

"Don't worry, that wasn't a suggestion that it should be you. What would be the point of you running away from Wellington, just to end up in the same boat in Toronto? Besides, it's not something that has to happen immediately, but I will have to do something before too long."

Martha managed to look both relieved and worried. "But what will happen to Mrs. Dunphy? If you find another housekeeper?"

"She'll pretend she's still in charge, I expect."

"No, I mean – she'd still live with you wouldn't she?"

"Of course she would. It's her house."

"Really?"

"She and Christie are cousins, so he was always prepared to look after her, but when she came to live with him he put the house in her name, so she'd still have a home if something happened to him. We're all of us there on her sufferance."

He didn't add that he had been apprised of this information during a very frank discussion with the old doctor, who, aware of his own looming mortality, outlined the arrangements he had made. The house was Mrs. Dunphy's, but the practice would go to Luke, on the proviso that he continue to provide for the aging housekeeper. The stipulation was unnecessary. Luke would have looked after her regardless.

"Dr. Christie is an awfully nice man, isn't he? Martha said. "In spite of the fact that he's so rude."

"He is," Luke agreed.

"Rude? Or nice?"

"Both."

And once again they were laughing as Luke handed her down in front of the school, much to the annoyance of the cluster of girls who waited at the side door.

"Get your coat and let's walk in the garden for a bit," Martha said to Bernice after they'd eaten the dinner she'd brought for them both. "I need to tell you what's been going on."

The sun glinting off the snow and the lack of wind made the garden a pleasant place to be in the middle of a February day. There were a handful of other people taking advantage of the fine weather, and Martha expected Mr. Sorbie to go jogging by, but she didn't see him anywhere.

As they walked along the path that had been cleared through the orchard, Martha told Bernice everything that had happened.

"I wouldn't like any of this to get around the school," she said, "but you deserve to hear it. We wouldn't have known who to look out for if you hadn't discovered who was spreading gossip about me."

Tears began to run down Bernice's face as Martha finished her story.

"Why are you crying?" Martha asked.

"Because you had all that to cope with and I was just being stupid and selfish and sorry for myself. You're the one friend I've made here and I didn't help you at all."

"Yes you did. That's what I'm saying. You were brave and wonderful and I'll always be grateful."

"Really?"

"Yes, really," Martha said. "Now, blow your nose because it's time to go back to class."

It didn't take long for the news to spread that a madwoman had broken into Dr. Christie's house and gunned down Dr. Lewis's father. It was impossible to keep a secret in a village as small as Yorkville, and the story made its way to the school by that afternoon, brought, Martha suspected, by Alice Gleeson. It would have been exciting enough gossip all on its own, but the fact that it involved the subject of so much previous gossip guaranteed its repetition.

Miss Clark stopped Martha in the hall as she was on her way to her geography class.

"I heard the news. Would you like to go home early today?" she asked.

"I almost didn't come at all, to be honest, but I thought it best to keep myself busy. More than anything my grandfather needs some peace and quiet right now. There are two doctors in the household to look after him, so it's not like I could do anything useful. Someone will come for me should he take a sudden turn for the worse." She softened her next words with a smile. "Should that happen, though, I'm afraid I won't take time to inform you directly. And I may even leave by the front door."

Miss Clark smiled back. "If you need anything – anything at all – you let me know, all right?"

The headmaster waylaid her as she was leaving the class.

"A word with you Miss Renwell?"

"Yes sir, I know. Unusual circumstances," she replied.

"Quite. We shall all be at a loss for anything to talk about once you graduate."

"It's a long story, sir, but I believe this is the end of it."

"Good. And I wonder if you might pass a message on to your grandfather? Tell him I'm expecting him for tea as soon as he recovers. No excuses, now."

She smiled. "I'll tell him. With any luck he'll be along soon."

Robertson nodded and went on his way.

She finally spotted Mr. Sorbie as she was on her way to the Model School. He was coatless, about to go outside to run through the frozen school grounds.

When she called his name, he stopped and waited for her to catch up.

"Miss Renwell," he said. "I'm so sorry to hear that you've had more trouble."

"The trouble is mostly over and done with, thank you. I don't know how much of the story you've heard, but you should know that the woman who shot my grandfather is the same woman we saw yesterday."

He frowned. "I had a feeling that she was up to no good."

"This doesn't seem to be general knowledge, and I'd like to keep it that way, but she meant to harm me too. You may well have saved my life when you walked with me to the bus stop yesterday. I just want to say thank you."

"You're welcome, but really, I would have done that for any student. I'm glad I just happened to be there at the right time."

"So am I. I'm almost beginning to see the point of running around outside in all weathers. You never know when it's going to be the right time."

Fortunately, he realized she was teasing him.

"Well," he said, "I guess I should carry on then. There may be someone else out there who needs my help."

He grinned at her and jogged out the door.

Thaddeus was awake and grumpy when Luke returned to the house.

"How are you feeling?" Luke asked.

"I've been shot, stabbed, hit on the head, nearly run over and almost poisoned," Thaddeus said. "How do you think I'm feeling?"

"You forgot the heart attack."

"I didn't forget. I just don't want to think about it."

"You didn't help yourself any by throwing yourself on the floor last night."

"I helped you," Thaddeus pointed out.

"Spicer and I had it in hand," Luke protested. "We were going to make our move at any moment."

"You'd have been in trouble if it hadn't been for me and Martha."

"Martha was very helpful. All you did was fall down."

"At least you didn't end up covered in blood this time."

"I didn't," Luke conceded. "And I'm grateful for it."

"Do you think the doctors at the asylum will be able to do anything?"

"For the Simms woman?" Luke said. "I don't know. I'm no expert on disorders of the nervous system, but I expect she'll be there for a very long time, provided, of course, she survives her injuries and her measles."

"Is that why she disappeared for a while? Because she was sick? I've been trying to piece things together."

Luke took a moment to consider this. "I expect so. The timing is right if she caught the disease from the youngest Gleeson boy. She'd have run a high fever for a few days, but would have started feeling better as soon as the rash broke out. But by then her eyes were probably affected. She may have thought she was going blind and decided to complete her mission even if it meant getting caught."

"Will she be disfigured? From the gun exploding in her face?"

"I expect so, yes. There was quite a loss of tissue and that doesn't grow back."

Thaddeus sighed. "She was a pretty girl once."

"Yes. She looked a bit like Sarah, didn't she?"

"And like Martha. And like your mother." Thaddeus seemed to be lost in the memory and Luke was about to leave him to it when he spoke again.

"I have one more tricky thing to get through and then I'll follow your advice to do nothing for a while."

"What tricky thing? This is over now, isn't it?"

"Not quite. And unless I'm very much mistaken it will happen sometime in the next couple of days."

Chapter 16

With a little help, Thaddeus made it up the stairs to his own bed that night, and in spite of the fact that he had slept for most of the day, he almost immediately fell into a deep sleep.

The next morning he managed to dress himself and make his way down to the breakfast table, but Luke shooed him into the parlour where he could sit with his feet up.

"I'll bring your breakfast to you," he said. "I'll even cut it up for you."

He reappeared a few moments later.

"Mrs. Dunphy says the twins are here and they have something important to tell you. Are you up to a visit?"

"Let them through," Thaddeus said. "If they're here, it's because they think there's something I should know."

They crowded through the door and shifted from foot to foot, ready to bolt as soon as they had imparted their information.

"There's more strangers in town," Mark reported breathlessly.

"Two of 'em," Matthew said. "Mark and me seen 'em down at the Red Lion last night."

"Saw them," Thaddeus corrected.

"Saw 'em," Matthew echoed. "They was askin' questions about you. They wanted to know if there'd been any strange ladies come to visit you."

"And what were they told?" he asked.

"That you was…were… shot down by a madwoman. That's all anybody's talkin' about."

"I want you to think about this very carefully," Thaddeus said. "Did they ask about two strange ladies, or only one?"

"Just the one," said Matthew.

"Did they mention any names?"

Mark and Matthew shook their heads in unison. "They just said "a lady".

"And where are the strangers now?"

"Eatin' their breakfast at the Red Lion," Mark said. "We skedaddled over here as soon as we knew they was…were…busy."

"And here's another question for you. What were you doing at the tavern so early in the morning?"

"Sometimes we get their horses for them," Matthew said. "We always get good pay."

"And we deliver beer sometimes too," Mark added.

Thaddeus could scarcely have chosen better spies. Everyone knew the twins – they were so extraordinary they had become a source of village pride, but at the same time they were so much a part of the scenery that no one ever seemed to question why they were in any given place at any given time.

"Thank you for coming to tell me this," he said. "And now, you'd better hurry or you're going to be late for school. Luke, do you have any spare pennies to see these fine children on their way?" Luke fished in his pocket and drew out a handful of coins.

"Be sure to share it amongst you all," Thaddeus cautioned.

"Yes, sir!" they chorused and then they tumbled out of the parlour again.

"What are you up to?" Luke asked when they'd gone.

"I'm not sure myself," Thaddeus said. "Maybe nothing. We'll have to wait and see."

But they didn't have long to wait. Martha had just left for school when there was a knock at the front door. Luke answered.

"We'd like to speak with a Mr. Thaddeus Lewis," a male voice said. Thaddeus could hear them clearly from his chair in the parlour.

"Mr. Lewis is indisposed," Luke replied. "I'm afraid he can speak with no one."

"It's important," the man said. "We've travelled a long way to see him. We're looking for a fugitive from justice."

"You'll have to look somewhere else," Luke said. "Mr. Lewis is not well."

Thaddeus wondered if it would seem suspicious to delay the encounter. It might. Better to send them in the wrong direction as soon as possible.

"It's all right," Thaddeus called, "as long as they don't stay long." Luke looked into the doorway. "Are you sure? You don't have to talk to them at all, you know."

"I like to be helpful where I can. But I'd like you to stay in the room, if you don't mind."

Luke looked at him for a long moment, then nodded.

"He says he feels well enough this morning to entertain a little company," Thaddeus heard Luke say. "But you can have only a few minutes with him. As soon as he begins to tire, you'll have to leave."

Thaddeus hoped he was up to this conversation, and wasn't so muzzy-headed from laudanum that he would make a mistake. But if it looked as though he'd gone astray, he could always call on Luke to put a stop to it on medical grounds.

Luke ushered two hard-faced men into the little parlour. They seemed taken aback when they saw Thaddeus propped up with pillows, pale and unshaven, his arm in a sling. They must have thought that Luke was just trying to put them off, in spite of what they had heard about Thaddeus being shot.

"We're detectives working on behalf of the Bellingham family of Philadelphia and Mr. Augustus Van Sylen of New York City," one of the men said by way of introduction.

So Clementine had assessed the situation correctly. Two "somebodies" had joined forces to come after her.

"I'm sorry, I didn't catch your name," Thaddeus said.

"My name is Smith and this is Mr. Brown," the man said. Thaddeus had no reason to believe that these were real names.

"And what do Mr. Smith and Mr. Brown want with me?"

"We're looking for information on a woman. A swindler who has bilked our clients out of a great deal of money. We have reason to believe that she may have tried to contact you."

"Why would she contact me?" Thaddeus asked. "I'm a clergyman. As you can well imagine, I have no fortune to be swindled out of."

"We know for a fact that you've had dealings with her in the past."

"You'll have to be a little more specific. I've had dealings with thousands of people over the years. Would she, by any chance, have been a member of my congregation?"

Mr. Brown snorted. "Not likely. She's known by a number of different names, but most recently she posed as an Englishwoman called Lady Flora Hargrave."

Thaddeus shook his head and then winced from the movement. "I'm sorry. That name means nothing to me. Perhaps you could furnish a description?"

In answer, Brown drew out a small carved wooden box that was similar to the one Thaddeus carried in his pocket. He opened it to reveal that it held an identical daguerreotype portrait of Clementine. Thaddeus hadn't known there was a copy. They must have got it from the daguerreotypist in London.

The detectives were watching Thaddeus closely to see what his reaction would be. "Oh," he said, "that's Clementine Elliott. Yes, I met Mrs. Elliott in Wellington a few years ago. And yes, you're right, she was a fraud."

He could scarcely deny any knowledge of her. After all, he had written to Van Sylen at the time, asking for information, and the Elliott case had subsequently been reported in all the newspapers.

"And you met up with her again in London," Brown said.

Thaddeus hesitated, but only for a moment. Clementine hadn't been mentioned in any of the newspaper accounts of Martha's kidnapping, but she had been the talk of the town. Even his son Will had heard all about her and he suspected that these men had too. He might just as well own to it right away.

"Well, yes, as a matter of fact. I was in London – and that's London in Canada West, by the way, not London, England, although the Canadian London has gone to extraordinary effort to pattern itself after its namesake. Have you ever been there?"

"Yes," Smith said shortly.

"She just turned up out of the blue one day," Thaddeus went on. "And then she did her best to interfere in my business. It was most annoying."

"Nonetheless, according to our information, you seem to have spent a lot of time with her."

"As I said, she did her best to interfere."

"It didn't occur to you to report a known criminal to the authorities?"

"No. I knew of no particular charge against her. No one would have paid any attention to me."

That seemed to flummox them, and Thaddeus relaxed a little. So far, so good.

"Do you know where she went from there?" Smith asked.

"Yes I do." Luke shot him a glance as if to ask what on earth he thought he was up to. Thaddeus ignored him. He had this in hand.

"Mrs. Elliott was involved in the terrible railway accident at Baptiste Creek. I'm sure you must have read about it, as it was reported widely. Dreadful number of fatalities."

Both Brown and Smith nodded.

"I'm fairly certain that her immortal soul would never be admitted to heaven, given some of the things she's done, so there is no doubt in my mind that you should look for her in the other place."

Smith frowned and Brown blinked a little, neither of them sure whether or not they were being mocked. Thaddeus hoped that neither of them would notice the look of amusement on Luke's face.

"I'm afraid you're mistaken," Smith said. "She's very much alive. She turned up again in New York City. Mr. Van Sylen – as I mentioned, he's one of our employers in this case – happened to see her in the street. That's why he reactivated the investigation. And then, of course, we discovered that the Bellinghams were looking for her too."

I made a mistake, Thaddeus. At least in New York City I still had some contacts.

Poor Clementine. A city the size of New York, and she had to cross paths with the one person she didn't want to see.

"Are you sure?" he said. "I was quite definitely told that she didn't survive."

"Fortunately," Brown went on, "we're familiar with the various aliases she uses. She's been leading us a merry chase, but eventually we tracked her here, to Toronto. Since she sought you out in London, it stands to reason that she might try to make contact here as well."

"May I ask what Mrs. Elliott has done to warrant such extraordinary efforts on your part? I know that she was practiced in small deceptions, but I wouldn't have classified her as anything but a petty criminal."

"You already know that she led Van Sylen to believe that his son was dead and duped him out of a pile of money," Brown said. "Subsequent to that she contracted a fraudulent marriage with a Mr. Frederick Bellingham. After he died, she disappeared with a number of items that quite rightfully belong to the Bellingham heirs."

"In what way was the marriage fraudulent?" Thaddeus asked. "Professional curiosity, you understand, having officiated at a number of weddings in my time." He allowed himself a wan smile.

"It wasn't so much that the marriage itself was illegal," Mr. Brown said. "It was the fact that she used a false name. That negated any claim she had against the estate. Even if she'd been mentioned in the will – which she wasn't – any inheritance would have been declared invalid under the laws of Pennsylvania. She must have known that would be the case, so she helped herself and ran."

Some people don't like what I did, but if it will set your pesky conscience to rest, I was perfectly justified in doing it.

She'd told him in London that she'd married again. And been widowed. This Bellingham must have double-crossed her and then the heirs had circled like vultures. She'd been left with nothing, and in her usual Clementine way, had taken steps to ensure her own survival. Any qualms Thaddeus had about what he was doing vanished. These people didn't deserve any help in tracking her down.

"Be that as it may, the information I was given is that

Clementine Elliott died in the train crash."

"They're saying down at the tavern that a woman shot you two days ago."

"Yes, that's correct."

"I don't understand why she would shoot you," Brown said. "By all accounts, the two of you were pretty friendly in London."

"It wasn't Mrs. Elliott who shot me. It was a woman by the name of Esther Simms."

Smith and Brown exchanged a glance. Thaddeus could see they didn't believe him. That suited his purposes just fine.

"Why did this Esther Simms shoot you?" Smith asked.

"She had an old score to settle. Or at least that's what she said."

"For a preacher you sure seem to have a lot of trouble with women. First Mrs. Elliott interferes with your affairs, then this other woman shows up and tries to gun you down."

"Yes, I know," Thaddeus said with a mournful sigh. "I've had nothing but trouble since my poor wife died."

"What happened to this woman after she shot you?" Brown asked.

It was Luke who answered. "She's been admitted to the Provincial Lunatic Asylum. I don't expect she will ever be released as she's quite mad."

"Where exactly is this asylum?"

"On Queen Street," Luke replied. "In the city."

Thaddeus knew that they would check. That they would travel down to Queen Street and ask to see her. He was also fairly certain that they would be unable to make an identification. Esther Simms' face would be swathed in bandages, and even after they came off, might well be altered forever. It didn't matter. Whatever the detectives concluded, they would have wasted at least a day in their pursuit of Clementine. With any luck an extra day was enough to let her get away cleanly.

But in the meantime, the detectives hadn't asked quite all of their questions.

"Do you know a Chauncey Hargrave?" Brown said suddenly.

"No," Thaddeus answered quite truthfully.

"He's apparently Mrs. Elliott's son."

"Yes, she did have a son, although I never knew him by that name."

"What name did you know him by?"

"Why, Elliott, of course." At least he had in Wellington.

"Do you know where he is?"

"No, I have no idea what's happened to him."

Brown leaned in close to Thaddeus. "There's a substantial reward, you know. If you can deliver up any information that leads us to the stolen property, you could set yourself up real nice for your old age."

Thaddeus didn't bother dignifying this with a response. He leaned his head back against the chair and closed his eyes.

Luke picked up on the signal. "I'm afraid you'll have to go now," he said. "My father tires very easily. You've worn him out."

The detectives rose to leave, but Smith turned back to Thaddeus as he reached the doorway. "If you hear from Mrs. Elliott, you'll let us know, right?"

Thaddeus opened his eyes again. "The information I was given is that Mrs. Elliott died in the train accident. And although I personally have every expectation of one day being received in heaven, in all honesty I really don't expect to see her there, nor could I report it to you if I did."

As Luke saw the detectives out the door, Thaddeus replayed the conversation in his mind, and decided that he had done everything he could. He'd hoped that the detectives were working from a general description and that he could persuade them that Clementine and Esther Simms were the same person, but the existence of the duplicate daguerreotype had complicated this strategy. They might believe it yet, depending on what they found at the asylum, but Thaddeus somehow doubted it. Clementine should never have had her picture taken in the first place. She'd done it for him, to help him solve his case.

He wondered what, exactly, she'd made off with. It must have been something spectacular to merit such a chase. She'd had to take it to New York to sell it. And it had been worth enough that she could afford to leave Joe a pile. No wonder she had run so hard. No wonder they were chasing her so far.

Clementine had told him the truth the last time they met. About everything. And she had risked everything to tell it to him. He was humbled by what she had done.

He watched the detectives go past the front window, and it was only then that he noticed the brown paper package on the table. Another bundle of money left for Joe, part of the proceeds from whatever Clementine had taken. It had been sitting there this whole time and no one had seen it. Thaddeus was glad he hadn't been aware of it during his conversation with the detectives. He might have given the game away by looking at it.

Luke came back into the room, a bemused expression on his face.

"How'd I do?" Thaddeus asked.

"It was masterful," Luke said. "For a preacher you're awfully adept at prevarication."

"I know. I sail awfully close to the wind sometimes. I guess I'll have to pray for forgiveness, won't I?" He sighed. "But later. Right now I think I'll take another nap."

Chapter 17
Toronto, Spring 1855

Thaddeus napped a great deal over the ensuing weeks, but as time passed he slowly regained his strength, helped along by Martha's fussing, Mrs. Dunphy's provision of tasty delicacies and the occasional dose of laudanum supplied by Luke.

Dr. Christie spent hours in the back room attempting to recreate the drawings that had been damaged and on the infrequent occasions that he emerged, he roundly berated Thaddeus for monopolizing the most comfortable seat in the parlour.

As Luke predicted, the newspapers picked up the story of the shooting, but as the woman had been apprehended and there were no further thrilling developments to relate, they soon turned their attention back to the shenanigans of Canadian politicians and news of growing tensions in the United States.

Martha reported that Alice Gleeson had a fit of hysterics when she learned that she had been sharing a house with a murderous madwoman, but the incident was a nine day wonder at the Normal School, soon eclipsed by the extraordinary news that Clara Parker and a male student had been expelled after they were caught passing love notes in the hallway.

Letters from both Will and Moses were quick to arrive.

Moses politely expressed the hope that Thaddeus would soon recover from his injuries, then went on at length about which fields he was putting in wheat next year, and which he was leaving fallow.

Will adhered to his usual breezy style of correspondence.

Dear Pa,

Honestly, if I could get into the papers as often as you do, I would have no difficulty getting elected for high public office based on recognition of my name alone. I would ask you to tell me how you do it, but as you seem unwilling to tell me anything at all about your personal affairs, I'll refrain from pestering you. Had Luke not written, I would have had no idea that you are with him in Toronto, never mind that you were gunned down in the street.

Suffice it to say that I hope you experience no permanent effects from your misadventure. Nabby joins me in wishing you a speedy recovery, and your grandchildren are eager to hear the grisly details.

Please start taking better care of yourself.

With much love,
Will

To Thaddeus's relief, there was no communication at all from Francis.

When he felt well enough to sit at the dining room table again, he returned to the task of writing his autobiography. He decided that the best way to move the project forward was to skip over his war experiences and the early years with Betsy, which were bittersweet sources of reminiscence. Instead, he concentrated on the extensive notes he'd kept from his years as an itinerant minister. As the winter wore slowly away to reveal the first stirrings of spring, he realized – with a certain amount of wonder – that he had crafted much of the middle section of his book, each chapter built around the church's yearly conference. He found familiar names in the lists of preachers ordained and those accepted on trial, old friends among the records of his meetings. Too many of them were gone now, and he learned that one of these was Caleb Webster, to whom he had written to ask for news of the Simms family. His son returned the letter, with a brief note stating that Caleb had passed away two days before it arrived.

April had already turned to May when they discovered why there had been no blistering note from Martha's father demanding her return. Francis had been far too preoccupied to read the newspapers. After so many disappointments, Sophie was delivered of a healthy baby boy, he wrote, "with as lusty a pair of lungs as I've ever heard." Charles Francis Renwell was keeping them all awake at night and, Francis claimed, "I have never been so happy to be sleepless."

"You aren't the youngest anymore," Luke teased when Martha shared the news. "You won't get away with anything now. You'll have to settle down and be the responsible older sister. Of course then you get to boss everybody around."

"Is that what my mother did to you?" Martha said.

"Constantly. She could be really annoying. Except when she made Will and Moses leave me alone. Then she was all right."

"Everyone danced to Sarah's tune," Thaddeus said. "Even me."

"Especially you," Luke said, but he laughed as he said it.

Martha hadn't ever considered her mother in relation to her Uncle Luke. It was an aspect of the family dynamic that was unfamiliar to her, but by all accounts, Sarah's death had cast a heavy pall of sadness over them all. How different things would have been if she had not been murdered. If she had lived happily ever after with Francis and they'd had more children. Martha would truly have been the older sister then, bossing and protecting the little ones.

Sophie's baby was a second chance for Francis, but Martha would not be part of the hustle and bustle of their busy household. She could certainly be someone that the new child turned to when he was puzzled or upset or needed advice - except that she probably wouldn't see him all that often. She wouldn't be in Wellington. Not if she was going to go off and teach somewhere. She was happy for Francis, but she wasn't sure anything much would change for her.

"As soon as the school term ends I'd like to go to Wellington for a visit," she said to Thaddeus. "I have a few weeks before the second session starts."

"I'd be happy to take you," Thaddeus said. "That is, if your father allows me anywhere near your new brother."

"It sounds to me as though they'd be happy to have us give them a hand, although I don't know much about babies. I may want to sleep for two or three days first, though. Then I'll be ready to travel."

Thaddeus also figured that the Christie household could do with their absence for a time. Dr. Christie hadn't said a word about the danger Thaddeus had put them all in, but he must have wondered whether he had been wise in inviting such chaos into his well-ordered existence. He hadn't yet called for Thaddeus to be hanged, but he must have thought it once or twice.

Luke upset their plans by finding Thaddeus a job.

"I have a twelve year old patient who was laid up with measles for a long time and missed a lot of school," he said one Saturday morning. "The father is quite well-to-do and hoping to get his son into Upper Canada College next year. The boy was no scholar to begin with, and now he's fallen badly behind in his studies. They're looking for a tutor. Are you interested?"

"Yes," Thaddeus replied, "depending on the subjects. I'm fine with the basics, but I wouldn't be much help with classical studies. I don't know any Greek or Latin."

"The father's primary concern is that the tutor be someone respectable who can make his son toe the line. The mother coddles him. Not surprising, I suppose. He was pretty sick."

"How often would they need me?"

"It would be only for a couple of hours a day to begin with, as he's not up to much more at this point. And that's probably about as much as you should be doing as well."

"I think I can manage a couple of hours."

"He's looking for someone to start next week, and he would want you through to Christmas."

"Oh," Thaddeus said. "I was going to go to Wellington with Martha."

"Martha can go by herself, can't she?" Luke said. "After all, by this time next year she may well be in charge of a whole school. Surely she can manage a trip to Wellington on her own."

"I suppose," Thaddeus said. He had been looking forward to

spending the time with her, but she would be gone only a few days and the income from the tutoring position was too important to pass up.

"Besides," Luke went on, "given your history with Francis, I think it would be a good idea for you to stand back a little. Give him his time in the limelight, so to speak."

Martha has always been yours. I was gone too long and missed my chance to be a father.

Luke was right. Best to let Francis have his whole family to himself. "I see what you mean," he said. "Yes, all right, I'd be more than happy to tutor the boy, and I can start whenever they want me."

As soon as the dining room table was cleared away from dinner, Thaddeus began drawing up a lesson plan. He had only just assembled an outline when Townsend Ashby arrived unannounced.

"Good to see you," Ashby said when Thaddeus answered the door to discover the young barrister he had been wanting to talk to for so long. "But what on earth have you been doing to yourself? You look quite the worse for wear."

"It's a long story," Thaddeus said, "but do come in. I hear you've been away."

"Yes, we took a tour through England."

Just then Martha came down the stairs, an unfortunate turn of events, as far as Thaddeus was concerned. He knew that she was likely to get snippy, and he would have preferred a private word or two with Ashby before that occurred.

"Oh, it's Mr. Ashby," she said.

"Good afternoon, Miss Renwell."

"May I congratulate you on your recent marriage."

"You may. And thank you. You must meet Jane. Perhaps you'd care to join her for tea some afternoon?"

"Why thank you very much for the invitation, Mr. Ashby. It's very kind of you, but I'm afraid I must decline, as my studies leave me with very little free time, especially in the afternoons."

"Your studies?"

"Martha is attending the Toronto Normal School. That's how we ended up here in Yorkville," Thaddeus explained.

"So you're going to be a teacher?" Ashby smiled at her, but managed to make it look patronizing.

"Yes," Martha said, a wicked gleam in her eye. "I'm afraid that young women like myself are infrequent guests at things like tea parties. We have weightier considerations to accommodate. I do wish you and your bride all the best, though. Was it one of those romantic, spur-of-the-moment affairs?"

Her shot struck home. Ashby looked embarrassed. "Umm…actually, no. We'd been engaged for quite some time. Our families are friendly, you see. It was a matter of waiting until my practice was established."

"I was surprised when I heard, that's all," Martha said. "I had no idea, as you never mentioned it. And now, if you'll excuse me, I promised Dr. Christie that I'd help him with the groundhog."

And with that inscrutable remark, she nodded her goodbye and walked away, conscious, Thaddeus was sure, of Ashby's eyes as they followed her down the hall.

"So…" he said, for lack of anything better to say. "Won't you sit down?"

"I can only stay for a few minutes," Ashby said. "There are a couple of things I need to discuss with you. I was surprised when I returned and was told that you were in Toronto. Given the state of my office, I was even more surprised when my clerk managed to give me the message. And then this turned up in my private correspondence." He handed Thaddeus a letter. "I'm afraid I read it – it was addressed to me after all – but I have no idea what to make of the contents."

Dear Mr. Ashby,

My sister and I are writing to you in the hope that you might know the whereabouts of a Mr. Thaddeus Lewis, a Methodist preacher who at one time was living in the Bay of Quinte area. He was mentioned in several newspaper articles in connection with a murder trial in London where you represented the accused. The reason we are writing is to warn him that our youngest sister Esther may pose a danger to him.

Mr. Lewis was involved in another trial many years ago that, unfortunately, had a very tragic outcome for us. Esther has always blamed him for her unhappy lot in life and frequently railed against him in a very unseemly and untoward manner, but until recently our mother was able to control her fits of rage. Sadly, mother died not long ago and Esther disappeared one night with all our money and without a word. She is quite unstable and we fear she plans to take some drastic action.

We really are at a loss as to how else we might contact Mr. Lewis. If you know where he is, would you please pass the information in this letter to him so that we can rest assured that we have adequately fulfilled our Christian duty.

Yours sincerely,
Matilda and Isabella Simms

P.S. Tell him that it involved Isaac Simms, in case he can't remember.

And with that, you consider your responsibilities at an end, Thaddeus thought when he finished reading. Pass it off on someone else and wash your hands of it. And of your sister as well. Sally Spicer had guessed correctly - the old woman who dominated her family died and there was no one left willing to control Esther. He reread the letter, shaking his head at the tone. The older Simms sisters seemed to think that all of the tragedy had been theirs. No wonder Sally hadn't liked any of them.

"I came as soon as I read it," Ashby said. "Are you in danger?"

"Not any more. The woman in question has been apprehended."

Thaddeus would write back to the Simms sisters and let them know what had happened to Esther. And then he would once again attempt to put it all behind him.

He set the letter aside. "I do appreciate you taking the time to deliver this," he said to Ashby.

"There's another reason for my call," Ashby said, "although I might not have made it quite as quickly if I hadn't been so concerned for your safety. I saw Mrs. Elliott in England."

"Really?" Thaddeus waited for Ashby to say something more. He was one of the few people who knew the truth about Clementine's supposed demise, but for some reason Thaddeus was suddenly wary of sharing the details of his most recent encounter with her.

"Yes, it was most peculiar," Ashby said. "We were waiting to board our ship in Liverpool when I spotted her. I called her name. She turned around. But then she denied that she was Mrs. Elliott and acted like she didn't know who I was."

Thaddeus could only follow her lead. "You must have been mistaken. They say everyone has a twin somewhere. I'm sure it was a woman who looked very like her, that's all."

"That's what I thought at first. I apologized for bothering her and she brushed it off very graciously. I asked if we might assist her in any way – she seemed to be travelling alone. She declined, and started to walk away - but she'd only gone a few steps when she turned around and said something very odd. She said she was trying to find her way to a place called otherwise enough."

It was a message meant to be delivered straight to Thaddeus, and Ashby knew it. Nevertheless, Thaddeus kept his expression as neutral as he could. It was safer to keep the inquisitive Ashby uninformed. About any of it.

"How strange," he said. "Perhaps the woman was mad. There seems to be a lot of that around this season."

Ashby regarded him for a long moment, but to Thaddeus's relief, chose not to pursue the issue. "Well, I thought I should let you know about the letter," he finally said.

"Yes, thank you, Towns. I appreciate the trouble you've gone to."

"I haven't been back long enough to sort out my docket yet, but you never know, I may need you in the future."

"You never know," Thaddeus agreed. "And now you know where to find me."

"In the meantime, I have mounds of paper waiting for me at the office." Ashby rose and shook Thaddeus's hand. "It's awfully good to see you again – and I'm glad that the letter isn't as ominous as it sounds. We should get together again soon. Maybe you can persuade your charming granddaughter to find a little room in her busy schedule."

"I'll try. But you know Martha."

Ashby looked a little rueful. "Yes. I do. And please give my regards to Luke," he added as an afterthought.

After he left, Thaddeus stood at the parlour window and stared out at the passing traffic. He was at both an end and a beginning, he reflected. The crimes of Isaac Simms had been a weight on his soul for a long time, but now he was fully and finally prepared to push it aside.

A time to weep and a time to laugh, a time to mourn and a time to dance.

Time to clear away whatever sorrow remained and make room for rejoicing – in his sons, who had grown into such fine men; in Martha and all of his other grandchildren; in his friends; in the new little life that promised to make Francis whole again.

And in Clementine.

For the present, it was enough to know that she had made it safely across the ocean. At some point, he was sure, he would receive an enigmatic message written in a strange mirrored hand mailed from some faraway foreign city. He would tuck it away with her picture in the little wooden box he kept in his pocket. He would look at it often, and content himself with the prospect that someday, somehow, they might meet again at a place that was otherwise enough.

It was good to be alive.

The End

ACKNOWLEDGEMENTS

Those wishing to delve into the background history of this tale of Canada West in 1855 will find the following sources particularly illuminating:

The article *Paupers and Poor Relief in Upper Canada* by Rainer Baehre, published in *Historical Essays on Upper Canada: New Perspectives*, Carleton University Press Inc. 1989, provided useful information on Toronto's House of Industry, as did web resources such as *Toronto Star's* article *Once Upon A City: Poor house helped Toronto's destitute* by Janice Bradbeer, August 27, 2017.

The essay *Friendly Atoms in Chemistry: Women and Men at Normal School in Mid-Nineteenth Century Toronto* by Alison Prentice, published in *Old Ontario, Essays in Honour of J.M.S. Careless*, Dundurn Press 1990 provided information on how the Toronto Normal School functioned, with further details provided by the Centenary Address delivered by Dr. J.G. Aulthouse, Chief Director of Education for the Province of Ontario at the Hundredth Birthday Dinner of Toronto Normal School in 1947, archived at the University of Toronto and available on-line.

Details of life in Yorkville were taken from *Seven Eggs Today, The Diaries of Mary Armstrong, 1859 and 1869*, Edited by Jackson W. Armstrong, Life Writing Series, Wilfrid Laurier University Press 2004.

And, once again, I returned to *The Autobiography of Thaddeus Lewis* published in Picton in 1865 to borrow the text written by the historical Thaddeus Lewis so the fictional Thaddeus Lewis could begin his memoirs.

The family of the real life Adam Sorbie honoured his memory by making the winning bid in a "name the character" auction at the 2018 Women Killing It Crime Writers' Festival, the proceeds of which were donated to Alternatives for Women, the Prince Edward County agency that provides support for abused women.

Many thanks to my agent Robert Lecker, my husband Rob, and to all the people who put up with me spending so much time with my imaginary friends.

Praise for the Thaddeus Lewis Books:

"Love the Murdoch Mysteries? Then you need to discover Janet Kellough's terrific series featuring preacher-detective Thaddeus Lewis. Who says Canadian history is boring?

Margaret Cannon, The Globe and Mail

"Kellough does a fine job of bringing life to the times and to her ministerial hero on horseback."

The National Post

"…it is hard to think of any crime fiction set in Canada's rich historical past. *On the Head of a Pin* by Janet Kellough is doubly welcome, since it is firmly historical and also extremely well done."

www.whodunitcanada.com

[*The Burying Ground*] "is an engaging historical mystery. Fans of Chesterton's Father Brown or Anne Perry…will find this Canadian variation much to their liking."

Booklist

[*Wishful Seeing*] "is an appealing look at life in mid-1800's Canada, full of historical detail, engaging characters, and a murder investigation that takes many surprising twists and turns before it can be solved."

Kirkus Reviews

[*Wishful Seeing*] "Kellough smartly brings her trails of intrigue and misunderstanding to a fine finish…suspenseful, complex, satisfying – and entertainingly instructive, as well."

Joan Barfoot, The London Free Press

Janet Kellough's novel *Wishful Seeing* was short-listed for the 2017 Crime Writers of Canada Arthur Ellis Best Novel Award.

306001

Made in the USA
Middletown, DE
22 May 2019